AN ECHO IN TIME

A Novel

Marco Antonio Varela

An Echo in Time

This is a work of fiction. Names, characters, places, and incidents are the product of the author's imagination or are used fictitiously. Any resemblance to actual events, locales, or persons, living or dead, is entirely coincidental.

First published 2026

Printed in the United States of America

ISBN 979-8-9956428-7-9 (paperback)

For everyone who built something in a difficult place

and had the grace to call it home.

Part One: Before

ONE

The Wall

Matt

Matt

The rock knew him by now. That was what it felt like — not a delusion, not the kind of thing Matt would ever say out loud to another person, but a private fact he'd accumulated over three years of coming back to this particular face on this particular granite wall in the high desert east of Wells, Nevada. The holds had positions his hands moved to before his eyes found them. The crux sequence twenty feet below the summit — a rightward traverse across a band of compressed sandstone where the rock changed character entirely, going slick and unforgiving after the generous roughness below — he'd mapped it so completely in his body that he sometimes solved it in his sleep, waking with chalk-dusted fingertips that were, of course, perfectly clean.

He was three hundred feet up and moving well.

Below him the valley floor lay flat and enormous, the kind of landscape that makes you understand the word vast in a physical way, not just an intellectual one. His jeep sat in the dirt near the trailhead — dark green, eleven years old, the back seats permanently removed to make room for gear. From up here it was a dark rectangle, indistinct, belonging to the valley the way the rocks and scrub belonged to it. The highway was a grey line unspooling west toward the mountains. There were no other cars. There were no other people. There was the hawk working the thermals somewhere above and to his right, and there was the granite under his hands and boots, and there was the particular quality of silence that you could only find this high up on a windless morning, a silence that wasn't absence but presence — the world's own sound when nothing human was in it.

Matt pressed his palm flat against the wall. Felt the warmth in it, the heat the rock had been storing since dawn. Felt the texture — not smooth, never smooth, but a kind of organized roughness, crystals of quartz and feldspar arrayed in patterns too small to see but large enough to hold a man's weight if he placed himself correctly.

He breathed out through his nose. Looked up at the remaining face. Seventy feet of granite between him and the summit, and between him and the summit was the traverse, and the traverse was why he kept coming back. He'd made it twice. He'd failed it eleven times. Each failure was instructive and each failure was also just a failure, a body-memory of the wrong sequence that he had to consciously overwrite before the next attempt. The traverse required you to shift your weight in a direction that felt wrong, to trust a friction hold that offered no positive edge, to move fast through the crux rather than slow because slowing was where you lost the momentum that was, in fact, the point.

His Bluetooth earpiece buzzed.

He closed his eyes for one second. Opened them. The traverse was thirty feet above him and he was breathing correctly and his forearms were good, not pumped, the blood moving freely through the muscles. He was exactly where he needed to be in his body and in his mind.

He answered.

"This better be worth it."

"It's me!" Charlie's voice arrived in his ear with the particular warmth of someone who believed his calls were always welcome. "How's it going up there?"

"You know I don't take calls on the wall."

"I thought you'd want to hear this. I invited Carmen to come with us."

Matt's fingers tightened on the ledge. His left foot shifted, searching for a better smear. He found it — barely. Above him the traverse waited like a problem he'd been solving for three years.

"She just got back from her last deployment," Charlie said. "Fourteen months. I figured she could use some desert air."

"Carmen's not fun, Charlie."

"She's Sophie's best friend!"

This was Charlie's complete answer to any objection about Carmen. She's Sophie's best friend. As though friendship were a credential that superseded personality.

Matt didn't say what he was thinking, which was: Carmen was exactly fun, in the way that a very sharp knife is useful, which is to say that she was impressive and occasionally alarming and most of her humor was delivered so deadpan you could miss it entirely if you weren't paying attention. What she was not was easy. She had the quality of someone who was always assessing the room and usually finding it wanting, and she communicated this through an economy of expression that most people read as indifference and that Matt had come to understand, over several years and a handful of camping trips, was actually something closer to its opposite.

He did not say any of this because he was three hundred feet off the ground having a conversation he should not be having.

A small chunk of rock broke loose under his left boot. He felt it go — a shift in the friction, a fraction of a second of wrongness — and his left hand moved before the rest of him caught up, reaching for the ledge above, finding it, gripping it. His right hand had been on a side-pull, a vertical crack, but the side-pull required downward pressure and the downward pressure required the left foot smear and the left foot smear was gone.

His right hand didn't hold him.

He went.

The wall passed him going upward. He'd been in this moment before — the body's instinctive recognition of the fall, the half-second where everything is very clear and very fast — and his hands were already moving, pushing off the rock, creating distance, because the worst thing you could do in a fall was cling to the wall and let it tumble you. He pushed off cleanly and his right hand found the ripcord and he pulled it and the parachute came out and opened above him with a sound like a large book being dropped on a hard floor, a flat crack, and then the harness went taut and the valley floor stopped rising toward him.

He swung gently in the harness, looking up at the wall, at the traverse thirty feet above where he'd been, at the summit above that.

"What's happening?!" Charlie's voice, which had been saying something Matt hadn't registered, suddenly sharpened with genuine alarm.

"I slipped."

"Was that — was that my fault? That was my fault, wasn't it."

He drifted down on the thermal, the valley floor rising slowly to meet him. The jeep resolved from a dark rectangle into a recognizable shape. The hawk was still up there, watching.

"Yes," Matt said.

"I'm so sorry. But don't worry about Carmen — we're going to have a great time. All of us. All four of us, plus Carmen, which makes five, which is —"

"Charlie."

"What."

"I'm landing."

He hit the valley floor cleanly, knees soft, and took two steps to absorb the momentum. The parachute settled behind him in the still air. He unclipped his helmet and looked up at the wall — all seven hundred feet of it, the traverse a barely-visible line of discoloration in the granite, the summit above that, clean against the blue.

"Sorry," Charlie said. "I really am."

"It's fine."

"Is it though?"

"Call me tonight. We'll go over the plan."

"Okay. Yes. Sorry about the climb."

"Charlie."

"What."

"It's fine."

He ended the call. Stood in the valley with the parachute spread behind him like something shed, and looked at the wall. The traverse. The problem he'd been working for three years.

"Next time," he said, to the mountain or to himself — the distinction felt academic.

The thing about the wall — the thing Charlie would never understand, the thing Matt had stopped trying to explain to anyone except in the most functional terms — was that it had nothing to do with the summit.

The summit was just the end of the problem. It was the point at which the problem became resolved, which was not the same as the point at which it became interesting. The interesting part was the traverse. The interesting part was the moment when the route required him to do something that felt wrong in order to do something right — to shift his weight in a direction his body didn't want to shift it, to trust a hold that offered no positive edge, to move through fear rather than around it.

He'd been a competitive climber until he was twenty-five, when he'd understood that competition was not the point. The point was the wall and the problem the wall presented and the slow, years-long process of learning to read what the wall was telling him about himself. Competition required you to solve the problem faster than another person. The wall just required you to solve it.

He gathered the parachute and stuffed it in its bag with the practiced efficiency of someone who has done this a thousand times. It was a BASE rig, modified for cliff-jumping, but he used it for the wall — it was faster than a rope system and it meant he climbed alone, which was how he preferred it. There had been a period, in his early twenties, when he'd climbed with partners. He'd liked it. He'd also noticed that he climbed differently with a partner — more cautiously, with more awareness of how the climb looked from the outside rather than how it felt from the inside. Alone, he climbed the way he thought. Alone was the better data.

He loaded the rig in the back of the jeep and took a long drink of water and sat on the tailgate looking at the wall. Three years of coming back to this face. The traverse was a sequence of six moves, and he had the first five locked, and the sixth was the one that kept throwing him. The sixth move required you to release a good hold with your right hand and move it across eighteen inches of nothing to a sloper — a rounded, featureless knob of granite — and commit your body weight to it before your left hand moved. The sequence only worked if you moved fast and trusted the sloper completely. Any hesitation transferred your weight the wrong way and you came off.

He understood this in his mind. He understood it in his body up until the sixth move, and then the body's understanding broke down and the mind tried to compensate by slowing things down, which was exactly wrong. The mind's instinct for self-preservation was the obstacle. The climb required him to be faster than his instinct.

He thought about this while he ate an apple and watched a pair of ravens cross the valley at altitude, riding the same thermals as the hawk.

He thought about Charlie's call. Not with irritation — the irritation had dissolved when the parachute opened, as it always did. Charlie called during climbs because Charlie was constitutionally unable to believe that anyone was doing something that couldn't be interrupted. It was not carelessness. It was a failure of imagination specific to people who lived primarily in the social world and could not quite conceive of an activity that was genuinely all-consuming. Charlie lived in the social world completely and happily, which was why Matt liked him. They were different in the way that complementary things are different. Matt made Charlie more thoughtful. Charlie made Matt more human.

He thought about the weekend. Leatherman Peak — the summit he needed to log for Club Nine, the semi-formal organization of extreme-altitude climbers whose membership would get him access to the Everest expedition he'd been angling toward for two years. The club's membership included a man named Graves who had summited Everest four times and who had, on each occasion, brought a different extreme athlete to attempt a different record. What Matt wanted to do had never been done: a base jump from the summit in a wingsuit, a full glide descent from the highest point on earth, riding the wind down the mountain rather than climbing back down it. The planning and logistics were complex and the cost was substantial and the danger was genuine and none of these things discouraged him at all.

What Charlie thought of this plan — genuinely one of the dumbest ideas he'd ever heard, as he had said, more than once — was not entirely irrelevant, because Charlie's opinion of things Matt proposed was a useful calibration tool. If Charlie thought something was dumb, it meant the risk-to-reward ratio looked unreasonable from the outside. This was useful information. It didn't change the plan.

Carmen, though. Carmen's reaction to the Everest plan had been: "I kind of want to do it myself." Which was a different category of response entirely. Matt had filed this away without quite knowing what to do with it.

He drove back toward Wells on the empty highway with the windows down, the desert air dry and hot and smelling of sage and something mineral and ancient. The landscape did not care about him, which he found restful. The mountains in the distance did not care. The sky did not care. He existed in it the way the ravens existed in it — passing through, subject to its conditions, navigating by its features. This seemed to him like the correct relationship to have with the physical world, and it was a relationship that required practice to maintain, because the social world was constantly asserting that it was the important world, that the things that happened between people were the things that mattered, that the sky and the rock and the silence were backdrop rather than content.

He didn't entirely disagree. He understood that the things that happened between people were, in fact, the things that mattered. He just found it harder to be good at them.

His phone showed seventeen missed calls from the last two hours, which was the standard toll for climbing without signal. Three from Charlie. Two from his sister in Portland. One from a number he didn't recognize, which was almost certainly someone selling something. The rest from work, because it was a Tuesday and he was supposed to be at his desk in Las Vegas — he was an athletic trainer and consultant for a private sports performance facility, a job he was good at and that paid well and that felt, most of the time, like the supporting activity that funded the actual work, which was the wall.

He called his sister back because she called less often than Charlie and when she called it usually meant something.

"How was the climb?" she said.

"Good. I slipped on the traverse."

"Again?"

"It's the same traverse. Yes."

"How many times is that now?"

"Twelve."

She paused. Not with sympathy — his sister had the family's capacity for bluntness, which was to say a complete one. She paused with what sounded like consideration.

"Maybe the traverse is telling you something," she said.

"It's telling me I'm not doing it right yet."

"Or it's telling you you're thinking about it wrong."

"Those are the same thing."

"Are they?"

He didn't answer because he was considering whether they were. The highway ran straight ahead of him into the heat shimmer. A hawk — possibly the same one from earlier, possibly a different one — held its position against the blue sky to his left, making no effort that was visible from the road.

"Are you going this weekend?" she asked.

"Yeah. Leatherman with Charlie and Sophie and Carmen."

"Carmen's back?"

"Apparently."

"Good," his sister said, which was interesting. He didn't pursue it.

"I'll call you Monday," he said.

"Be careful on the traverse," she said, with a tone that suggested she was talking about more than the traverse. He chose not to ask.

★★★

He was back in Las Vegas by six, showered and eating leftover rice at his kitchen counter when he let himself think about the weekend properly. Not the climb — the climb he'd been thinking about for weeks, every detail of the approach and the summit and the long ridge to the peak mapped in his mind with the completeness of something memorized. The weekend. Charlie and Sophie and Carmen and four days in the desert and the particular social architecture that those four people created when assembled, which was: Charlie and Sophie at the center of it, a unit with its own internal logic that the other two orbited. Carmen and Matt as satellites. Carmen and Matt, who were not a unit and never had been and probably never would be, making conversation on the periphery of Charlie's enthusiasm while Charlie arranged things around them and called it a plan.

This was not a complaint. It was just the shape of things.

He ate his rice and looked out the kitchen window at the parking lot and thought about the traverse. Thought about his sister's question: maybe the traverse is telling you something. Maybe you're thinking about it wrong.

He'd been thinking about the sixth move — the release and the commitment to the sloper — as the problem. What if the sixth move wasn't the problem. What if the problem was in the fifth move, or earlier, something he was setting up wrong that compounded through the sequence until it expressed itself as a failure at the sixth.

He thought about this until the rice was gone.

His phone buzzed. Charlie.

He answered.

"I've been thinking," Charlie said, "about what to bring for Sophie. She mentioned once that she loves those little individual cheese things, the kind wrapped in wax? Do you think they have those in Wells?"

Matt looked at the ceiling.

"I don't know, Charlie."

"I'll just bring some from here. Better to be safe. Also — and tell me honestly — do you think Sophie will be okay with Carmen coming? I know I already invited Carmen but I forgot to think about whether Sophie would want her there and then I invited her and Sophie says she's happy but she said it in the voice she uses when she's not entirely happy and I —"

"Charlie."

"What."

"Sophie loves Carmen."

"Right. Yes. I know. I just —"

"Everything is going to be fine."

He said it with the conviction he usually felt when he said it, which was most of the conviction in the world plus the private awareness that he had no actual evidence for it. Everything was going to be fine. He believed this the way he believed in the traverse — not because it was provably true but because committing to the belief was the only way to move through the crux.

"Okay," Charlie said. "Okay. Yes. You're right. See you Friday."

Matt put his phone on the counter. The parking lot outside was orange in the evening light. A woman was loading groceries into a white SUV, a child in the cart seat watching the sky with the absolute absorption of someone encountering clouds for the first time. The sky was doing something extraordinary in the west — the color that happened sometimes in the desert when the light came through at exactly the right angle, turning the air itself a shade that didn't have a name, something between amber and gold and the particular orange of a fire seen from very far away.

He looked at it for a while.

Then he went to bed, because Friday was three days away and there were things to do before Friday, and also because the traverse was waiting for him in his sleep — the sixth move, the sloper, the question of whether he was setting it up wrong from the beginning — and he wanted to get to it.

TWO

The Photograph

Emma --- Greenbriar Gulch, Nevada, 1886

Emma — Greenbriar Gulch, Nevada, 1886

She had been writing on the back of the photograph for twenty minutes, which was longer than the photograph deserved and shorter than the feeling required. The feeling did not have a name, which was part of the problem. It was adjacent to grief but grief was too large a word for a Tuesday evening in a saloon office in a mining town. It was adjacent to loneliness, but she had been lonely in larger rooms than this and the loneliness here had a different texture — not the hollow kind, not the kind that echoes, but the dense kind, packed with the small furniture of a life she'd built herself, table by table and chair by chair, and which was entirely hers and which was, she understood on evenings like this one, also entirely silent.

She was writing to her sister Linda.

The photograph was from five years ago, taken by a man with a large black camera who had come through Greenbriar Gulch on his way west. He had set up his equipment in the main street and charged two bits for a sitting and the whole town had queued up in their Sunday best with the self-conscious stiffness of people who understood that they were becoming permanent for the first time. Emma had sat alone, because James had died the previous spring, and she had worn the dress she'd brought from home — pale blue silk, not practical, worn twice since she'd arrived in Nevada, kept in tissue paper at the bottom of her trunk. She had looked at the camera with the expression she practiced in the small mirror above the washstand, which was to say: composed, which is to say: whatever was beneath the composure stayed there.

She looked at the photograph now. She was writing on the back of it because the front was already complete and because Linda would want a letter and Emma could not quite muster a letter — could not manage the cheerful inventory of news that letters required, could not write the saloon is doing well and Rusty finally found his seam and the new sheriff seems to be a decent man in the voice she would have used a year ago. A year ago the voice had come easily. A year ago she had believed, with the specific conviction of someone who has made a large decision and committed to it entirely, that Greenbriar Gulch was the right place and the saloon was the right work and the life she was building was the one she was supposed to build.

She still believed most of this. The doubt was not about the place or the work. The doubt was about the silence at the end of the day, which expanded each evening in the same way the dark expanded across the valley — gradually, and then completely.

She wrote on the back of the photograph:

To my dear sister Linda. Love, Emma.

It wasn't much. It was what she had tonight.

She set the pen down and looked at what she'd written. Then she looked at the front of the photograph again. At her own face, composed and in silk, looking at a camera that was recording her into permanence in a town her family had never heard of. The feeling that did not have a name moved through her chest like weather.

She put the photograph face down on the desk.

The saloon was quiet at this hour, which was the hour just before the last drinkers left and the hour just after the piano player had given up and gone home. The oil lamps on the tables had burned down to a warm amber. Through the thin wall of her office she could hear the occasional creak of the building settling — the Drunken Coyote was twelve years old and had been two other things before she bought it, a feed merchant's and briefly a dentist's office, and the wood remembered all of this, sighing and contracting through the night with the memory of everything it had held.

She had renamed it when she bought it, five years ago. The previous owner had called it simply The Saloon, which seemed to her a failure of imagination. She had thought of several names — the Rose, after herself, which she dismissed as vain; the Coyote, which she liked for its particularity, the coyotes being the most reliably present sound of the Nevada desert, their calls threading through the dark every night with a kind of cheerful persistence she found admirable. She had added the Drunken because a saloon that didn't acknowledge its essential nature seemed dishonest. The Drunken Coyote: a creature doing what it was made to do, somewhat louder than necessary.

She had the rifle leaning against the wall beside her desk because she had always had it there and had always slept better for it. James had taught her to shoot the spring before he died — had insisted on it, had taken her to the flat land east of the plantation and stood patiently behind her while she learned the kick and the sighting and the particular discipline of waiting. He had been a patient man. The rifle was not his — hers was a later acquisition, purchased in Sacramento on her way west — but she had learned on his and the learning had stayed in her hands.

She was not afraid of the rifle, which put her in a minority among the women she'd known. She was not afraid of much, which was a fact about herself she'd arrived at empirically rather than by temperament. She had been afraid of James dying and he had died. She had been afraid that she could not make the saloon work and she had made it work. She had been afraid of the desert and it had become, over five years, the landscape she knew best in her body — its heat and its scale and its silences and the way the dark fell here faster and more completely than anywhere she'd lived before. You feared things until the thing happened or until you'd lived inside it long enough that it became simply the world. This seemed to her not a philosophy but a fact.

She picked up the pen again. Set it down. Picked up the photograph and looked at Linda's address, written in her own hand on the back. Thought about Linda in Georgia — the house, the children, the husband who sold agricultural equipment and who was decent enough in the way that men were decent when they didn't have to try very hard. Thought about the question Linda had put in her last letter, carefully, sideways, in the register of a question that was really a concern:

Are you well, Emma? And I mean really well. I mean the other kind.

Emma had read this three times and written back:

I am the other kind of well too. Don't worry about me.

Whether this was true depended on the evening.

★★★

She heard Rusty before she heard him, which was always the way. His voice carried ahead of the rest of him like a herald — loud, unmodulated, belonging to a man who had spent decades in conversation with empty spaces and had calibrated his volume accordingly. She pushed back her chair and went to the door of her office and looked through the gap into the saloon.

Rusty was at the bar, which was where Rusty was always to be found at this hour, but tonight there was something different in the set of his shoulders, something higher and looser, and when he turned to speak to the barkeep she could see it in his face as well — a brightness that was not the whiskey kind, or at least not only that.

"Gut warmer!" he was saying. "And the beef! Tonight I'm celebrating!"

She came out of the office and walked to the bar.

"Well, look who decided to show up," she said. "I thought we might have to send a search party."

"Miss Rose!" He turned to her with the full force of his brightness and she saw, yes, that there was something real behind it. "Look here." He reached into his coat and she put her hand on his arm before he could produce whatever he was reaching for.

"Not here, Rusty."

He lowered his voice to a register that was, for Rusty, merely loud instead of very loud. "I found some. Bigger than the last ones. I was on Black Water Creek, going upstream, and there was a new stream I hadn't seen before —"

"Rusty." She kept her hand on his arm and her voice even. "I'm glad for you. Truly. But you know better than to crow about it in here."

She glanced at the room. Four tables occupied. Three she knew by name — Hendricks, playing patience alone, and the Morrison brothers having a quiet argument about something that was not her business, and Old Pete asleep in the corner as he had been asleep in that corner on and off for three years. The fourth table she didn't know: three men, sitting together in the back, away from the lamps. They'd come in an hour ago and ordered whiskey and not said much. One of them was very large, with a white-red beard and a black hat. She had looked at him when he came in because she always looked at the men who came in, and she had put him in the category of men who required watching rather than the category of men who required assistance, which was a distinction she'd developed a reliable instinct for over five years of running a saloon.

She had not looked at him again, which was a choice. Looking again would have told him that she'd noticed something worth noticing.

"Put it away," she said to Rusty, and Rusty, who had known her for three years and understood certain things about her without requiring explanation, put it away.

"Yes, ma'am." He settled on his stool. "You'll let me have the beef, though?"

"I'll let you have the beef." She nodded to the barkeep. "And give him whatever he wants to drink. He's earned it."

She went back to her office but she did not close the door. She stood beside it, just out of the lamplight, and listened.

The large man's voice, when she heard it, was low. He had an accent she couldn't place precisely — Irish in its bones but worked over by years of somewhere else, somewhere rougher. He was talking to his companions in a murmur she couldn't resolve into words, but the murmur had a particular quality, a kind of lateral stillness, the sound of a man who was listening more than he was speaking.

She went back to her desk. She picked up the pen. She did not write anything.

After a while she heard the three men get up and leave. She counted to sixty before she went back out to the bar.

"Those men," she said to the barkeep. "Did you catch a name?"

He shook his head. "Paid in coin. Didn't say much."

"If they come back, you come find me."

He nodded. He had worked for her for four years and he had learned to treat statements like this as instructions rather than suggestions.

She went back to her office and she cleaned the pen and she looked at the photograph on the desk and she thought about Linda's question:

Are you well, Emma? And I mean really well. I mean the other kind.

She picked up the pen and on a fresh piece of paper she wrote:

Dearest Linda. I am well. There was something I wanted to tell you tonight and I find I cannot locate it. The saloon is in good order. I have taken on a new barkeep who is reliable. There is a prospector named Rusty who has been finding gold in the hills to the north, which is good for him and good for business. The new sheriff seems to be a serious man, which is what the town needs. I think of you often. Give my love to the children. Write when you can.

She read it over. It was perfectly adequate and entirely incomplete and it was what she had, and Linda would read between its lines with the accuracy of someone who had known her for forty years and would not press further, which was what Emma had always loved about her sister — that she understood what was said and what was unsaid and she kept them both without making you account for either.

She folded the letter. Addressed it. Set it with the photograph.

She put out the lamp and sat in the dark for a moment, listening to the building settle around her, and to the coyotes beginning their night business out in the valley, and to the silence that lived underneath all of it, the desert's own silence, which was not an absence but a presence — the sound of a very large thing not moving.

She was not afraid.

She went out to check the locks on the front door.

The morning was the same as all the mornings. She rose at five, made coffee on the small stove in her quarters behind the office, drank it standing at the window that faced the alley between the saloon and the feed merchant's. The alley was full of the flat grey light that preceded the sun by half an hour in the high desert, the light that had no warmth yet but plenty of clarity — she could see every rock in the alley, every board in the feed merchant's wall, with a precision that the warmer light of midday wouldn't match.

She dressed. She went out to assess the previous night's damage, which was modest — three broken glasses, one table that needed a leg tightened, and a stain on the floor near the bar that she could not entirely account for but which was brown and not red and so was probably not her problem in any serious sense.

She sent the morning boy to fetch the bread from the baker on Third Street and she made the inventory and she noted that they were short on the good whiskey, which would need to be ordered from the supplier in Elko, and she wrote this down in the ledger that tracked every bottle that came in and went out and at what price because money was the mechanism by which the saloon stayed open and the saloon staying open was the mechanism by which she stayed here and staying here was what she had decided to do.

She was thinking about the three men as she did all of this. Not with alarm, exactly. With the particular attention she gave to things that had not yet resolved into a category.

The large man with the beard. The way he'd listened more than he'd spoken. The way she had looked at him once and then deliberately not looked again, and the way she'd felt, even with her eyes on Rusty, that his eyes had not moved from wherever they'd settled.

She had served difficult men for five years. She had served men who were drunk in the angry way and men who were drunk in the sad way and men who were looking for trouble and men who were looking for company and men who were simply tired and wanting to sit somewhere warm before they went back to the cold work of the mines. She had developed, over five years, a taxonomy of difficult men, and she knew which category required which response and she had never, in five years, had cause to question the taxonomy.

The large man didn't fit it.

He was not drunk-angry or drunk-sad or trouble-seeking in the obvious way. He had the quality of someone who was already decided — already past the stage of wanting something and into the stage of planning to take it. She had met this quality before, once, in a man on the road west from Sacramento, and she had moved to the other side of the road and kept moving and had not looked back, and it had been the right thing to do and she had known it was the right thing to do even as she'd done it, in the way you sometimes know things before the evidence is complete.

She would tell the sheriff.

She would tell him this evening, she decided. It was possible she was wrong. It was possible the man with the beard was simply a large, quiet traveler with somewhere to be. It was possible that the quality she'd read in him was a projection of the evening's mood — the photograph, the feeling without a name, the letter she couldn't quite write. She allowed for this.

She would tell the sheriff anyway. It cost nothing to say:

three men came in last night, one of them very large, black hat, didn't say much, I didn't like the feel of it.

The sheriff was a serious man. He would hear it and weigh it and tell her she was probably right to mention it and do whatever he thought should be done. This was what serious men were for.

She went on making the inventory. Outside, the morning was arriving in the usual way — light, then warmth, then the sound of the town waking up, boots on the boards, the distant percussion of the mine operations starting their day, the particular rattle of the ore wagons heading east. Greenbriar Gulch in the morning was a functional and purposeful place, and she was part of its function and purpose, and she found this, most mornings, to be enough.

She found her pen and wrote the whiskey order for Elko.

She did not think about the photograph again until that night, when she sat down to write and found it still on the desk, face down, with

To my dear sister Linda. Love, Emma. in her own hand, and the feeling moved through her chest again, the one without a name, and she sat with it for a moment before she put the photograph in an envelope and sealed it and set it with the letter and told herself she would mail both of them on Thursday.

She did not mail them on Thursday.

She did not mail them at all.

By Thursday evening, the men had come back.

★ ★ ★

Three days after the burial, the priest wrote in the parish ledger what he had not said aloud at the graveside, because gravesides required comfort and the ledger required honesty.

Emma Rose, aged 41 years, departed this life the 14th of September, by violence. She came to us from Georgia five years past and conducted herself with grace and industry in all the time she was among us. The town is diminished.

He paused. Set the pen down and looked at what he'd written and then picked the pen up again and continued.

A peculiar season. The Morrison family departed for Salt Lake three weeks past, without farewell, which is unlike them. The Hendrickses left the week prior. I count seven families gone from the congregation in the past month, which is more than any comparable period since I came to this place.

He stopped again. Outside the window of the church office the afternoon was very still, the air dry and metallic in the particular way it sometimes was in the valley, not like the smell of rain but like the smell of something else entirely, something he had no word for and which he'd noted before, on other dry still afternoons, but had never troubled to record.

He recorded it now.

Brother Thomas tells me he has had a persistent bitter taste in his mouth these past weeks, which he attributes to the water from the north well. I have had the same, though I had not mentioned it. Old Harlan the assayer has been unwell — a strange fatigue, he says, as though the weight of the air has increased. I have recommended rest.

He looked out the window. On the far side of the valley, at the edge of the flat land where the scrubland thinned before the foothills, there was sometimes a light in the evenings — he had seen it three times in the past month, a low amber glow with no identifiable source, gone by the time he went to find it. He had mentioned it to no one. He mentioned it now.

I have seen lights on the valley floor at night, three occasions. Low, amber, not fire. I cannot account for them. I have prayed for discernment and found none forthcoming, which I take to mean the answer is not yet available to me.

He read over what he'd written. It seemed to him the kind of entry that a future reader might find either very significant or very ordinary, depending on what they were looking for. He did not know which it was. He was a man who had learned, over many years, to sit with not-knowing and to record what he observed while the knowing resolved itself, or failed to.

He wrote the date at the top:

September 17th, 1886.

He closed the ledger. He said a prayer for Emma Rose, whom he had known five years and found consistently admirable — her practicality, her steadiness, the way she ran the saloon as though it were a kind of stewardship rather than merely a business. He asked that she be received with the welcome she'd earned.

Then he asked, more quietly, for guidance about the lights on the valley floor, and for an explanation of the bitterness in the air, and for the understanding of why the town was emptying itself this autumn in a way he could not account for.

No answer came, which was not unusual. He had been in this work long enough to know that the answers came on their own schedule, and that the correct response in the meantime was to keep writing down what you saw.

He kept writing.

THREE

Lucky Timing

Charlie

Charlie

The booking confirmation came through at 11:47 on a Tuesday morning and Charlie minimized it immediately, the way you minimize something you've been waiting for and don't want to jinx by looking at too directly. He finished the report he was drafting — projections for the Henderson account, a pleasant enough piece of work that required the appearance of careful analysis and the reality of about forty minutes — and then he maximized the confirmation window and read it properly.

Campground: reserved. Check-in Friday, check-out Monday. Two sites adjacent, which meant he and Matt would have one and Sophie and Carmen — he was already thinking of them as a unit, which he understood was optimistic but chose to believe was also simply correct — would have the other. He'd paid extra for the sites with shade structures, because Sophie burned easily and would not appreciate burning, and he'd noted in the reservation comments that they were celebrating a birthday, which was not technically true but had reliably produced a complimentary bag of firewood at three different campgrounds in his experience and he saw no reason not to try.

Flight confirmation: Sophie's flight from Paris landed Thursday at two-forty. He had already mapped the drive from the airport to his apartment. Thirty-one minutes without traffic. He would leave at one-fifteen, which gave him a twenty-minute buffer, because Sophie's luggage always arrived last — not because the airline was targeting her specifically, which he'd once gently suggested, but because she traveled with bags of a weight and dimension that required special handling, a fact she received as a compliment.

He maximized the third window: the gear list he'd been building in a notes file for three weeks. Tent, sleeping bags, camp stove, the small percolator Sophie preferred to the pour-over because the pour-over, in her assessment, made camping feel like a chore. His telescope, the new one — a four-inch refractor he'd bought in March and had used twice, once in his apartment parking lot and once at Red Rock, both times with results that were extraordinary and that he had described to Sophie in probably too much detail via text message at the time. The wooden case from the back of his closet.

He looked at the wooden case line and then deleted it. Added it back. Deleted it again.

Left it.

He'd bought the wooden case at an estate sale in Henderson two years ago, on a Saturday when Sophie was in Paris and Matt was climbing somewhere and he'd had nothing particular to do and had driven around the city in the way he sometimes did on empty Saturdays until he ended up somewhere. The estate sale was in a small house on a street of small houses, the lawn crowded with card tables and the card tables crowded with the accumulated particulars of a life he knew nothing about. He'd bought a lamp he didn't need and a set of mid-century highball glasses he'd used once and a wooden case, roughly the size of a large briefcase, with brass fittings and a clasp that needed a firm push to release. He'd asked the woman running the sale what was inside and she'd shrugged and said she didn't know, it had been found in the attic, and he'd paid twelve dollars for it and put it in his car and driven home.

The case was empty. He'd been mildly disappointed and then decided the case itself was the point. It was well made — real joinery, a cedar lining that still carried a faint smell — and it had clearly held something important for a long time. He'd put it in his closet and looked at it occasionally and felt, each time, the particular fondness you feel for things that have a history you can't quite access.

He'd told Sophie about it on the phone one evening and she had said:

"You paid twelve dollars for an empty box?"

And he'd said yes, and she'd said:

"Charlie."

And he'd said he knew, and they'd both been quiet for a moment, and then she'd said:

"Bring it camping. It should have some air."

Which was such a specifically Sophie thing to say — the precision of it, the unexpected tenderness of the reasoning — that he'd fallen a little more in love with her in that particular moment and had not told her so because he was trying to be better about the frequency with which he said that kind of thing. Sophie loved him. He knew she loved him. He also knew, in the way you know things you're not entirely ready to examine, that love was not a single substance but a category, and that what lived inside the category shifted and changed its consistency over time, and that monitoring these shifts too openly was not the same as understanding them.

He finalized the gear list. Added the wooden case.

The photograph on his desk was from Chamonix, three years ago. He and Sophie, behind them the Mont Blanc massif making everything else in the frame feel provisional. Sophie was looking at the camera with the precise composure she brought to all photographs — she knew exactly what her face was doing at all times, which he had always found both impressive and slightly opaque, like watching someone speak a language you almost understood. He was looking at her.

He was always looking at her in photographs. He'd noticed this pattern a year ago, going through old pictures on his phone, and had felt briefly self-conscious about it and then decided it was simply accurate documentation. Sophie was the more interesting thing in any room she entered. It made sense to look at her.

He turned the photograph slightly so it caught less glare from the window. His office had a window that faced east, which meant good light in the morning and a slow dimming through the afternoon that sometimes made him feel, at four o'clock, that the day was more finished than it was. It was a Tuesday at four o'clock. The Henderson report was complete and sent. The Vasquez account had called twice and he'd let it go to voicemail both times, not from avoidance exactly but from the particular calculation of someone who understood that the Vasquez account's concerns were rarely as urgent as the Vasquez account believed them to be.

He had three days.

He said this to himself the way you say things that are pleasant: three days. Three days until Sophie landed and the weekend started and the four of them were in the desert together under whatever stars his telescope could find and Matt was occupied with his climbing and therefore less likely to make everything feel like a logistics problem and Carmen was back, which was a relief he hadn't let himself fully feel yet because Carmen coming back from deployment meant Carmen was safe, and he'd worried about Carmen in the specific low-grade way he worried about things he couldn't affect, which was to say constantly and quietly, in the background of his other thoughts.

He'd known Carmen since college. She and Sophie had been roommates sophomore year and she'd been part of his life ever since in the peripheral but permanent way of the people you don't see often but whose existence in the world makes the world feel more stable. Carmen had a quality he'd never quite been able to name — a reliability, but not the passive kind. The active kind. The kind that meant if things went genuinely wrong, Carmen would be the person in the room who knew what to do next.

He hoped things didn't go genuinely wrong. He also felt, honestly, slightly more comfortable going camping in the middle of the Nevada desert knowing Carmen was coming.

He called Matt.

Matt answered on the fourth ring, which was Matt's standard — never the first, never the fifth.

"Hey," Charlie said. "How was the wall?"

"Good."

"Did you make the traverse?"

A pause. "No."

"Ah." Charlie had learned, over seven years of friendship, that there was nothing useful to say about the traverse. Matt would make it or he wouldn't and he would think about it until he did, and the thinking was not the kind that benefited from company. "You feeling okay about Friday?"

"Yeah. I might go up one more time Thursday morning if the weather holds."

"Before we leave?"

"Early. I'll be back by noon."

This was so entirely Matt that Charlie didn't question it. "Carmen's flying in Thursday afternoon," he said. "She lands at four. I told her we'd swing by and get her."

"That's fine."

"I invited her, by the way. To the camping trip."

A pause of a different quality than the traverse pause. "I know," Matt said. "You told me this morning."

"Right. On the wall. Sorry about that."

"It's fine."

"Is it though?"

"Charlie."

"What."

"Stop apologizing. It's fine. Carmen's fine. The trip will be fine. Stop."

Charlie smiled at his desk. This was also entirely Matt — the patience under the economy, the genuine reassurance delivered in the fewest possible words. He'd once asked Sophie what she thought Matt actually felt, underneath all the restraint, and Sophie had said, without hesitation:

"Exactly what he shows you. He just doesn't waste the showing."

He thought about this a lot.

"See you Friday," he said.

"Friday," Matt said, and hung up.

★ ★ ★

He stayed late to finish the Vasquez account and left the office at seven, which was the receptionist's usual sign-off time though she was not there to deliver it, and took the elevator down and walked to his car in the parking garage and sat in it for a moment before starting the engine.

Three days.

He was aware, in the way he was aware of most things he preferred not to examine too closely, that Sophie had been different since January. Not distant exactly — Sophie communicated with too much warmth and too much precision for distance. But something had shifted in the calibration. The jokes came at the same frequency and the calls came at the same frequency and she said

mon cher the same way she always had, with the slight French curve on the vowel that he'd been trying and failing to replicate for three years. But underneath the frequency there was something he couldn't name. Something that was the same in texture as the thing he felt at four o'clock when the light in his office went flat — not wrong, but less bright.

He had considered asking her about it directly. He had composed several versions of the question in his head, tried them out in different registers — casual, serious, the sideways approach — and discarded all of them because each version, when he ran it through the simulator of his imagination, produced one of two possible responses: Sophie reassuring him warmly and everything being fine, or Sophie confirming that there was something and everything not being fine. And he could not quite determine which of these he was more afraid of, which suggested that the fear was not really about the answer but about the asking, which suggested that he already knew something he hadn't officially acknowledged yet.

He started the car.

The weekend would help. It always helped, the desert — the scale of it, the way it made the small worries feel proportional to the actual size of the world, which was very large. Sophie laughed differently outside. She moved differently, was less carefully assembled, let the sand get in her shoes without commenting on it. He liked her best in the desert, which was interesting because she was not, by any reasonable measure, a desert person. She was Parisian by training and disposition and had the Parisian's considered skepticism about anything that required sleeping on the ground. But she came, every time he asked, and every time she came she became, by degrees, more herself — or a different self, a less curated one, and he loved both versions but the less curated one most.

He drove home through the Tuesday evening traffic, which was substantial because Las Vegas traffic was always substantial, and thought about the telescope. He'd been reading about the sky above the Ruby Mountains, east of Wells, and it was genuinely extraordinary — almost no light pollution, at an elevation that thinned the atmosphere usefully, the kind of sky you could spend a whole night inside without getting to the bottom of it. He had a list of things he wanted to find: the Andromeda galaxy, which was the furthest thing visible to the naked eye and which always made him feel a specific kind of vertiginous that he could only describe as

good-scared, the way the traverse made Matt feel presumably, or the way great heights made some people feel — afraid and fully alive in the same breath. He wanted to show Sophie Andromeda. He wanted to be standing next to her when she understood how far away it was.

This seemed to him, as he drove, like the most important part of the weekend.

★ ★ ★

He did not tell Sophie about the telescope plans when she called that night, because Sophie called every night and the calls had a particular rhythm he'd learned not to disrupt — she led, he followed, they arrived somewhere comfortable and stayed there for a while and then said good night, and inserting the telescope plans felt like it would require a different rhythm, more enthusiasm on his end than the call's natural temperature allowed.

Instead she told him about the meeting she'd had that afternoon, with a client she found difficult — a gallery owner who wanted everything he asked for and then changed his mind about what he'd asked for, which Sophie tolerated with the particular patience she reserved for people who were paying for something.

"He kept saying

"but what I actually envisioned,"" Sophie said, "and then describing something completely different than what he'd told me he envisioned. Three times. Three."

"Did you tell him?"

"I showed him the notes from our first meeting. He looked at them very carefully and said,

"Hm, yes, but I think my thinking has evolved since then."

"What did you say?"

"I said,

"Wonderful, shall we start fresh?" And he said yes. So we started fresh. So now I have twice as much work as I started with." She paused. "I need the desert, Charlie."

"Three days," he said.

"Three days," she repeated, with a quality in her voice that he chose to interpret as anticipation.

They talked for another twenty minutes about small things — the weather in Paris, which was wet; a film she'd seen; a restaurant near his apartment he'd been meaning to try. Comfortable inventory. The landscape of a relationship that had found its topography.

He almost asked about January. Almost let the question form enough to escape.

Instead he said: "I'm glad you're coming."

"I'm glad too," she said. He heard something real in it and held it.

After the call he sat on his couch for a while in the dark without turning on a light or the television, which was not something he normally did but which felt, tonight, like the right thing to do. The apartment was quiet. Outside the window the Las Vegas night was doing what it always did — glowing, humming, insisting on itself — but he'd been here long enough that it was background now, the city's version of the silence under the silence, the desert's own dark.

He thought about the Andromeda galaxy. Two and a half million light years. When you looked at it, you were looking at light that had left it before humans existed, before

Homo sapiens was anything, when the thing that would become us was still some earlier version of itself moving through an earlier version of the world. The light had been traveling for two and a half million years and it had arrived now, tonight, at his retinas, at this specific moment of all the moments it had passed through. That seemed to him significant in a way he couldn't articulate but that he felt, sitting in the dark, in his chest.

He thought: I want to show Sophie that.

He thought: I want to be standing next to her when she looks at it.

He turned on one lamp. He went to bed. He set his alarm for six-thirty, which was earlier than he needed to get up for work, but which would give him time to check the weather forecast for Wells before he had to do anything else, and to refine the gear list if the forecast required it, and to be ready.

He was, he understood as he fell asleep, genuinely happy.

He did not take this for granted. He knew enough to know it was a thing that could change, that did change, that was in fact changing in ways he was not quite ready to see. But tonight it was true, straightforwardly and completely, and he lay with it the way you lie with something good — not holding too tightly, just close enough to feel the warmth.

Three days.

He slept well. He always slept well.

FOUR

Mon Cher

Sophia

Sophia

She knew before she booked the flight. That was the honest version, the one she told herself in the small hours of Tuesday morning, lying in the dark of her Paris apartment listening to the rain on the zinc roof and the particular silence of the sixth arrondissement at three a.m., which was the silence of a city that had retired but not entirely, a city keeping one eye open. She had lain there for an hour and looked at the ceiling and done the accounting that she had been avoiding since January, and the accounting was not complicated once she let herself do it, and at the end of it she had understood that she was going to Nevada, and she was going to end things with Charlie, and she was going to do it in person because he deserved that, and she was going to find the right moment, which she understood even as she formulated the plan might not exist, might have to be made rather than found.

This was the honest version.

The version she told herself in the daylight was softer — she was going because she missed Charlie, which was true; she was going because she missed Carmen, which was also true; she was going because Paris in March was wet and grey and the wet and grey had settled into her in a way that required something vast and dry and ancient to displace it, and the Nevada desert was all of these things in a quantity that Paris could not match. She was going because she needed to think, and thinking in Paris was compromised by Paris being everywhere — its beauty and its noise and its very specific demands on your attention, the way it required you to be present to it or feel that you were missing something. The desert asked nothing. You could think in the desert without the thinking being interrupted by something lovely.

Both versions were true. The daylight version was true. The three a.m. version was also true. They coexisted the way that uncomfortable truths and comfortable ones often coexist — not contradicting each other exactly, but not quite compatible, like two objects that occupy the same space only if you don't look at them simultaneously.

She booked the flight on Wednesday. She packed on Thursday morning with the methodical efficiency she brought to all practical tasks, which was the efficiency of someone who had moved apartments seven times in ten years and had learned that the cost of disorganization was always paid on the far end, when you were unpacking somewhere unfamiliar and the thing you needed was at the bottom of the wrong bag. She packed the silk scarf because the desert was cold at night and also because it was the scarf Charlie had given her two Christmases ago, which she was aware was a complicated reason to pack a scarf but which she packed it for anyway.

She put the saber case on the bed and looked at it.

The saber had belonged to her grandmother's grandfather, a cavalry officer who had served in the Franco-Prussian war and who had come home from it changed, according to family legend, in ways that the family had never quite specified but that Sophia had always understood to mean: marked by violence in a way that made certain rooms feel smaller than they were. The saber had come to her through her mother, who had come to it through her grandmother, each woman inheriting it without quite knowing what to do with it — it was too significant to discard and too martial to display — until it had arrived in Sophia's hands at twenty-two, when she'd been living in a studio apartment with barely enough room for her own furniture, and had leaned it against the wall in the corner and looked at it for a week before she'd enrolled in the fencing club at the Université.

She had been fencing for eleven years. She was good at it — not competitive, not especially interested in competition, but genuinely good in the technical sense, precise and economical, with a point control that her instructor had described, once, as almost surgical. She fenced the way she did most things: with full attention and no performance. The performance was for the spaces where performance was required. The fencing was for herself.

She put the saber case in the bag.

Charlie would ask about it. She would say it was a surprise. He would accept this because Charlie accepted most things she told him, which had always been one of the things she found most disarming about him — the absence of suspicion, the open-handed way he received whatever she offered, taking it at face value and not looking for the seams. It was generous. It was also, she had come to understand over three years, a kind of faith that required reciprocation, and she had not always reciprocated it as fully as it deserved.

This was part of the accounting.

The apartment was on the rue Saint-Jacques, on the fifth floor with no elevator, which she had stopped noticing three years ago and which visitors still mentioned with an expression that she'd come to think of as the Staircase Face — a brief rearrangement of features that communicated both complaint and the decision not to complain. The apartment itself was small by any standard that was not Parisian, which meant it was considered generous by Parisian standards: a main room that served as living and dining, a kitchen the width of a large person standing sideways, a bedroom with a window that faced the courtyard, a bathroom with a claw-foot tub that was the apartment's primary luxury and for which she had paid more than she'd intended when she'd signed the lease.

She had lived here for four years, which was the longest she'd lived anywhere since leaving her parents' house at eighteen. The apartment had accumulated her in the way apartments do when you stay long enough — small interventions that were each trivial and that together composed something. The print above the kitchen door that she'd bought at the Marché d'Aligre for eight euros because the colors were exactly right. The row of cookbooks on the shelf above the stove that she used rarely but liked having visible, the way you like having certain things in your field of vision without quite being able to explain why. The photographs on the small table in the main room — her mother and father at the sea, Carmen in uniform with the platoon, the Chamonix photograph that was also on

Charlie's desk in Las Vegas, a fact she found symmetrically painful in a way she couldn't entirely account for.

She was going to leave this apartment eventually. This was not new knowledge — she'd known it since she'd signed the four-year lease, which was itself an unusual commitment for her, someone who'd always moved with the slight restlessness of a person looking for the place that was fully right rather than nearly right. Paris was nearly right. It had been nearly right for four years with no sign of becoming more than nearly. She liked Paris deeply and lived in it as though it were temporary, which was also part of the accounting.

She made coffee. She stood at the courtyard window with the coffee and looked at the grey morning and thought about Nevada.

She had been to Nevada twice — once with Charlie to Las Vegas, which was Nevada in the way that Times Square was New York, which was to say it was an extreme expression of something real that was also, if you drove twenty minutes in any direction, nothing like the thing it claimed to represent. And once, three years ago, when Charlie had taken her to the Valley of Fire, which was an hour outside the city and which was, she had thought then and still thought, one of the most serious landscapes she had ever stood inside. The red sandstone formations rising from the flat valley floor with no preamble, no transition, no apology for their scale. She had stood in it and felt, for forty minutes, very precisely located — not small exactly, but accurately sized, which was something different and something she rarely felt in the city.

She wanted that feeling. She wanted to be accurately sized for a few days before she did the thing she needed to do.

She finished the coffee. She washed the cup. She carried her bags down the five flights and called a taxi and sat in it watching Paris go past the window — the Boulevard Saint-Germain, the Pont de la Tournelle, the river doing what the river always did, which was to move through the city as though the city had been built around it as an afterthought, as though the river had been there first and had graciously allowed the rest of it. She watched it and felt the thing she always felt leaving Paris, which was: I will miss this, and underneath that, quieter: but I am ready to go.

The flight was nine hours and forty minutes, which she had learned over many transatlantic crossings to treat as a specific category of time — neither day nor night, neither productive nor restful, a suspended state in which the normal accounts of how time was being spent were temporarily suspended. She had a window seat, as she always requested, and she looked at the clouds below the plane for a while and then she looked at nothing and let her mind do what it did in this category of time, which was to move without her specifically directing it, from one thing to another, following connections that she would not necessarily have followed in the clear daylight.

She thought about the moment in January.

It had not been a dramatic moment. That was the thing about it — she had been prepared, in some theoretical way, for a dramatic moment, for something that arrived with the weight of significance she could point to afterward and say: there. That was when. But the moment in January had been a Thursday evening in the apartment of a man named Olivier, who worked in architectural preservation and who had been trying to have dinner with her for two months and whom she had finally agreed to have dinner with and whose apartment was in the Marais and very beautiful in the way that architects' apartments were often beautiful — considered, precise, everything exactly where it should be.

They had eaten and had wine and talked about his current project, which was the restoration of a nineteenth-century arcade in the third arrondissement, and she had found him intelligent and interested and interesting, and at some point in the evening she had understood that she could, if she chose, stay. That the evening contained that possibility and that he was aware of it and that the choice was entirely hers.

She had gone home.

Not because she hadn't found him interesting. Not because the evening hadn't been good. But because sitting across the table from Olivier in his considered apartment she had become aware, with a clarity that was almost uncomfortable in its precision, of the specific quality of Charlie's attention. The way he listened — not politely, not strategically, but completely, the way you listen when you are genuinely trying to understand another person rather than positioning yourself in relation to them. She had been with Charlie for three years and she had always known he listened this way but she had not, until that Thursday evening in the Marais, understood what it meant to be in a room with someone who didn't.

She had gone home and called Charlie and they had talked for an hour about nothing in particular, the easy inventory of their separate days, and she had not told him about the dinner because there was nothing to tell — she had had dinner and come home, which was the complete story — but she had felt, after she hung up, something she could only describe as relief, which immediately raised the question of what she had been afraid of and whether she was relieved because she'd chosen correctly or because she'd avoided something she wasn't ready for.

She had not resolved this question. She had, instead, spent three months carrying it alongside everything else, taking it out occasionally to look at it and putting it back when looking at it became uncomfortable.

The plane crossed the Atlantic. Below the window the clouds moved.

She thought: Charlie deserves to know what he has.

She thought: I am not sure I have been showing him.

She thought, after a while, of Carmen — who had told her once, on a camping trip two years ago, sitting by a fire while Charlie and Matt argued about the best route for the next day's hike:

"You know what your problem is? You're so busy deciding whether you're happy that you forget to actually be it."

Sophia had said, with the precision she brought to her own defense:

"That's an oversimplification."

And Carmen had said:

"Yes."

And that had been the end of the conversation, which was how Carmen operated — she said the thing and then she left you with it, without the cushioning of qualification or the softening of context, because Carmen had decided that the cushioning and the softening were your job, not hers.

Sophia had been annoyed at the time. She thought about it regularly.

She slept for three hours somewhere over the middle of the ocean and woke up with the specific alertness of someone who has slept hard and briefly and whose body is not sure where it is. The cabin was dim. The man in the aisle seat was asleep with his mouth slightly open in the way that made everyone look temporary. She looked out the window. Below the clouds the Atlantic was a dark nothing, which was accurate — it was a dark nothing down there, miles of dark water, and they were flying over it in a pressurized tube at thirty-five thousand feet because someone had decided, a hundred years ago, that this was a reasonable thing to attempt, and had been right.

She thought about what she was going to say to Charlie.

She had rehearsed it, the way she rehearsed things — not scripted, not word for word, but mapped, the way you map a route: the starting point, the general direction, the significant turns, the destination. The destination was honesty, which was always easier to locate on the map than in the territory. In the territory there were his eyes, which were the eyes of someone who trusted her completely and who would receive what she said with the same open-handed faith he brought to everything, and she would have to watch that faith process what she was telling it, and she did not know, with any precision, what that would look like or how she would manage it.

She had been managing things for three years — managing the distance, which was real and logistically complex; managing the question of the future, which neither of them asked directly but which was present in every conversation about the present; managing her own ambivalence, which she was aware she did not have the right to manage indefinitely. Ambivalence was a private condition. After a certain amount of time it became something you owed to the other person.

She was aware that she had passed that point.

The cabin brightened as they crossed into the day. The flight attendant came through with coffee and she took it and held it with both hands and looked at the brightening window and thought about the desert. The Valley of Fire. The feeling of being accurately sized.

She thought: use this trip. Watch him.

This was Carmen's voice in her head, which was where Carmen often was — practical, unadorned, cutting through the parts of her own thinking that were decorative rather than structural.

Use this trip. Watch him. Remember why you said yes in the first place.

She had said yes three years ago at a restaurant in the eighth arrondissement, a Tuesday in October, rain on the windows and the particular amber warmth that Parisian restaurants had in October, the way they turned the rain outside into something you were grateful to be sheltered from. He had not asked the question in the way she had expected — she had expected, if she was honest with herself, something grander, something prepared, because Charlie was someone who prepared things. Instead he had simply looked at her across the table at a moment in the conversation that was not remarkable, a Tuesday in October, and said:

"I'd like us to be together. Properly. I know the distance is real and I know you have your life here and I know it's complicated. I just thought you should know that's what I want, and you should decide accordingly."

And she had said yes. Not immediately — she had looked at him for a moment first, long enough that he'd started to say something else, and she'd said:

"Yes. Alright."

And he had smiled the way he smiled when he was genuinely happy, which was not the social smile — the social smile was wide and easy and very Charlie — but the other one, the smaller one, the one that happened before he could compose himself, and she had thought:

there it is. That's what this is.

She had not stopped thinking it was what it was. That was not the problem. The problem was the distance, which was real, and the question of the future, which was unresolved, and the accumulation of small absences that distance produced — not his fault, not hers, simply the arithmetic of two people living on different continents who loved each other and could not quite solve the problem of the geography.

She drank her coffee. The Atlantic finished itself and the eastern seaboard appeared below the clouds, grey-green and intricate, the coastline she recognized from every transatlantic approach, always a relief.

She thought: he deserves the honest version.

She thought: I don't know yet what the honest version says.

She put her head against the window and closed her eyes and listened to the engine noise, which was the sound of a great deal of force being applied in a single direction, and thought that this was probably also a description of what she needed to do, and that the force was available to her, and that the direction was the thing she was still finding.

Charlie was at the curb when she came out of baggage claim. He always arrived early — she had never once exited an airport to find him not already there, not in three years, and she had never told him what this meant to her because it was the kind of thing that was easier to receive than to acknowledge. He was leaning against his car in the particular way he leaned against things, arms crossed, watching the doors with the alert patience of someone who has learned that the thing they're waiting for is worth waiting for.

He saw her and climbed off the car and came toward her and she felt the thing she always felt when she saw him after an absence — a warmth that was not excitement exactly but something older and quieter, a recognition, the specific pleasure of a face you know well arriving in your field of vision after it has been absent from it.

He opened his arms and she went into them and he held her the way he always held her, with his whole self, unguardedly, and she put her face against his neck and breathed and let the flight and the accounting and the three a.m. honesty and all of it recede for a moment into the background where it could be held while she held this.

He went in for the lips. She pivoted, gave him both cheeks, which was habit and also, tonight, distance management, and she felt him receive it with the particular stillness that meant he had noticed and chosen not to say anything.

"I've missed you so much," he said.

"Thank you," she said. "Now we can enjoy some time together, yes?"

She heard it as she said it — the slight formal quality, the

yes that was a linguistic habit but that tonight sounded like something else, like a question she was putting to herself rather than a punctuation mark. She got in the car. She touched the dashboard because it was new and she liked new things and because touching something concrete helped when the things in your head were not concrete.

"I love your car," she said.

"Last one on the lot," he said. "Lucky timing."

She looked at him. He was smiling at the road, and the smile was the social one, the wide easy one, and underneath it she could see, because she knew him well enough to see it, the careful architecture of someone who was being cheerful on purpose.

She thought: three days.

She thought: watch him.

She thought: you already know why you said yes. Stop pretending you need the desert to remember.

She looked out the window at the Nevada afternoon — the flat sprawl of the valley, the mountains ringing it at a distance, the sky very large and very blue and doing nothing subtle. She thought about the Valley of Fire and the feeling of being accurately sized.

She looked out the window at the valley as Charlie drove.

This was always the part she found strangest — the return to the familiar after the familiar had been absent long enough to become strange again. Las Vegas from the highway was Las Vegas from the highway: the signs, the density, the way the city insisted on itself against the desert with a completeness that left no room for ambiguity. She had been here seven times in three years. She knew the drive from the airport. She knew the specific quality of the afternoon light on the mountains east of the city, which was a better quality of light than the city deserved, or perhaps exactly the quality the desert always had regardless of what had been built in it.

She had been watching Charlie since they left the airport. Not conspicuously. She had always been a person who observed without appearing to observe, a skill developed over a childhood in which reading the room was a survival competency and refined over years of working with clients who needed to feel that they were not being assessed while they were being assessed. She had been watching the way he held the steering wheel — both hands, easy, the specific comfortable relationship to a car that came from years of living in a city where you drove everywhere. She had been watching the way he talked, which was the way Charlie always talked when she had just arrived from a long absence: a little too fast, covering a lot of ground quickly, the conversational equivalent of showing someone a house room by room so that the showing feels complete and no one has to say the thing that is not in any room.

She knew what was not in any room. She had known since January.

She thought: he has been managing his happiness since January. He has been calibrating it in my presence the way he always calibrated it in my presence when he sensed that the calibration was necessary, and it has been necessary since January, and he has been doing this for four months without asking why.

This was the thing she had been carrying that was the heaviest. Not the ambivalence — the ambivalence had been real and she was not going to pretend it hadn't been real, because pretending was not her way and also because whatever came next had to be built on what was actually true, not on a revised version of the past that was more comfortable. But heavier than the ambivalence was the knowledge that he had seen the change in her and had chosen, four months ago, to wait for her rather than press her, and that the choosing had not been passivity but the specific active generosity of someone who understood that the space to arrive at your own conclusion was a thing you could give to someone you loved.

He had given her the space. She had spent four months in it. She had arrived.

"Last one on the lot," he said, about the car. "Lucky timing."

She looked at him. He was smiling at the road with the social smile, the wide easy one, and underneath it she could see the architecture of someone being careful.

She thought: not much longer. She thought: tonight, if there's a moment. She thought: or the desert. The desert will make room for it.

She reached over and touched the back of his hand where it rested on the gear shift. Just briefly. A point of contact, nothing more. She felt him go slightly still under the touch, the same way he went still when he was receiving something he hadn't expected and was deciding what to do with it.

She took her hand back.

"Good," she said, about the car. "It suits you."

He looked at her, just for a second, at the light. She looked back. Something passed between them that was not a conversation and not nothing — the specific frequency of two people who knew each other well enough to communicate in registers below speech.

Then the light changed and he drove and she looked out the window at the mountains.

She thought: be honest. Be honest and be kind and do it in person and let whatever happens happen.

"Tell me what we're doing this weekend," she said, and he told her, and she listened, and she was here.

FIVE

The Blade Check

Carmen

Carmen

The first thing she did when she got home was check the blade.

Not because it needed checking.. The knife had been on her person or in her kit for fourteen months and she knew its condition the way she knew the condition of everything she depended on — continuously, without needing to look. The blade was fine. The blade was always fine because she maintained it the way she maintained everything: on a schedule, without waiting to be reminded, without letting the small deteriorations accumulate into a problem. She checked it anyway, standing in the doorway of the apartment she hadn't been inside in fourteen months, her backpack still on her shoulder, the hallway behind her smelling of the building's particular combination of old carpet and other people's cooking and the faint chemical note of the cleaning service that came on Thursdays.

She checked the blade because it was the first familiar thing available to her, and the familiar thing was what you reached for when you stepped back into a life you'd left in a specific configuration and returned to find had continued without you, rearranging itself slightly in the way that things rearrange themselves when no one is watching them — not dramatically, just enough to remind you that the world was not, in fact, paused while you were away.

The apartment was as she'd left it. She had a cleaning service come once a month while she was deployed — the same service as the building, arranged through her neighbor Mrs. Petrakis, who had a key and who checked the mail and who had sent her, over fourteen months, eleven emails, each containing a photograph of the mail pile with a brief inventory of its contents, which Carmen had found both touching and slightly melancholy, the mail of an absent person being such a complete record of how completely the world continued to issue demands regardless of whether you were available to receive them.

She set her backpack down. She did not sit. She stood in the main room and looked at it — the couch, the small table, the bookshelf that was organized by size rather than subject because she had never been able to commit to organizing by subject, the categories always seeming arbitrary at the edges. The photograph on the dresser in the bedroom doorway. She didn't look at that yet.

She went to the kitchen and ran the tap until the water was cold and drank two full glasses standing at the sink. Then she went to the bathroom and stood in the shower for eleven minutes, which was longer than she usually showered, but the water in the forward operating base had always been either too cold or too hot and never quite the right temperature to feel like anything other than a functional necessity, and this shower was exactly the right temperature, and she let it be that for eleven minutes.

She dressed. She went to the bedroom doorway and looked at the photograph.

Her platoon, eighteen months ago, before the deployment that had just ended. Twenty-two people in full gear, squinting into the desert sun of the training base in the Mojave, arranged in the way military photographs were always arranged — tallest at the back, shortest at the front, everyone's expression calibrated to something between serious and not-serious, the expression of people who had been told not to smile and were trying to comply while also being human. Carmen was in the second row, off-center. She knew everyone in the photograph by name, by the specific way they moved, by the particular quality of their attention under pressure — who got faster when things went wrong and who got slower, who needed to talk and who needed silence, who you put on the left flank and who you kept close.

Eight of the twenty-two were still there. The rest had rotated out, transferred, in two cases been injured, in one case been killed — Specialist Torres, twenty-four years old, in the fourth month of the deployment, an IED on a road they'd driven seventeen times before without incident. She had written the letter to his parents herself, which was not required of her but which she had done because she had a theory, arrived at over three deployments, that the letters written by people who actually knew the person were read differently than the letters written by people who were performing the knowledge of a person they didn't have. She had written two such letters in her career. She hoped to write no more, which was the same hope she'd had before writing each of them and which experience had not yet been able to extinguish.

She looked at Torres in the photograph. Second from the left in the back row. He was laughing at something that had happened a half-second before the shutter, his face caught in the residue of it, the laugh mostly gone but not completely. She had always liked that about the photograph — that it had caught him in that particular moment, the laugh receding, the face settling back into the serious expression he wore for most things but not quite there yet. He looked, in the photograph, like someone between two states.

She went and made coffee.

Charlie had texted while she was in the shower:

Hey! Welcome back. So glad you're home safe. Trip is Friday — you're in if you want to be in. No pressure. Sophie is coming. Matt too. Desert, hot springs, Leatherman Peak (Matt's thing). Four days. Let me know.

She read it twice. She thought about Charlie — his texts were always like this, the information and the warmth and the assurance that there was no pressure, which was itself a kind of pressure but a gentle kind, the pressure of someone who wanted you to come and was willing to not-want-it-too-openly in the service of giving you room.

She texted back:

I'm in.

She thought about adding something. She didn't add anything. The two words said what needed saying.

She drank her coffee and looked out the window at the street below. It was a Thursday morning in Las Vegas, which was a category of time with a specific quality — not the full weekend energy and not the dead-center weekday flatness, something in between, the city at a moderate register. She had grown up here. She had lived here her whole life except for the time she'd spent deployed and the year she'd spent at Fort Benning for training, and she'd come back each time to the same apartment on the same street and resumed the civilian version of herself with the practiced fluency of someone who had learned to move between registers without losing either one.

This was not as simple as it sounded. She knew people who couldn't do it — who came back from deployment and found that the civilian version of themselves had become inaccessible, sealed off by what the deployed version had experienced, and who then lived in a kind of anteroom between the two, belonging fully to neither. She had known this was a risk going in. She had spent considerable effort making sure it didn't happen to her, which she understood was a strange thing to say — that you could effort your way out of certain psychological outcomes — but which she believed was at least partially true, in the same way that you could effort your way out of certain physical outcomes if you were honest about what was coming and prepared for it rather than hoping it wouldn't arrive.

What she had not been prepared for, and what she had not been able to effort her way out of, was the specific quality of the quiet.

The apartment was quiet. The street outside was quiet in the way that streets in residential Las Vegas neighborhoods were quiet — a background hum, traffic at a distance, the sound of someone's air conditioning unit on the building next door. It was, by any objective measure, not quiet. But after fourteen months in a place where silence meant either that nothing was happening or that something was about to happen and you didn't know which, the undifferentiated quiet of a Thursday morning in her apartment had a quality she couldn't quite categorize. It wasn't peaceful exactly. It was legible. She could read it. She knew what it meant, which was: nothing is happening, and nothing is about to happen, and this is the correct state of affairs.

She was working on believing that.

She called Sophie at noon.

Sophie answered on the second ring, which meant she was at her desk and not in a meeting, because Sophie in a meeting let everything go to voicemail with the completeness of someone who had decided that meetings deserved your undivided attention and voicemail could wait.

"You're home," Sophie said. Not a question — she'd seen Carmen's text to the group thread, the brief

landed, customs, see you Friday that Carmen had sent from the baggage claim.

"I'm home," Carmen said.

"How was it?"

"Fine."

Sophie paused. This was one of the things Carmen valued about Sophie — she knew when

fine meant fine and when it meant something that wasn't fine but that the person saying it wasn't ready to discuss, and she received both versions without pressing, which was a rarer quality than it should have been.

"Are you sleeping?" Sophie asked.

"Yes."

"Are you eating?"

"I ate on the plane."

"Carmen."

"I'll eat. I'm going to the market this afternoon."

"Good." A beat. "I'm glad you're back. I've been thinking about you."

"How's Paris?"

"Wet. Cold. The usual March."

"Are you looking forward to the desert?"

A pause that was slightly different from Sophie's usual pauses. "Yes," she said. "I think I need it."

Carmen noted the pause and the particular quality of the

need and filed it without comment. Sophie would say what she needed to say when she was ready to say it, and pressing before that point produced not the information but a more defended version of the non-information, which was less useful than the original silence.

"I'll see you Friday," Carmen said.

"Friday," Sophie said. "I'm glad you're back, cherie. Really."

After the call Carmen sat at her small kitchen table with the empty coffee cup and thought about Sophie's pause. She thought about the three years she'd been watching Charlie and Sophie from the outside — the way Charlie looked at Sophie, which was the way people looked at things they were afraid of losing; the way Sophie looked at Charlie, which was warmer and more complicated and which had been changing, in Carmen's assessment, since approximately January, when something had shifted in the register of Sophie's references to him, a slight increase in the carefulness of what she said and didn't say, which in Carmen's experience meant that the things not said had become more significant than the things said.

She hoped they worked it out.

She thought this with the sincerity she brought to most things: completely, without much drama. She liked Charlie. She had always liked Charlie, in the way you liked people who were genuinely good at being a person — who had figured out, through some combination of temperament and effort, how to be in a room with other people in a way that made the room better rather than more complicated. This was rarer than it should have been. She appreciated it.

She hoped they worked it out. She did not think about what would happen if they didn't, because what would happen if they didn't was that Sophie would be sad for a while and then not sad, and Charlie would be sad for a while and then not sad, and the four of them would rearrange around the change the way friends rearranged around changes, which was with a combination of loyalty and tact and the ongoing negotiation of which things needed to be said and which were better left unsaid. She had been through this before with other configurations of people. It was manageable. Most things were.

She went to the market in the afternoon. She went to the gym. She cooked — not a complicated meal, just rice and black beans and the chicken that had been in her freezer since before she'd left, which she'd defrosted in the morning with the vague plan of cooking something, which she now executed with the mechanical efficiency of someone who cooked not for pleasure but for maintenance.

While she ate she thought about Matt.

She did not, as a rule, think about Matt at length. She had a policy, arrived at approximately two years ago and maintained with the discipline she brought to most things she'd decided to maintain, of not dwelling on things she had no intention of doing anything about. Matt was one of those things. He was in the category of: acknowledged, filed, not acted upon. She had put him there deliberately, and she kept him there deliberately, and she was aware that keeping him there required more deliberate effort on some days than others, which was itself information she received and logged and did not particularly act on.

The situation was simple enough. She liked Matt. She had liked Matt since the camping trip three years ago when she'd watched him build a fire in the rain with the focused competence of someone who had decided the rain was not a relevant variable, and had thought:

hm, and then filed that thought under its proper heading and continued with her evening. She was not someone who acted on hm. She was someone who noted it and moved on. She had been noting and moving on for two years.

The complicating factor was not the liking, which was straightforward. The complicating factor was that Matt did not, in her assessment, know she existed in that category. She was not sure he had a that-category in the way she meant it — not because he was incapable, but because Matt's attention was organized around different things, and those things absorbed him so completely that the space available for the other kind of attention was limited. This was not a criticism. She found it, if anything, clarifying. A man whose attention was that organized was a man who, if he ever pointed it at you, would point it completely.

She ate her rice and beans and chicken and thought about this and then stopped thinking about it because thinking about it for more than a certain amount of time produced no new information and consumed attention she could spend on other things.

She washed her plate. She cleaned the kitchen in the precise way she cleaned all spaces — not compulsively, but completely, starting at one end and finishing at the other, leaving nothing half-done.

She went to bed at nine-thirty, which was earlier than she usually went to bed in civilian life but which her body had decided was the correct time regardless of what she thought about it, and she did not argue with her body about these things because her body was right more often than she was.

She lay in the dark.

The apartment was quiet — legibly quiet, the quiet that meant nothing was happening. She lay in it and did her usual inventory: what needed to be done tomorrow, what needed to be done by Friday, whether she had the right gear for the desert, whether the butterfly knife needed any maintenance before the trip — it didn't, she'd maintained it before packing, she always maintained her equipment before packing — and then she let the inventory go and lay in the quiet without filling it.

She thought about the desert.

She had been to Nevada desert a dozen times and found it, each time, to be the kind of landscape that didn't argue with you. It had a quality she could only describe as indifference, but not the cold kind — not hostile indifference but simply the indifference of something very old and very large that had been there before you arrived and would be there after you left and had no particular stake in what happened to you in the interim. She found this restful. After fourteen months in a landscape that was full of stakes — where every variable had potential consequences and every decision was load-bearing — the desert's lack of stakes felt like the correct corrective.

Four days. Sophie and Charlie and Matt and the desert and the hot springs and whatever Matt needed to do on Leatherman Peak, which was the kind of thing Matt needed to do and which she respected even when she didn't entirely understand the specific appeal of climbing a mountain in order to qualify for a club in order to get access to an expedition in order to jump off the highest point in the world in a suit.

She had told him she wanted to try it herself.

She had meant it.

She closed her eyes. The quiet continued to be legible. Outside, far away, a car passed. The air conditioning unit on the building next door cycled on and hummed its neutral hum.

She thought: four days.

She thought: it'll be fine.

She slept.

She went to the market in the afternoon. She went with a list — she always had a list, the civilian habit she'd never lost, the need to know before she arrived at a place what she was there for. The list was reasonable: rice, black beans, chicken, coffee, the individual cheese things wrapped in wax that she had mentioned to Charlie in passing once and which had since appeared at every camping trip, as though he'd filed it under permanent preferences rather than offhand comment. She bought two. She stood in the cheese aisle of the Vons on Eastern Avenue for a moment looking at them and feeling, unexpectedly and briefly, the specific texture of being looked after.

She moved on. She bought what was on the list and nothing else, which was the discipline she'd arrived at over three deployments of managing resources carefully and which applied to groceries the same way it applied to ammunition — you took what you needed and you didn't take what you didn't need, because excess was weight and weight had consequences.

At the register she got behind an elderly woman with a very full cart and a very specific system for unloading it, which involved setting each item on the belt in a particular orientation and then checking each one after. The woman took her time. The cashier waited. Carmen waited. The woman ahead of her did not apologize for her pace and Carmen respected this completely.

She thought about the pace of things here.

This was the transition she always had to make — the recalibration from a tempo that was high and load-bearing and oriented entirely toward the immediate problem, to a tempo that was lower and more diffuse and that had room in it for an elderly woman's particular system for unloading a grocery cart. Both tempos were real. Both required something from you. The first required alertness and the compression of everything irrelevant. The second required patience and the willingness to let irrelevant things exist without classifying them as threats.

She had learned, returning from each deployment, that the second tempo was harder. Not because it was worse — it was better, unambiguously, by every metric she had — but because the first tempo was one she knew how to do, and the second was one she had to relearn each time, the way you relearned the feel of a language you hadn't spoken in a year, the grammar still there but the ease of it gone.

The woman ahead of her finished. Carmen unloaded her own cart. The cashier was young, maybe twenty, with the specific quality of someone who was here between things — between school and the next thing, between one version and another. She smiled at Carmen without particular meaning and rang everything through.

"Anything else?"

"No," Carmen said. "Thank you."

She meant it. It was a small transaction and she had made thousands of them and the gratitude for the smallness of it — for the transaction that was just a transaction, for the cashier who was just a cashier, for the afternoon that was just an afternoon — was real and present and she received it without analysis.

She carried her groceries to her car. She sat for a moment before starting it.

Around her the parking lot did what parking lots did — people moving through it, cart return, a child in a stroller pulling at a balloon, a man talking on his phone beside a red truck. The ordinary machinery of an ordinary Thursday. She watched it with the particular attention she had trained into herself, which was the attention that assessed everything and registered it as information, and then she let it just be a parking lot on a Thursday afternoon in Las Vegas, Nevada, and she was home, and she was going to the desert on Friday, and everything was fine.

She started the car.

She had learned, over three deployments, to sleep when sleep was available, without negotiating with it. Sleep was available. She took it.

SIX

All of Us

Matt

Matt

He was the last one ready, which was not a thing that happened to him often. He was ready at six. He was packed at six. The gear was organized on the porch in the order it needed to be loaded — heaviest items first, tent and sleeping gear in the middle, the day-use things accessible at the top — and he had done this at six and then had three hours to stand in his kitchen and drink coffee and not need to do anything else, which was the consequence of being the kind of person who was ready at six.

Charlie arrived at nine-fifteen, which was fifteen minutes late, which was Charlie being slightly late rather than significantly late, a distinction that mattered. He came around the back of the SUV and looked at the gear on the porch and said, "Help me with that will you?" meaning that he wanted Matt to carry it to the vehicle, which was also Charlie — the comfortable assumption that people wanted to help, delivered without embarrassment, in the same register as asking someone to pass the salt.

Matt helped. The gear loaded cleanly. He had a system.

Sophie was in the passenger seat with the window down, which she always did when weather permitted — she liked air on her face, which was a small and specific thing he knew about her from three years of being in Charlie's vicinity. She had her sunglasses on and she tipped them at him when he came around to say hello, which was the Sophie greeting — the small elegant gesture that conveyed warmth without expenditure.

"Morning, pretty girl," he said.

"Bonjour, pretty boy," she said. "How's France these days?"

"I'll let you know when I get there."

He opened the back of the SUV. The cargo area contained: Charlie's camping gear, a telescope in a leather case, two suitcases that were Sophie's, a long wooden box he didn't recognize. He looked at it. He looked at the cargo area as a whole. He made the rapid calculation he made every time he loaded a vehicle for a multi-day trip, which was: weight distribution, access order, volume versus necessity.

"What's in the wooden box?" he said.

"A surprise," Sophie said. "Be good and I'll tell you."

He thought about pressing and decided against it. Sophie's surprises were always either genuinely surprising or designed to appear surprising while being quite ordinary, and in either case the appropriate response was to wait. He loaded the vehicle efficiently and got in.

★★★

Carmen's building was twelve minutes from his house. He'd been there twice before — once for a dinner party she'd thrown the year before her last deployment, which had featured very good food and very sparse conversation because Carmen's idea of a dinner party was food and people who didn't need to fill silence, which had suited Matt considerably and which had apparently been the whole design — and once to help her move a piece of furniture that required two people, which Carmen had approached with the same focused efficiency she brought to everything and which had taken eleven minutes including the parking.

He waited in the SUV while Charlie went to the door. Sophie had the window down again. She was looking at Carmen's building with the particular attention she brought to the physical details of people's lives — the neighborhood, the building, the small contextual facts that told her something she hadn't been told directly. Matt had noticed this about her over three years: she read spaces the way some people read faces.

Carmen came out before Charlie reached the door, which was typical. She had her backpack and no other bags, which was also typical. She moved at a pace that was not hurried but covered ground efficiently, the gait of someone whose relationship to walking was functional rather than leisurely.

She saw Sophie and a real smile happened on her face — the one that was different from the public-facing expression Carmen usually wore, which was neutral with a slight forward quality, the expression of someone who was paying attention and not particularly concerned with being caught doing it. The real smile was something she apparently reserved for Sophie and, Matt had noticed, occasionally for moments when something struck her as genuinely funny in a way she wasn't going to announce.

He got out and they did the version of a greeting that he and Carmen did, which was:

"Hey, shorty."

"Hey, meathead." She looked at him. "How was the climb this morning?"

"Could've gone better."

"There's always next time."

He took her backpack without asking. She let him, which was how it worked — she didn't ask for help and she didn't refuse it when it appeared, and he gave it without announcement because announcing it would make it a thing when it wasn't a thing.

She climbed into the back seat next to Sophie. He got in.

Charlie, from the driver's seat: "Everybody ready?"

Three people said nothing, which was yes.

The drive north out of Las Vegas was one of the things Matt liked about living here — the way the city ended. Most cities tapered: the density decreased, the buildings got smaller, the commercial strips thinned out into suburbs and then exurbs and then eventually something that was not quite the country. Las Vegas ended differently. It ended. You drove through the valley and then you were past it and the desert was simply there, offering no transition, no apology for its scale. The highway went from four lanes to two. The road stretched ahead into the distance and the distance was very large and the mountains ringed it on all sides and the sky above was the specific blue of the Nevada desert in the morning, a blue that had no warmth in it but a great deal of clarity.

He liked clarity. He found it restful in the way that some people found warm rooms restful — as a corrective to whatever the previous condition had been.

Classic rock on the radio. Charlie drove slightly faster than he needed to, which was Charlie's way of managing a schedule — he had a destination time and a plan for arriving at it and the plan expressed itself, unconsciously, as a slight compression of everything on the approach. Matt had pointed this out once, three years ago, and Charlie had been genuinely surprised and had said,

"Do I? I don't think I do," and then driven at exactly the same speed for the rest of the trip. He had not mentioned it again.

Sophie said he was driving fast. Charlie explained about Wells by eight. Sophia asked why Wells. Matt explained about Leatherman Peak and Club Nine.

Sophie said: "And then what — have a beer with the other mountain men?"

He had heard this kind of response before and had developed a method for receiving it, which was to give the actual answer rather than the defensive version. He explained about the Everest expedition and what he wanted to do off the summit. He explained it clearly and in a specific amount of detail — enough to be understood, not enough to invite the extended skepticism that too much detail produced.

"That is genuinely one of the dumbest things I've ever heard," Sophie said, with a quality in her voice that was not hostile. She said dumb the way some people said remarkable.

"I kind of want to do it myself," Carmen said from the back seat.

He turned to look at her. She was looking out the window at the desert going past, her expression neutral, her statement apparently complete.

"You're not invited," he said.

"I don't need an invitation." Still looking out the window. "I'd race you. Be the first woman to jump."

"Ha."

She looked at him then, briefly. The expression was the one she used when she meant something she wasn't going to underline.

He turned back to the road. The desert did its thing — the scrubland, the rock formations, the occasional Joshua tree standing with the particular dignity of something that had been here much longer than anything around it. He thought about what Carmen had said and whether she meant it. He thought she meant it. He filed this under the heading of things that were interesting and left it there.

Charlie threatened to turn the car around. Carmen and Matt both noted that they hadn't started it. Charlie said they'd both started it. This was not accurate and also probably true.

The rest stop appeared at two-thirty, a low concrete building beside a gas station beside a parking lot that was mostly empty in the way that Nevada rest stops were mostly empty on a Friday afternoon — a couple of truckers, one family with children at the far end of the lot, a man walking a very old dog in slow circles near the grass strip. Charlie announced chips and Sophia announced coffee and the car deposited them at the entrance and Matt stayed in the passenger seat because he didn't need anything and there was something agreeable about sitting in a stationary vehicle in the desert with the window down and the engine off, the heat dry and still outside and the shadow of the overhang across the hood.

Carmen stayed too. He heard the door open and close on her side — not getting out, just settling.

They sat in the quiet for a moment. The man with the old dog was completing another slow circuit. The dog moved with the careful deliberateness of an animal that had learned to allocate its energy.

"How long were you over there?" he said.

"Fourteen months."

"You good?"

"Yes."

He waited. He had found, over several years of knowing Carmen, that waiting produced more than asking. She was not someone who withheld — she was someone who organized, who decided what was ready to be said and said it when it was ready, and pressing before that point produced the same result as pressing on a gate that was still latching: resistance and a slight backwards movement.

"The quiet is different," she said. "Coming back. I can read it now. I know what it means when it's quiet. I'm working on being okay with that."

He thought about this. He thought about what it meant to be in a place where silence was information rather than simply silence, and what it did to you to live in that place for fourteen months, and what happened to the silence-reading faculty when you came back to a place where silence was, most of the time, nothing.

"Makes sense," he said.

"Does it?"

"Yeah."

She looked at him. He looked at the dog completing its circuit. The dog's owner had stopped moving and was standing in the middle of the lot with his face tilted up toward the sun, eyes closed, not doing anything in particular except being in the sun.

"That thing you want to do off Everest," Carmen said.

"Yeah."

"I meant what I said. About the race."

"I know you did."

"Would you actually want that? Someone there with you for it?"

He thought about this honestly. He had always imagined the jump alone — the summit, the suit, the step off. He had not imagined a second person. He tried it now, the image of Carmen in the frame somewhere, and found that it changed the image without wrecking it. Changed it in a way he didn't have language for yet.

"Maybe," he said.

Carmen nodded. Filed it. They sat for another minute in the good quiet of two people who didn't need to fill silence.

Charlie and Sophie came back. Charlie had chips and two waters. Sophie had coffee, both hands around the cup, and the expression of someone who had found the one necessary thing.

They got back on the highway.

The light changed around four. This was the thing about desert light in the late afternoon — it didn't dim the way it dimmed elsewhere. It shifted registers instead, going from the high clear blue of midday to something lower and warmer, the sun moving to an angle where the rock faces caught it differently, where the shadows had length, where the landscape stopped being simply visible and became something more editorial. The Joshua trees cast shadows thirty feet long. The roadside formations went amber and then orange and then, for about ten minutes around five o'clock, a color that didn't translate to language well — something between the rock itself and whatever light existed before the rock.

He watched it. He didn't take photographs. He had learned early that photographs of this kind of light were always slightly wrong — not because the technology failed but because the camera recorded what was there and what was there was not, precisely, the thing he was looking at. The thing he was looking at involved his own presence in it, the light arriving in his eyes from that specific angle at that specific time, and the camera could not include that.

Sophie had fallen asleep against the window. He knew this because he heard her breathing change — slower, with the particular release of someone who has finally allowed themselves to stop being awake. He had noticed, without remarking on it, that she'd been slightly more assembled than usual all day — the performance calibrated slightly higher, the warmth slightly more deliberate. This was probably nothing. He was probably projecting.

Carmen was reading on her phone with the focused absorption she brought to anything she decided to pay attention to. Charlie was driving and occasionally humming along to the radio in the private way he hummed, just under audible, as though he'd forgotten there were other people in the car.

Matt looked at the light. He thought about the traverse.

His sister's question had stayed with him:

maybe you're thinking about it wrong.

He had been treating the sixth move as the problem — the release and the commitment to the sloper — because the sixth move was where he fell. But falling happened at the end of a sequence and sequences had architectures, and the failure of a sequence often lived not at the point of failure but earlier, in some assumption that was made correctly for the first five moves and incorrectly for the sixth. He had been assuming the same footwork through the entire traverse. What if the sixth move required different footwork — not a smear but a heel hook, a subtler weight distribution that committed the body differently to the final hold.

He sat with this. The light continued to change. Outside, the desert was doing what the desert did in this hour, which was to become briefly more itself — the colors more saturated, the distances more legible, the whole landscape organized around the low sun in a way that felt, if you let it, intentional.

Sophie stirred against the window. Didn't wake. Charlie hummed.

Matt thought: heel hook. He thought it felt right. He thought he would know on Thursday whether it felt right in his body the way it felt right in his mind, which were not always the same thing and which the wall was very good at distinguishing between.

The storm announced itself the way storms in the high desert announced themselves — not with gradual overcast but with a sudden change in the sky's quality, the blue going from clear to dense, clouds building in the west with the speed of something that had been gathering elsewhere and had now arrived with its mind made up. By seven o'clock the clouds had taken the upper third of the sky. By seven-thirty they had the rest of it. The radio began to fracture — signal coming and going as the ionosphere did whatever it did in advancing weather, the music swallowing itself and returning changed.

Sophie woke up and noted that he'd said it would be clear all weekend. Charlie said it had been clear when he'd checked. This was true and also beside the point, because weather in the Ruby Mountain foothills was locally generated in ways that no online forecast consistently captured, which Matt knew from four previous trips to this area and which he had not mentioned to Charlie when Charlie had shown him the weather projections because the projections had been good and because mentioning the caveats to good weather forecasts when someone was excited about a trip was exactly the kind of thing that made people not want to invite you on trips.

He should have mentioned it.

The weather service broke through on the radio in a flat official voice: dangerous thunderstorm, flash flood potential, high wind advisory. Charlie asked for the map from the glove box. The map was wrong — two states over, which told you something about how long it had been in the glove box and whether anyone had ever expected to use it. The phone signal went to nothing.

He looked out the window. The clouds were the color of something very decided. The first lightning appeared to the northwest, a branching white against the dark grey, the thunder arriving twelve seconds later — two and a half miles, he calculated automatically, the storm moving southeast at a rate that put it over them in forty minutes or less.

"Sign coming up," he said to Charlie. "Slow down."

The sign read: GREENBRIAR GULCH — 4 MILES.

He had never heard of Greenbriar Gulch. He knew this part of Nevada reasonably well — he'd driven through it a dozen times over the years, had climbed in the foothills to the east, had camped in the valley — and he had no memory of a town by that name. Which meant it was either very small or very disused or both.

Charlie wanted to keep going. Sophie wanted to keep going slower. The lightning came again — closer, the thunder less than ten seconds behind it. And then they came around the curve and the headlights found the water: the flash flood, brown and fast and absolutely definitive, moving across the road with the unhurried confidence of water that had decided the road was its now and was not interested in negotiation.

Charlie stopped. Everyone looked at it.

The flood was three feet deep across the road and moving fast. Fast enough to take the vehicle if they tried it, and the vehicle was large. Matt made the calculation in two seconds and it came out negative.

"We go back to the town," Carmen said from the back seat. It was not a question.

Charlie turned the car around.

The Greenbriar Gulch exit was unmarked except for the sign they'd already passed. The road it deposited them on was the kind of road that existed to connect two places that were both, by the standards of the paved world, not quite places — packed dirt, narrowing, the headlights cutting about thirty feet into the dark before losing confidence. The rain had started in earnest. It hit the windshield in the sudden complete way that desert rain always started, no preliminary, just full volume.

Carmen made the observation about Starbucks. He agreed internally and said nothing.

The road narrowed. The clay went slick. The SUV fishtailed — Charlie corrected, it corrected again, fishtailed again. Matt tracked the corrections in his peripheral attention. Not alarmed yet. Watchful.

"Can we turn around?" Sophie said.

"No room," he said.

This was accurate. The road had narrowed to one vehicle width and there were no turnouts and the vegetation on both sides was close and the terrain on the driver's side dropped away from what he could see of it. Turning around here meant reversing blind in the rain, which was worse than continuing forward at low speed.

"There has to be something ahead," Carmen said. "And if there isn't, we walk back."

This was the correct tactical assessment. He said nothing because she had said it and it didn't need to be said twice.

The rear end swung. Not a fishtail this time — a genuine loss of traction, the back wheels going sideways as the clay gave out, and the vehicle moving off the road's edge in the slow definitive way that physics produced when you ran out of friction. It hit the boulder — a solid, unhurried impact, the kind that meant both the boulder and the vehicle were staying exactly where they were — and then the wheels found mud and found nothing useful in the mud, and they were stopped.

He got out. The rain was cold and immediate. He walked around the vehicle and assessed: rear end embedded in mud, the right rear wheel in the deepest of it, the front wheels on harder ground but the angle wrong for the engine to generate any useful pull. He walked back. He opened the door.

"Charlie," he said.

"I know."

They looked at each other. Seven years of friendship produced, in moments like this, a kind of efficiency — the situation was understood, the options were limited, and the question was simply which of the limited options to take.

"We walk ahead," Matt said. "Find whoever's in the town. Come back with help."

Charlie processed this. "In this."

"In this. It's a mile at most."

"In this," Charlie said again, in the tone of someone confirming a fact they find unbelievable but have decided to accept.

He looked at the dark ahead. He looked at the rain. He looked back at the red lights of the SUV behind them, Sophie and Carmen inside it, and felt the particular discomfort of leaving them there — not fear exactly, more an alertness, the feeling of a variable he wasn't fully in control of.

"We'll be fast," he said.

"Fast," Charlie agreed, and opened his door.

They walked into the dark. The rain was cold and the road was worse on foot than it had looked from the vehicle and the dark was very complete about twenty feet past the headlights. He set his pace and Charlie matched it. Behind them the headlights receded.

Ahead, nothing visible. Ahead, wherever the road went.

He thought about the traverse. The heel hook hypothesis. He thought about it because it was available and because thinking about something solvable was useful when you were in a situation where the immediate problem was simply endurance — rain and mud and dark and the unknown quantity of whatever was at the end of this road.

The town appeared ahead. He stopped.

Gas lamps. Amber light, not electric, burning with a quality that was distinctly not the quality of electric light — a warmth and a movement, a slight variation, the flame's own breath in the glass. The buildings dark. The main street visible in the lamp glow, the mud on it catching the light and returning it changed.

He looked at the mud on the main street. He looked at the road they'd come in on, behind them, where the rain was heavy and the ground was saturated.

The mud on the main street was dry.

He stood in the rain looking at dry mud under gas lamps in a town he'd never heard of, and the traverse left his mind entirely, and something else came in its place — not a feeling he had language for yet, something pre-linguistic, something his body was doing before his mind had caught up.

"Those lamps look old," Charlie said beside him.

"Very old," Matt said.

There was light in one building. A sign above the door that he read twice to make sure he was reading it correctly: THE DRUNKEN COYOTE.

He stood in the rain for another moment. The lamp flames breathed. The dry mud on the main street held its condition with the serenity of something that had no reason to be otherwise.

"Come on," he said.

They walked toward the light.

Part Two: The Town

SEVEN

The Town at Night

Emma --- Greenbriar Gulch, Nevada, 1886

Emma — Greenbriar Gulch, Nevada, 1886

They came back on Thursday, which was three days after she'd first seen them, and she knew they were coming before she heard the horses. This was not intuition in any mystical sense. It was pattern recognition. She had watched, over five years of running the Drunken Coyote, a sufficient number of men in a sufficient number of states of intention that she had developed, without meaning to, something like a catalogue. Men came in wanting drink and warmth and company and she knew what that wanting looked like. Men came in wanting trouble and she knew what that wanted looked like. Men came in with purposes that had nothing to do with drink or warmth or company and they sat apart and spoke to each other in voices too low to carry and she had learned to identify those too.

The three men on Monday had been the last kind. She had known it when she saw them and she had been correct, as she generally was about such things, and she had gone home on Monday night and double-locked the front door and put the rifle within reach of her bed and lain awake for an hour doing the thing she did in her worst moments, which was to assess what she had and what she didn't have and whether what she had was sufficient.

What she had: the rifle, loaded; the barkeep, who was steady; the knowledge of every exit from the building and the time required to reach each one; the sheriff, who was two miles out of town and who had not yet been told what she suspected.

What she didn't have: certainty, which meant she could not go to the sheriff with anything more than a feeling about three travelers who had come in, had one drink, and left without incident.

She had decided to wait one more day. She had not told the sheriff. She had not told anyone. This was the decision she would revisit many times in the days that followed, though revisiting it did not change it — it was the decision she made with the information she had, and the information she had was insufficient, and waiting for sufficient information was often the only reasonable thing to do and was also sometimes the thing that cost you everything.

She heard the horses on Thursday evening at twenty minutes past seven. Three horses, moving at a walk, the particular sound of iron on the dry main street that she had learned to distinguish from the mud-muffled sound of the side roads. She was in her office. The rifle was leaning against the wall. She heard the horses and she put the pen down and she sat for a moment and breathed.

Then she stood up, smoothed her dress, and went out to the bar.

★ ★ ★

The saloon was running at its Thursday evening pace, which was moderate — a dozen men at various stages of the evening's work, which was to say the work of being done with the day and not yet required to sleep through it. Hendricks was at his usual table. The Morrison brothers were at the bar. The piano player was doing something unhurried in the key of F, which was where he tended to settle when there was no particular request. The oil lamps were burning at their evening level, warm and adequate, the shadows behind the tables deep but not oppressive.

She moved to a position behind the bar from which she could see the front door and the side entrance and most of the room. The barkeep caught her eye and she gave him the small nod that meant: alert but normal. He was a man who communicated well in small signals, which was one of the primary reasons she had kept him on four years.

The front door opened.

They came in the same order they had on Monday — the lean one first, Tommy Boy she would later learn his name was, with the rifle across his back and the coiled quality of a spring too long compressed. Then the large one with the red bandana, who they called Frog, a name so wrong for the size of him that she assumed it was a joke that had outlasted its occasion. Then the one who went last because he had learned, over a long and evidently eventful life, that arriving last in a room was a form of authority — that the room oriented to whoever arrived last if that person carried themselves with sufficient weight. This one did. He filled the doorway the way certain men filled doorways, not with physical bulk alone but with something less nameable, a gravitational quality, the sense that the room had reorganized itself around his entrance without being asked.

He had an accent she could now place more precisely than she had on Monday — Irish in its bones, buried under years of the American frontier, the vowels flattened and the consonants hardened by a decade or more of a different country's weather. It was the accent of someone who had left Ireland young and had been moving ever since.

His name, she would eventually learn, was James O'Donnell. She never called him that. She called him nothing at all, because names were a form of acknowledgment and acknowledgment was a form of relationship, and she had no intention of having a relationship with this man of any kind.

They took the same table they had taken on Monday. Away from the lamps. Backs to the wall. Tommy Boy and Frog sat with the particular alertness of men who were covering the room without appearing to cover it. O'Donnell sat facing the bar and looked at her across twenty feet of lamp-lit saloon floor with the same expression she had seen on Monday, the expression of someone doing arithmetic.

She looked back at him for exactly as long as she had looked on Monday, which was one count, and then she looked at the barkeep and said,

"George, check the Elko order, will you?"

This was not a question that required checking. It was a way of indicating to George that she needed him in the back room for a moment. George understood this and went. She followed.

★ ★ ★

"Those three men," she said, in the back room, in a voice pitched for the back room only.

"I know," George said.

"They were here Monday."

"I know."

She looked at him. He was a composed man — forty-three, had worked saloons in three different territories before arriving in Greenbriar Gulch, had seen things she hadn't and had organized them into a working philosophy of professional detachment. He was not detached now. She could read it in the set of his jaw.

"What do you know about them?" she said.

"The big one. I've heard his name."

"Where?"

"Reno, last time I was through. A man named O'Donnell. They say he's been working his way east through the mining towns. Takes what he wants, leaves when it suits him." He paused. "They say the law has been trying to get ahead of him for two years. They say nobody who's gotten in front of him has stayed in one piece long enough to testify."

She absorbed this. "Why didn't you tell me Monday?"

"Monday I wasn't sure. Now I'm sure."

She thought about the sheriff. Two miles out. She thought about sending for him and what would happen in the time it took to get word to him and for him to return, which was a minimum of forty minutes even if she sent right now.

"Go now," she said. "Find Patterson — the boy who runs errands for the mine office. Give him half a dollar and tell him to ride to the sheriff's house and not stop for anything. Tell the sheriff what you told me. Tell him O'Donnell."

"And you?"

"I'll run the bar. If they ask where you are, I'll say you're receiving a delivery."

George looked at her with the expression of a man deciding whether to say the thing he was thinking. He said it: "Miss Rose, if O'Donnell is what they say he is —"

"George."

"Yes, ma'am."

He went out the back. She gave herself three breaths. She went back out to the bar.

The three men had not moved. O'Donnell was watching the room with the patience of someone who was accustomed to waiting and found waiting neither difficult nor unpleasant. Tommy Boy was cleaning his nails with a knife, which she noted as both a display and a threat and also, possibly, just a man cleaning his nails with a knife — the problem with men who displayed threats was that sometimes the display was the whole thing and sometimes it was the announcement of an intention, and you could not always tell which.

Frog was looking at her.

She had known he was looking at her since she came back from the back room, and she had managed it the way she managed all unwanted attention in the saloon, which was by making the thing being looked at less interesting than the things around it. This required a particular quality of motion — not avoidance, which communicated anxiety, but a kind of easy purposefulness, the look of someone too occupied with their own work to notice anyone else's. She moved along the bar filling orders. She kept her back straight and her hands busy and her face in its working expression, which was warm and slightly preoccupied.

Rusty came in at quarter past eight.

He came in the way he always came in, which was with velocity and volume, his voice arriving before the rest of him, already celebrating something she didn't yet know about. She heard him and felt a complicated gratitude — Rusty was a distraction, and distraction was useful, and also Rusty in his current state of apparent excitement was likely to draw the room's attention, which was the opposite of what she needed with three men at a back table who were already paying more attention to the room than was comfortable.

She crossed to him before he could get fully into his stride.

"Well, look who decided to show up," she said, and took him by the arm and walked him down the bar to the quieter end of it. "I thought we might have to send a search party."

He was radiant. She had seen Rusty in many moods over three years — discouraged, philosophical, resigned, moderately drunk — but she had not seen this particular brightness before and she understood immediately what it meant.

"Look here, Miss Rose —" He reached into his coat.

"Rusty." She kept her voice warm and her hand on his arm. "Not here."

He read her meaning and lowered his voice to what was, for Rusty, a moderate register. He told her about the stream he'd found, the pool of deep blue water, the sand at the bottom of it. He was not able to fully contain his excitement, which was understandable — he had been looking for this for three years and it was the kind of looking that most people stopped before they found anything, and he had not stopped, and he had found it, and the finding was real and permanent and his.

She was happy for him. She was also aware that Rusty, in his current state, was a liability in a room that contained O'Donnell's table.

"Put it away," she said. "And don't speak of it again tonight."

"But —"

"Rusty." She looked at him steadily. "Do you trust my judgment?"

"Yes, ma'am. Always have."

"Then put it away and eat your supper and go home the same way you came in, which is to say quietly."

He put it away. She squeezed his arm once and went back to the bar. She did not look at O'Donnell's table. She didn't need to. She could feel the quality of the attention coming from that direction the way you could feel a draft from a gap in the wall — not see it, not hear it, but know it was there from the effect it had on the air.

He had heard enough.

She knew it the way she knew things about men in her saloon: with the conviction of someone who had paid attention to the same category of information for five years and had learned to trust the conclusions it produced.

She kept working. She kept her face in its expression. She refilled Hendricks' glass and asked after his wife, who had been unwell, and she listened to what he said about his wife with the full attention it deserved because Hendricks' wife deserved full attention and also because the performance of normalcy was the only asset she had right now and she was not going to squander it.

They left at nine o'clock, all three of them, without ordering anything further and without speaking to her again. O'Donnell stood last, and he looked at her across the room with the arithmetic expression that she had now seen twice, and she met it with her working expression, which was warm and slightly preoccupied, and then he turned and they were gone.

She let out the breath she'd been managing since quarter past seven.

George had not yet returned, which meant he was still with Patterson, or Patterson was already riding, or something had gone wrong, and she did not let herself think about the third possibility because there was nothing useful to be done with it. She told herself he was still with Patterson. She served the remaining customers. She waited.

George came back at nine-thirty. He came in through the back and found her in the office and said, low and fast: "Patterson's gone. He'll be back with the sheriff in an hour, maybe less. Are they still here?"

"They left twenty minutes ago."

George released something in his shoulders. She understood this — the particular physical relief of a threat that had receded, even temporarily.

"Miss Rose," he said, "you should lock up tonight. Close early. Don't be here when they come back."

She thought about this. She thought about the gold behind the panel — not a large amount, but her amount, the savings of five years of careful work, and it was in her building and she was not going to be displaced from her building by three men with bad intentions, because if she was displaced once the displacement would be permanent, because the world of the mining frontier had a long memory for weakness and a short one for everything else.

"No," she said.

George looked at her.

"I'll lock up at the regular time," she said. "I'll have the rifle loaded and within reach. And if the sheriff arrives before they come back, all the better."

"And if he doesn't?"

She thought about the rifle. She thought about James O'Donnell's arithmetic expression and the conclusion it had clearly reached. She thought about the feeling of having built something that was hers and the particular quality of that feeling, which was not pride exactly but something quieter and more durable — the feeling of having done the work, of having stayed when it would have been easier to leave, of having made the thing that now existed in the form of a saloon with a name she'd chosen and a cedar door she'd chosen and a piano player she'd chosen and a barkeep who was loyal and a clientele who were mostly decent and a back room with a panel in the floor behind a flower pot that no one else knew about.

"Then I'll handle what comes," she said.

George was quiet for a moment. He was a man who understood that certain statements were not the beginning of a negotiation and this was one of them.

"Yes, ma'am," he said.

She went to check the rifle.

They did not come back that night. She stayed until eleven, which was her usual closing time, and she locked the front door and checked every window and set the rifle beside her bed and lay in the dark listening to the coyotes in the valley and the building settling around her and the silence that lived underneath everything, and she was afraid, which was appropriate, and she did not allow the fear to make any decisions on her behalf, which was the only thing she had ever asked of it.

She slept, eventually. She was a person who had learned, through the specific curriculum of the years since James died and the plantation was sold and she had packed what fit in two trunks and pointed herself west, that sleep was not a reward for the resolution of difficulty but simply a requirement of the body, available on most nights regardless of what the mind was doing, and that lying awake all night solved nothing and cost you the next day.

She slept.

In the morning she rose at five and made coffee and stood at the alley window in the flat grey pre-dawn light and thought clearly and without drama about what might happen and what she would do in each case. She thought about the sheriff and whether he would arrive in time and what time meant in a situation where the other party set the schedule. She thought about the gold behind the panel. She thought about her sister Linda and the photograph she had not yet mailed.

She had a thought she had not previously allowed herself to have, which was:

if something happens to me, I would like someone to know I was here.

Not grief for herself — she was not, by temperament, someone who grieved for herself. But a recognition, plain and factual, that she had spent five years building something in this valley and that the building mattered and that she wanted the record of it to exist somewhere beyond the Drunken Coyote's ledger books.

She finished her coffee. She went to her desk. She took out the photograph — herself, five years ago, in the pale blue silk dress, looking at the camera with the composed expression she had practiced — and she turned it over and picked up her pen.

She wrote on the back:

To my dear sister Linda. Love, Emma.

It wasn't much. It was true. She set it down and looked at it for a moment and then she picked up the pen again and began a letter she had been putting off, the real one, the one that said:

I am well and the saloon is well and there is something I need to tell you, which is that I have been happy here. Not every day and not in every way, but in the way that counts, which is: I have been the person I meant to be in the place I chose to be it, and that is a thing not everyone gets to say, and I want you to know that I know I am lucky to say it, and I am saying it now so that if there is ever a time when it cannot be said, it will have been said.

She wrote until the morning boy came with the bread.

Then she set the pen down. She put the letter in the envelope with the photograph and sealed it and addressed it to Linda and set it on the corner of the desk where she would see it.

She did not send it that day.

By evening they had come back, and she had not sent it, and there was no longer time.

EIGHT

Greenbriar Gulch

Matt

Matt

The mud on the main street was dry.

He stood in the rain looking at it and the rain continued doing what the rain was doing, which was arriving at a rate that should have made the street a problem, and the street was entirely indifferent to this and to the rain and to the fact that they were standing in it. He looked at the buildings. He looked at the gas lamps. He looked at the sign above the nearest lit door: THE DRUNKEN COYOTE. He looked at the mud again. It was not damp-dry, the way ground went dry in an hour of sun. It was the dry of something that had not been wet.

Charlie said the lamps looked old. They did. They were not electric — the light they threw was not the flat even light of electricity but the warmer, variable light of flame, the kind of light that moved slightly even when nothing was moving, as though the light itself were breathing.

"Come on," he said.

He wasn't sure what he was moving toward. He was moving toward the light because the light was what was available and they needed to be indoors before the storm got worse and there was a building with light in it and so they moved toward it. This was the complete analysis. He was aware, in the way he was aware of the traverse when he was in the wrong part of the sequence, that something was not right — a pre-linguistic awareness, the body's intelligence arriving ahead of the mind's — and he held it and moved toward the light anyway because the alternative was to stand in the rain indefinitely, which was not a plan.

The door of the Drunken Coyote was solid wood, cedar, fitted cleanly — someone had built it with care. He pushed it open. The floorboards under his feet were old growth, worn smooth by years of use, darker in the patterns of traffic. The bar was to his left, long and made of the same dark wood as the door, with a large mirror behind it that was tarnished to a warm amber. The oil lamps on the tables were the source of the light they'd seen from the street — there were six of them, each burning with the same steady care, maintained by someone who understood that a lamp allowed to burn wrong was a lamp that became a problem.

The room smelled of wood smoke and something savory from the kitchen and a faint resinous quality he couldn't place — not tobacco, not pine, something older and less nameable.

He heard Charlie behind him, the particular quality of Charlie entering a room — he always made a slight adjustment at the threshold, a physical gathering of himself, as though rooms required a brief orientation before they could be properly entered. Charlie had been doing this for as long as Matt had known him and had no idea he did it.

A woman came through the door behind the bar.

His first clear thought, when he saw her, was that she was not from here.

This was not a judgment about the place. It was an observation about the person — the way she moved, the quality of her attention, the clothes she was wearing, which were period-specific in a way that stopped him before he could identify exactly what he was looking at. Not costume — they were working clothes, worn and clean, with the particular fit of things that had been worn often enough to conform to the body wearing them. But they were not the clothes of this decade or the previous several.

She stopped when she saw them, and the stop was controlled — not a flinch but a managed response, the halt of someone who had been surprised and had decided, very quickly, how to be surprised. She said they'd scared her half to death and the saloon was closed, and the voice matched the rest of her — warm, with a Southern latitude in the vowels, composed.

He apologized. Charlie explained about the road.

She listened with the full attention of someone who was assessing information rather than simply receiving it. She asked if they were alone. Charlie said no, two women waiting at the car. She noted the coyotes. She suggested they go get them, and then she offered them supper first, which was the organization of a person who understood that cold and hungry people made worse decisions than warm and fed ones.

He accepted and they sat down and she went to the back.

He looked at the room. He looked at the bar. He looked at the sign behind it — CREDIT IS THE ROOT OF ALL SORROW — which was a sentiment he found both cynical and probably accurate. He looked at the piano in the corner, which was an upright, its keys the yellow-white of old ivory. He looked at the window, which showed the main street and the gas lamps and the rain hitting the dry mud.

He looked at the mud again. He was going to have to think about the mud.

"Embalmed beef," Charlie said

He thought about what he knew.

He was a person who made his living, in part, from understanding physical states and anomalies — the way a body moved when something was wrong, the small deviations from normal that predicted larger problems if left unaddressed. He applied the same faculty now to the room. To the information the room was providing.

Gas lamps, not electric. Correct for before 1900, wrong for after it. An upright piano with ivory keys, real ivory, which had been regulated in the 1970s. A bar mirror tarnished in the way of old silver. Embalmed beef on the menu, which was an advertising category that had not been used since refrigeration made it irrelevant. A woman in working clothes that were period-correct for 1880s Nevada.

He had been in the physical world long enough to know what it did and did not do. It did not produce anachronistic combinations. It did not produce dry mud in a rainstorm. It did not produce gas lamps in a town serviced by modern highways.

He had also, in seven years of base jumping, learned something about the moment when the situation departed from the planned parameters in ways that required a recalculation. The moment when you knew the planned scenario was no longer the actual scenario and you had to work with the actual one. He had had this moment on a wall in Kazakhstan, a year ago, when a hold that should have been solid had not been solid, and the calculation had been fast and the outcome had been correct and the outcome being correct had required, first, that he accept what was true rather than what he had planned for.

He looked at the dry mud through the window. He accepted what was true.

He did not know what was true, precisely. He had insufficient data for precision. But he had enough data to know that the category of explanation for the data was narrow, and that the narrow category contained, as its most parsimonious member, a possibility he was not going to examine in the saloon over broth because examining it required more quiet and more time than he currently had. He filed it. He kept it filed. He was going to come back to it.

The woman came back with the broth.

, reading something.

"Probably jerky."

"Probably."

He looked at Charlie. Charlie was reading the menu — there was a small chalkboard near the bar with items written in a hand he could see was careful from across the room. Charlie had the expression he wore when he was processing something without wanting to flag that he was processing it, which was a slight neutrality, a deliberate withholding of reaction.

"She's something," Matt said. He said it before he'd decided to say it.

Charlie looked at him. "She's definitely looking at you."

Matt said nothing. He thought about the mud on the main street. He thought about the gas lamps. He thought about the clothes Emma Rose was wearing and the quality of the furniture in the room and the piano and the sign and the smell and the lamp light, which was not electric, and had never been electric, and was burning the way it burned because someone had trimmed the wick with a specific kind of care that you only had if you'd been trimming wicks your entire life.

"Girls don't usually look at me like that," he said.

This was true. He was aware of it in the practical way he was aware of most things about himself — not with embarrassment, not with particular feeling, simply as a fact about the landscape of his life. He was not the kind of person people looked at in that way. He was not sure why, exactly. He was not bad-looking. He was not unkind. He was simply, he suspected, too absorbed in other things to be fully available in the way that made people look at you in that particular way, and people could sense this and made their looking choices accordingly.

Emma Rose had looked at him in that way. He didn't know what to do with this and so he set it aside, the way he set aside anything he didn't yet know what to do with, and went back to thinking about the mud.

She came back with two bowls of broth.

The broth was the best thing he'd eaten in recent memory, which he recognized was a strange response to an undetermined liquid in a bowl in a saloon in a town he'd never heard of in the middle of a storm he hadn't anticipated, but which was nevertheless his honest assessment. It tasted of something slow-cooked and real, the kind of taste you only produced with time and attention and the willingness to not rush the process.

She sat down at the table with them. Not behind the bar — at the table, which was a different kind of hospitality. She asked their names. He told her. She told him hers and it was the name on the sign above the door — EMMA ROSE — which was either a remarkable coincidence or an explanation.

She said he looked familiar.

He said he didn't think they'd met. He said he would have remembered. He said this without thinking about it, which was how he said most things that were true. She smiled and the smile was real — not the social smile, the other one, the smaller one that happened before you had time to compose.

Charlie was drinking the broth in the focused way he consumed things he liked, which was with complete attention and no commentary. Charlie's most sincere appreciation was always silent.

Emma asked about Leatherman Peak. He told her the short version. She asked what base jumping was and he explained, and she listened with the genuine interest of someone encountering a new thing and finding it worth understanding rather than simply cataloguing.

"That sounds either very brave or very foolish," she said.

"Those aren't always different things."

"No," she said. "I suppose they aren't."

She looked at him and he looked at her and something was happening that he couldn't put language to and he was not going to put language to it, because language was a way of making things smaller and this thing, whatever it was, was the correct size and he didn't want to reduce it.

Charlie cleared his throat.

He asked Charlie to stop.

Charlie said nothing, which was how Charlie said a great many things.

★★★

The question about the main street came out of him sideways, the way questions did when you'd been thinking about them long enough that they stopped feeling like questions and started feeling like things you simply needed to say.

"The mud on your main street," he said to Emma. "It's dry."

She looked at him. Something moved through her expression — very fast, controlled, gone before it fully arrived.

"Weather in these mountains does strange things," she said. "Always has."

This was not an answer. It was true and it was not an answer. He received it and noted that it was not an answer and did not press, because pressing on a gate that wasn't fully latched produced the same thing every time: resistance and a slight backwards movement. He would think about it later. He would think about it a great deal later.

The sound of horses on the street stopped the conversation.

Three horses, moving at a walk. He heard them through the cedar door and through the rain and he heard them because he had been in enough places where ambient noise was information to have learned to listen through it.

He heard them and he looked at Emma and he saw that she had heard them too and that her response to hearing them was not the response of someone hearing ordinary travelers arrive on an ordinary evening.

The response was: stillness. The specific kind that was not relaxation but its opposite — a gathering, a containment.

He thought: she knows who this is.

The door opened.

The first one through was lean and tightly constructed, with a rifle across his back and the quality of a man whose physical ease was the ease of someone who had learned to be still in all the ways that made stillness dangerous. He came in and stopped one step inside and his eyes went around the room in the fast involuntary circuit of someone who had trained themselves to know where everything was before they decided where they wanted to be.

The second was very large — six-foot-one at least, with a red bandana and the unhurried physicality of someone for whom size had always been sufficient. He moved with the slight deliberateness of a large man who had learned that deliberateness communicated something useful.

Then the third.

He came last and he stayed in the doorway for a moment — not from uncertainty but from the opposite of it, from the understanding that a man who arrived last in a room and paused in the doorway was communicating something about the room and his relationship to it, and the communication was: this is mine now. The pause was not long. Two seconds. Long enough.

He was fifty or near it, with a white-red beard that had the quality of something that had been red once and was becoming white the way certain things became white — gradually and without apology. He wore a black hat with the brim pulled low. His eyes, when they moved to Matt and Charlie's table, were the color of overcast sky — neither grey nor blue, the color that was both and committed to neither.

The accent when he spoke was what Matt had expected from the look of him, which was to say Irish — but not the stage-Irish of vaudeville imitation. The real thing, buried deep under years of the American West but present in the bones of every sentence, in the particular music of the vowels and the compression of the consonants, the rhythms of a language underneath the English that could not quite be concealed no matter how many years of other weather had passed over it.

He spoke to the large one — called him Frog, which was a name so wrong for the scale of the man that Matt assumed it was either a very old joke or a very specific one — and then he looked at the room the way he had looked at the doorway: as something already decided.

Matt looked at Charlie. Charlie looked at his broth. The message was clear and mutual:

do not engage, do not attract, do not be interesting.

Emma came out from the back with coffee. Matt watched her face when she saw the three men. He watched her recover in the space of a breath — watched the fear arrive and be managed and be put somewhere internal where it would not show in her hands or her walk or her expression. She set the mugs at their table without looking at him, which was information too, because she had been looking at him all evening and now she was specifically not.

He thought: she told him about the saloon being closed.

He listened.

The large man — O'Donnell, he would learn the name later, from the sheriff, too late for it to be useful — spoke with a surface politeness that was the kind of politeness that was worse than no politeness, the kind that made the threat visible precisely by clothing it. He asked for whiskey. He asked for gold. He said Emma's name in the way that some men said women's names, which was as a demonstration that they knew it.

Emma said no.

She said it in different ways and in different registers and she said it with the composure of someone who had decided before this conversation started what the answer would be regardless of how the question was phrased. He had seen this kind of composure before, in people who had made a decision before a situation arose and were therefore not making one during it. It was one of the things that made people either very effective or very dead, depending on the situation.

"We have to do something," he said to Charlie, very low.

Charlie, very low: "Don't stare at them."

He was not staring. He was watching, which was different. He was watching O'Donnell step around the bar and take Emma's arm, and he was watching Emma slap him, which was the action of a woman who had run out of other options and had chosen the available one, and he was watching O'Donnell's face in the half-second after the slap.

What he saw in that face was not anger. Anger came after. What came first was something colder and more considered — a recalibration, the expression of a man who had just been given new information and was integrating it into a plan that had already accounted for most possibilities and was now accounting for this one.

He hit her. She went down.

Matt picked up the chair.

He threw it because it was the thing his hands found. He threw it across the room at the broadest available target, which was O'Donnell's back as he stood over Emma, and the chair crossed the room in the fraction of a second that it took and connected with a sound that was larger than he expected and O'Donnell went sideways into the bar and the bar gave slightly and took three bottles with it.

"Matt!" Charlie was on his feet. "Run! RUN!"

He had already pulled Emma up from the floor. She was lighter than he expected and she was on her feet faster than he expected and she was moving toward the back door before he had fully oriented himself to the fact that they were running, and he ran.

A gunshot. The lamp behind them exploded. The room went darker and the dark was now full of running and the sound of O'Donnell on the floor saying something with a quality that was not pain and not anger but a flat directed fury, the fury of someone issuing instructions to subordinates in an emergency.

The back door. Cold air and rain and the alley and then the street.

He ran. Emma ran beside him, her hand for a moment finding his arm not for support but for direction — she knew where they were going, she knew this street in the dark and the rain in a way he did not, and he followed her lead without thinking about it, the way you followed the lead of someone who knew the terrain when you were moving fast through it.

"There." He spotted the low building — dark, door ajar. He went to it. He pushed through. He turned and pulled the door shut behind them and put his back against it and felt the weight of the door, which was solid, and felt his own breathing, which was fast and not quite under control, and let it slow.

Charlie came through beside him. Breathing hard.

Emma was already below the window. She moved with the practical speed of someone who knew what she was doing, which was: stay below the line of sight, assess the situation, wait for the situation to resolve or force you to resolve it. He had the strong impression, in the dark of the small building, that Emma Rose had been in difficult situations before and had come out of them not by luck but by the application of something more reliable.

He got below the window. Charlie got below the window. Outside, rain. Inside, their breathing. Somewhere in the dark, the old wooden cross he could only barely see, and the single cracked pew, and the particular quality of a room that had been built for a specific kind of quiet and still held that quality even though no one had used it for that purpose in what felt like a very long time.

A chapel.

He had run into a chapel.

He would think about this later — about what it meant or didn't mean to run from violence into a chapel in a town he hadn't known existed an hour ago. He would think about it later. Right now outside there were horses and gunshots and Sophie and Carmen were out on the road in the SUV and he did not know what was going to happen next and he needed to think.

He thought.

"Sophie and Carmen are still out there," Charlie said, low.

"I know."

"We have to—"

"I know." He held up one hand. Outside the galloping faded west. He listened until he couldn't hear it. Then he listened to what replaced it, which was the rain and the silence underneath the rain and nothing else.

"Whatever happens," he said to Emma, "I'm not going to let them hurt you."

She looked at him in the almost-dark. The gas lamps from the street threw a little amber light through the window and it caught her face and the face was exactly what it had been at the table — warm and composed and seeing him with a directness that most people didn't bring to looking at anything.

"I know," she said.

She said it the way she'd said most things — simply, with the weight of someone who meant what they said and didn't need to say more than they meant.

He believed her.

Which was strange, he thought. He had known her for approximately forty minutes. He had thrown a chair at a man on her behalf. She had run beside him through a dark wet street in a town that was apparently older than electricity and had mud that the rain didn't touch. And she had said

I know in response to a statement about not letting anyone hurt her, and he believed her, and not because she had given him reasons to and not because forty minutes was enough time to establish trust, but because of something simpler and harder to name — the sense of a person being fully present in themselves, without performance, without management, without the gap between what was being shown and what was actually there.

He had met very few people like that. He was, he suspected, one of them himself. Maybe that was why.

Charlie made the sound that meant he wanted to say something.

"Not now, Charlie."

"I wasn't going to say anything."

"Good."

Silence. The rain. The faint sound of horses at a distance, moving, not approaching. He waited.

Beside him in the almost-dark Emma Rose breathed steadily. Her shoulder was an inch from his. He could feel the warmth of her in the cold chapel the way you felt a fire before you could see it — not the heat itself but the suggestion of it, the air changed by the presence of something that had heat to give.

Outside the night held its shape. Inside the chapel held its older quiet.

He began to think about what to do next.

NINE

Five Guys

Carmen

Carmen

When the SUV went into the mud she was already working the problem.

This was how her mind operated under pressure — not sequentially, not step by step in the way that emergency training sometimes described it, but simultaneously, running multiple assessments at once the way a processor ran multiple threads, each one independent and all of them feeding into a conclusion that arrived whole rather than assembled. She was assessing: the vehicle's position relative to the road's edge, the depth of the mud at each wheel, the angle of the chassis, the weight distribution, the available materials in the cargo area, the distance to the town that had to be ahead of them because the road had to go somewhere, and the question of whether Charlie and Matt were safe and how long they'd been gone and whether the gunshots she'd heard twenty minutes ago meant what gunshots usually meant or something else.

She had decided, provisionally, that the gunshots meant something else. The provisional decision was based on the absence of a second volley, which in her experience meant either that the situation had resolved or that it had not yet escalated beyond a warning, and she was going with the former because the latter produced an action — leaving the vehicle immediately, on foot, in the rain — that she was not yet ready to take.

Sophie had said: this really sucks.

Carmen had said: they'll be back soon.

Both of these were true and neither of them was the most useful thing to say, which was:

the SUV is stuck and we have two options, wait or act, and waiting is only useful if help is coming, and if help is not coming then waiting costs us time we don't have.

She did not say this because Sophie was not in soldier mode and soldier mode required a certain context to be useful, and the context was: shared understanding of the situation's parameters, shared acceptance of the chain of command, shared willingness to do whatever the situation required without negotiation. Sophie was in civilian mode, which was a different set of capabilities, and the civilian capabilities were real and she respected them — she had seen Sophie read a room and a person and a relationship with a precision that Carmen could not match — but civilian mode was not what the current situation was optimized for.

She kept her own counsel and waited and listened.

Sophie asked if she had thought about what she was going to say to Charlie.

Carmen said: I'll find the right moment.

She had not been thinking about Charlie and Sophie. She had been thinking about the road and the mud and the gunshots. She filed the conversation under:

ongoing, address later, and kept her eyes on the road ahead, which was dark and told her nothing useful.

★ ★ ★

Sophie said: can I tell you something.

The shift in register was small but Carmen caught it — the formality of asking permission before saying a thing, which Sophie did when the thing she wanted to say was something she'd been carrying for a while and had decided the current moment was as good as any other. Carmen had known Sophie for nine years and had learned to hear the difference between her spontaneous disclosures and her prepared ones. This was a prepared one.

"Always," Carmen said.

"I like Matt."

Carmen kept her eyes on the dark road. She thought:

of course you do. She thought:

this is not new information.

She said: "Since when?"

"A while."

This was Sophie being honest and also Sophie being Sophie, which was precise about everything except the things she most wanted to be precise about, where the precision failed her and she retreated to approximation. A while. Carmen translated this: two years, which was when she'd started noticing Sophie watch Matt at the camping trips — not obviously, not in the way Sophie looked at things she wanted people to see her looking at, but in the sideways way of someone who had decided not to want something and was not entirely succeeding.

"Does he know?" Carmen said.

"No. I'm not going to walk up to a man and spell it out for him."

"Carmen. It's the twenty-first century."

"I'm aware." She looked out the window at the dark. "I still don't do that."

"Why not?" Sophie said. "You do everything else that takes nerve."

Carmen thought about this. It was a fair point and she recognized it as such and also recognized it as the point that had a flaw in it, which was the assumption that all nerve was the same nerve. The nerve required to walk into a room where someone might shoot you and the nerve required to walk up to a person you respected and say

I like you were not the same nerve. They came from different places and they cost different things. The first kind she had in abundance. The second kind she had in theory and not in practice and she had spent two years being unwilling to examine why this was.

She was about to say something that was approximately honest when the gunshots came — not distant this time, not the muffled far-away sound of the last ones, but closer, sharper, the sound of a pistol fired in what could not be more than half a mile.

"That's close," Sophie said.

Carmen was already out of her seat.

★ ★ ★

The rope was in the cargo area, behind the second row, coiled in the emergency kit that she had quietly restocked before the trip because she had looked at Charlie's emergency kit in the hotel lobby and found it to contain: a foil thermal blanket, a box of granola bars, and a phone charger. She had gone to a sporting goods store and bought what was actually needed and put it in without comment, and Charlie had not noticed, and this was fine.

She got out in the rain. The mud was deep at the rear wheels — she could see this in the red of the taillights, the back end sunk to the axle, the angle of the chassis tilted left where the wheel had gone deeper than the other. She walked around the vehicle and made the full assessment in about eight seconds, which was faster than eight seconds felt from the inside.

The technique she needed was from the third month of her first deployment, a morning in early spring when one of the supply trucks had gone off the road into soft ground and they'd had a load that needed to be at the forward position by noon and no heavy equipment available and eight people who were cold and tired and in possession of a rope and a grove of dead scrub pine twenty feet from the vehicle. Their master sergeant had shown them the log-and-tire technique — a piece of wood tied to the rim of the stuck tire, long enough to dig into the ground behind it and give the tire something solid to push against. It was not elegant. It worked.

She went back to the cargo area. She found the rope. She found what she needed to make a log — a section of aluminum tent pole from Matt's kit, which was not ideal but was rigid and available and approximately the right dimensions. She tied it to the right rear rim with the knot that held tension under lateral load, which was the knot that mattered here.

"Get in," she said to Sophie through the window. "When I say go, give it gas. Not a lot. Steady."

"How does this —"

"Go."

Sophie gave it gas. Carmen stood to the side and watched and felt the moment the pole engaged the mud, felt it through the sound of the engine and the way the chassis shifted, and she said

"More," and Sophie gave it more, and the SUV wrenched free with a sound like something releasing a breath it had been holding since the boulder and the mud let it go.

Carmen got in.

"That was impressive," Sophie said.

"It was a technique," Carmen said. "Drive."

★ ★ ★

The town appeared ahead in the way that things appeared when you'd been driving in the dark for long enough that you'd stopped expecting to arrive — suddenly, without preamble, there in the windshield where nothing had been.

Gas lamps. She noted them without remarking on them. She noted the quality of the light, which was not electric. She noted the buildings, which were dark except for one. She noted the main street, which was — she looked more carefully — dry. She noted the absence of rain on the main street while the rain was active and present on the road they'd arrived on and on the windshield of the vehicle she was in.

She filed all of this under:

anomalous, address when situation allows.

Then the headlights found them.

Matt on the ground, one hand on his leg, jaw locked in the expression she recognized as pain being managed rather than expressed. A woman kneeling beside him — unknown, unfiled, assessed immediately: civilian, competent, not a threat. And Charlie standing with his hands at his sides and a man she did not know pointing two revolvers at him from a distance of about twenty feet.

She processed this in approximately one second.

"Oh, hell no," she said.

Sophie said Charlie's name.

Carmen put her foot down.

The impact was clean. She had aimed for the man's center of mass, which was the largest available target, and she had calculated the speed required to remove him from the situation without killing him, which she could not actually guarantee but which she had aimed for — enough force to displace him, not enough to be certain of the rest. The vehicle hit him at approximately twenty-five miles an hour and he went fifteen feet and landed in the manner of someone who had lost the argument with physics.

She got out. Sophie got out.

She went to Matt first because he was on the ground and on the ground meant injury and injury had a priority that superseded the other assessments. She took stock: the leg, the blood, the fact that he was on his feet faster than she expected given the blood, which told her the wound was not arterial. She felt something she did not name — something between relief and anger, the two states that were closest together in her internal taxonomy and that she had learned, over deployments, to let exist side by side without resolving them prematurely.

Then she saw the woman.

Unknown. Kneeling beside Matt with her hand under his arm, helping him stand, with the fluency of someone who had decided to help and was helping rather than deciding whether to help. The woman was dressed in clothes that Carmen's mind filed immediately as:

wrong era, the same way your eye caught a color that was slightly off before your brain identified which color it was.

"Who is she?" she said.

The woman began to say something. Carmen cut her off. She asked Matt.

This was not rudeness. This was information management — she needed the account from someone whose assessment she had a baseline for, and she had no baseline for the woman in the wrong-era clothes, and she needed the information fast because the man she had hit with the SUV was on the ground twenty feet away and she did not know if he was the only threat or one of several.

Matt said: Emma. He said: she's with us. He said it the way he said things that were simple facts and also, apparently, something more than simple facts, in the tone of someone who had decided something in the last hour that he hadn't expected to decide.

She had questions about this. She filed them.

She told him they needed a doctor. He said it was a flesh wound. She said he could not walk. He was, in fact, walking, with Emma's help, which she noted and also noted was not the same as walking independently. She added this to the file.

Sophie had found Charlie. Sophie and Charlie were doing the thing they did when they'd been separated in a frightening situation, which was to stand close enough that their shoulders were touching and talk quietly and quickly. Carmen had seen this before and found it both reassuring and something that made her feel, briefly, the particular shape of the space in her own life that was not filled by that kind of thing. She noted this feeling and also filed it.

She had a lot of open files.

Emma said: we need to move. She said: the others may be close.

Carmen said: what others.

Emma said: run.

It happened fast.

Fast in the way that things happened fast when they were over before the mind had fully registered that they'd started — no build, no anticipation, just the sound of horses and then the horsemen and then everything changed in the space of two seconds.

The large man came out of the dark at a gallop and she had time to register

incoming and the absolute uselessness of running from a horse in an open space before the horse hit her. Not the horse exactly — the man on the horse, the impact of a large person moving fast connecting with her and taking her off her feet. She hit the ground on her right side with the full force of it and the ground was dry — inexplicably, absurdly dry, in the middle of what had been a wet night — and the dry was somehow worse than mud would have been because mud absorbed and this just hit.

She got her hands under her and pushed. She was getting up. She was almost up.

He dismounted. He was faster than she expected for his size, which she had known abstractly but was now learning specifically, which was the way you learned things about opponents — abstractly first and then specifically and the specific was always instructive and not always in the direction you'd hoped. He lifted her before she had full purchase on the ground and she got one good elbow into his ribs and felt it land and felt him absorb it with the completeness of a man who had been hit before and had long since decided that being hit was simply a variable he operated with rather than a thing that stopped him.

He got her onto the saddle.

She heard Sophie scream and then the sound of galloping and then Charlie calling Sophie's name and the sound receded because they were moving and she was on the saddle and the man had her wrist and she was taking stock: hands free, legs free, no restraint except the grip and the speed and the man's size, which was substantial, and the horse, which was faster than she was.

She was working the problem.

The town went past her on both sides — the gas lamps, the buildings, the dry main street — and then they were past the buildings and into the dark on the far side and she was still working the problem and the problem was: escape from a moving horse without killing yourself, which was a niche competency she had not specifically trained for but which shared enough variables with other problems she had trained for that she was not, despite the circumstances, especially afraid.

Afraid and afraid were different things. She had learned this in the first deployment and confirmed it in each subsequent one. There was the afraid that was useful — the adrenaline and the narrowed focus and the accelerated processing — and there was the afraid that was not useful, the kind that locked you up and produced inaction. She could feel the useful kind doing its work right now: the clarity of the processing, the way each second was thick with information, the absence of anything except the present problem.

She noted, without particular emphasis, that the man smelled of horses and tobacco and something else she couldn't identify — something slightly wrong, a chemical quality she had no framework for, like nothing she'd encountered before. She filed this too.

He pulled up in front of a building she couldn't see clearly in the dark. He dismounted with her still gripped at the wrist and she went with it — no point fighting a dismount on a horse, the leverage was all wrong — and he pulled her through a door and into a room and pushed her into a chair and she was filing everything: room dimensions, one door behind her, one window boarded, one lamp, the chair's construction, the rope he was producing from somewhere.

He had a name. She would learn it later. O'Donnell — she would hear the sheriff say it with the weight of someone saying a name that had consequences, and she would catalog it then alongside everything else.

Right now he was tying her to the chair and she was letting him, because letting him was the option that kept her hands in front of her rather than behind her, which mattered, and because letting him conserved energy she was going to need, and because the man who had just galloped her across a ghost town in the rain while she made a mental map of the route they'd taken was a man she intended to escape from and the escape was going to require that she be in good condition when the opportunity arrived.

She was always in good condition.

He pulled the rope tight. He sat down across from her with the patience of someone who found waiting neither difficult nor unpleasant.

She looked at him.

He had the accent she would later understand as Irish — not performed, not imitated, but real, present in the bones of his speech the way a language learned in childhood stayed present even when it was no longer the primary language, the rhythms and the vowels and the particular music of it underneath the American surface, indelible.

He told her what he wanted.

She told him she didn't know.

He told her she was lying.

She told him she wasn't.

He stood up. He walked toward her. She watched him come with the focused attention she brought to incoming threats, which was the attention of someone making calculations rather than someone experiencing fear, though from the outside they might have looked the same.

He slapped her face.

Her lip split. She tasted blood. She worked her jaw. She looked at him.

"Untie me," she said, "and try that again."

She meant it. She meant it the way she meant most things — completely, without decoration, without the ironic distance that made statements like this mere bravado. She had two years of close-quarters training and a deep and personal investment in the outcome of the next few minutes, and she was currently restrained and therefore could not demonstrate any of this, but she was aware of it as a standing fact about the situation and she believed, on balance, that making him aware of it was useful.

He walked behind her. He pulled her head back by the hair.

She spat in his face.

It was the right move. Not strategically — strategically it was probably suboptimal, likely to escalate rather than to de-escalate, not aligned with the goal of maintaining the low-conflict posture that kept opponents underestimating you. But it was the right move in the sense that it was true to the moment and to herself, and she had learned that the moves that were true to yourself had a consistency that purely strategic moves lacked, and consistency was important when what you were doing was keeping a man off-balance.

He raised his fist.

The door opened.

TEN

The Chair's Other Side

Carmen

Carmen

The man in the doorway was not O'Donnell. This was the first thing she registered, ahead of all the other things she registered, because O'Donnell had just raised his fist and the man in the doorway was not him.

He was younger — thirties, maybe, lean in the way of someone who moved a great deal rather than someone who trained for it, with the particular upright quality of a person who had been in uniform long enough that the posture had become structural. He had a revolver. He had it pointed at O'Donnell, which was the most important information in the room.

She processed the scene in the time it took for the deputy — she understood immediately that he was the deputy, the way you understood certain things about certain people before they told you — to say:

"Still hitting women, Jim."

O'Donnell turned. He moved his bulk with the economical ease of a large man who had, over a long life, learned to turn without telegraphing the turn — no winding up, no preparation, simply rotated. She noted this.

She also noted the revolver on the floor. The deputy's revolver, which had flown from his hand when the man she'd run over with the SUV — Tommy Boy, she heard the name later, Tommy Boy, which was a name she had no framework for in the context of a person of his particular violence — kicked the deputy in the back. She heard the impact and heard the revolver hit the floor and she stretched her arm and her fingers found it and the rope on her wrists had enough slack, just enough, because O'Donnell had tied her in a hurry and hurrying was where people left margin.

She had the revolver.

She aimed and fired in the same motion, the way training produced — not thought, not decision, but the motion that thought had been compressed into over enough repetitions that it ran below the level of deliberation. The shot hit O'Donnell in the shoulder. She saw him take it — the impact, the way his body absorbed it without going down, the way his face registered it as information rather than as pain. He retreated through the back door. She fired twice more through the wall in the direction he'd gone, which was both correct and incorrect: correct because it kept him moving and incorrect because she had no sight picture and was spending ammunition she didn't know she could replace.

She filed this assessment and stopped firing.

The deputy had dealt with Tommy Boy. She heard this more than saw it — the struggle, the glass, the particular silence that followed someone going through a window. She turned and found the deputy looking at her with the expression of a man who had just intervened in a situation and found the situation more complex than anticipated.

She pointed the revolver at him.

This was not, on reflection, entirely fair. But the revolver was in her hand and he was an unknown quantity in a room where the only quantities she had verified were hostile, and pointing a firearm at an unknown quantity while you established his category was standard procedure and she was operating on standard procedure because standard procedure existed for exactly this kind of situation.

"Ma'am," he said. "I'm on your side."

She assessed him. The posture, the delivery, the way he'd said

ma'am — not with condescension but with the particular inflection of someone who had been taught to say it and had been saying it long enough that it was genuine. She assessed the fact that he had kicked Tommy Boy through a glass window rather than shooting him, which suggested either a shortage of ammunition or a preference for not killing, and she didn't know which but both were operationally relevant.

"About damn time," she said. "Untie me."

He untied her and helped her stand and she tested her weight and her shoulder and her hands and found everything functional. Bruised. Functional. She kept the revolver.

"I ran over that man outside," she said. "With a vehicle. Why is he standing?"

The deputy looked at her with a quality she couldn't immediately categorize. Not evasion — something more careful than evasion, more considered. The look of someone who had information they were deciding how to portion.

"Let's find your friends first," he said. "Can you walk?"

"I can run." She said it flatly, as a statement of capability rather than bravado. "Where are they?"

"The last I saw them they were making for the chapel. If they stayed —"

"Show me."

They went out through the front door and into the main street. The rain had lightened — still present but not the solid curtain it had been an hour ago. She looked at the main street. The dry mud. The gas lamps burning with their amber breath. The buildings silent on both sides.

She looked at the man she'd hit with the SUV — Tommy Boy — who was not there. The street where he'd landed was empty.

"The man I hit," she said. "He was right there."

"Yes," the deputy said, with that careful quality again.

"He went fifteen feet. He wasn't moving."

"I understand."

She looked at the empty street. She looked at the deputy. She had spent fourteen months in a landscape full of things that required explanation and had learned to operate effectively within the gap between the thing and its explanation — to let the inexplicable sit in its category, filed and unresolved, and to continue functioning. This was a skill and she employed it now.

She filed:

man struck by vehicle at speed, apparently no longer incapacitated. Cross-reference: the gunshots earlier, the dry mud, the chemical smell. File: priority unknown, address when situation allows.

She followed the deputy to the chapel.

The chapel was where she expected it to be — the small low building she'd noted when they'd driven into town, which was the kind of building that existed in the oldest part of a frontier settlement, built first because people built chapels first, before the saloon and before the assay office and sometimes before the well.

She heard them through the door before she reached it — movement inside, the particular quality of people trying to move quietly and not quite succeeding. She went around to the side and put her back against the wall and said, at the volume she used for communicating through walls without alarming occupants:

"It's Carmen. Don't do anything."

A beat. Matt's voice, flat and controlled: "Come in slowly."

She went in.

They were in the positions she'd have predicted for each of them — Matt near the window with his back to the wall where he had a view of the street without being visible from it; Emma beside him with the posture of someone who had decided to stay close and had been told this was appropriate; Charlie by the door with a piece of timber in his hand, which told you everything about Charlie's approach to a crisis, which was: find the nearest available object and position yourself between it and whatever needed positioning between; Sophie behind the pew with the saber, which told you everything about Sophie's approach to a crisis, which was: find the one thing she was actually good at and hold it.

Carmen looked at the saber. She had not known about the saber. She noted it and updated several assessments simultaneously.

"There you are," Charlie said.

"There I am," she said.

Matt looked at her — the quick comprehensive look he used to assess whether someone was okay without asking whether someone was okay, which was how Matt asked that question. She gave him the small nod that meant: functional.

He gave her the small nod that meant: understood.

Sophie was looking at the deputy, who had come in behind Carmen. Sophie's expression moved through several states in rapid succession — surprise, assessment, provisional acceptance. Sophie assessed people the way Carmen assessed rooms: quickly, comprehensively, reaching conclusions she mostly kept to herself.

"What deputy?" Sophie said.

Carmen turned. The deputy was not in the doorway. The doorway was empty.

She looked at the empty doorway for a moment. Then she turned back to the room.

"He was right here," she said.

Nobody said anything immediately, which was the response she would have given in their position.

She turned to Emma.

She had been building the Emma file since the headlights found her in the main street, kneeling beside Matt, and the file had accumulated a number of entries that required reconciliation. The clothes — wrong era, consistently wrong era, not costume but actual clothes of a period she was estimating at late nineteenth century. The speech patterns — formal in the way that was period-specific rather than individual, the vocabulary and the rhythms of someone who had learned to speak in a different century. The knowledge of the town — comprehensive, instinctive, the knowledge of someone for whom the town was not a place visited but a place inhabited, every alley and exit known without thought.

And: Emma had not been surprised by the gas lamps. She had not been surprised by the horses. She had not commented on the SUV or on the phones or on anything that should have required comment from someone encountering them for the first time.

Carmen looked at Emma and Emma looked back at her and Carmen said, in the direct and undramatic way she addressed most things:

"You almost got me killed over your gold. I was in that chair because of you. That man wanted me to tell him where you keep it."

She said it without heat. Heat was imprecise and imprecision was wasteful. She said it because it was true and because true things needed to be said when they were true, and because the relationship between Emma's gold and her own current physical state was a direct one and Emma deserved to understand that relationship.

Matt said: stop.

She looked at him.

He was right. This was not the moment. The moment was: their current position, the threat that remained outside it, the resources available to them, the options for what to do next. She was letting the adrenaline downstream into speech when it was better employed as fuel.

She nodded. Filed it.

"Where's the gun?" Matt said.

She held up the revolver. He looked at it. She looked at it. They both understood simultaneously that it was the deputy's revolver, which meant it was not hers, which meant she had no established claim to it, and also that the deputy had just disappeared from a doorway she'd been watching, which raised questions about the deputy's revolver that she was not ready to answer.

"Back to the chapel," Matt said. "We make a plan."

"We're in the chapel," Charlie said.

"I know. We stay in the chapel and we make a plan."

They stayed in the chapel and they made a plan.

★ ★ ★

The plan, as it developed through a conversation conducted in low voices over about ten minutes, was thin. This was because their resources were thin. What they had: one revolver of uncertain remaining ammunition — she checked, three rounds — her butterfly knife, Sophie's saber, Matt's training and her training and Charlie's good intentions and Emma's knowledge of the town's geography. What they didn't have: a clear picture of how many of O'Donnell's people remained operational, a way of contacting anyone outside the town, a vehicle they could get to without crossing open ground that was presumably watched, and any information about the sheriff or whether help was coming.

Emma said the sheriff would come. She said it with the conviction of someone who had sent for him and believed in him, which was a kind of faith Carmen neither shared nor dismissed — it was data, the faith itself was data, and data didn't have to be comforting to be useful.

Sophie said: we can't wait here.

Carmen agreed, but she didn't say so yet. She was still working through the tactical geometry. They were in a building with one entrance and one window. The entrance and the window were both exposure points. Moving from the building to any other position in the town required crossing the main street, which was open. O'Donnell was somewhere, shot in the shoulder, which meant he was injured and operational — a combination she had learned to treat with particular care, because injured and operational meant angry and less calculating, and anger and diminished calculation in a man of O'Donnell's type meant an increased willingness to take actions that pure calculation would have prevented.

She thought about the man she'd hit with the SUV. Tommy Boy. Who was not where she'd left him.

She thought about the man she'd put a knife through — twice — in the street outside, who had also not been where she expected him to be when the horses came.

She filed these two data points together for the first time, placed them in the same file, and looked at what they produced when placed together, which was a question she did not yet have the architecture to answer:

what is the category of a man who does not stay down?

She set the question aside. She would come back to it. Right now there were more immediately useful things to think about.

Matt said: "Here's what we're going to do." He said it the way he said things he'd decided — not a proposal, not a suggestion, a statement of intention that was open to modification but clear about its direction. "Come close."

They came close. Even Emma, who seemed to understand that the geometry of the situation had changed and that she was now inside it rather than adjacent to it, came close.

She stood at the chapel window while Matt talked. She kept one eye on the street — the gas lamps, the empty stretch of main street between the chapel and the saloon, the deeper dark beyond the lamp circles where O'Donnell was somewhere with his arithmetic. Nothing moving. She listened.

The plan, as Matt described it, had the shape of a plan built from genuine scarcity: they had one revolver with three rounds, the saber, her knife, Charlie's good intentions, Emma's knowledge of the town, and the sheriff, who was somewhere in the dark doing what sheriffs did when their town was being systematically taken apart. They had the chapel, which had one entrance and one window and was defensible in the limited sense of any position that you could see coming toward it.

She thought about what they didn't have. No communication out. No vehicle accessible without crossing fifty yards of open street. No clear picture of O'Donnell's remaining numbers — Frog was down, Tommy Boy was in the jailhouse if the jailhouse had held, and O'Donnell himself was somewhere with a shoulder wound that would have slowed a lesser man and would not slow him at the rate she'd prefer.

She thought about the man she'd hit with the SUV.

She came back to this, as she had been coming back to it at intervals throughout the night, with the persistence of a variable she had not yet been able to close. She had hit him at twenty-five miles an hour. She had watched him land. She had assessed the landing as non-survivable for any sustained operational capacity. She had then watched him not be where she had left him. She had filed this under the category she had been building all night, the category without a name, and she was aware that the category was getting crowded.

She thought: whatever the town is doing, it applies to them. She thought: that is relevant to the plan.

She said: "There's something you need to factor in."

Matt stopped. Emma looked at her. Matt looked at her in the specific way he looked at things he was ready to update on — open, direct, waiting.

"The men we've put down tonight," she said. "They haven't stayed down. I hit Tommy Boy at speed. He was gone. He was operational twenty minutes later. I put a knife in Frog twice before the horses came. He was the one who took Sophie." She paused. "Whatever is keeping this town in

1886 is keeping them too. I don't know what that means for the plan but I know it means something."

The room was quiet.

Emma said, with the matter-of-fact quality that was, Carmen had come to understand, her default register for information she had spent a long time managing: "They have always been difficult to stop. Since O'Donnell came to Greenbriar Gulch. The sheriff has noted it. We have — attributed it to constitution. To the kind of men they are."

"It's not constitution," Carmen said.

"No," Emma said. "I don't believe it is."

Sophie was watching this exchange with the attention she brought to things she was integrating — not reacting, not yet, just receiving and filing it in the same careful way Carmen filed things, which was one of the things Carmen had always valued in Sophie even when Sophie's filing speed was slower than the situation preferred.

"So we can't count on injury stopping them," Matt said.

"We can count on it slowing them," Carmen said. "And I would rather have three rounds than none. But we plan for them getting up."

Matt nodded. He adjusted the plan accordingly — two modifications that improved its probability without fundamentally changing its architecture. She approved of both. She offered one more: Sophie at the far left rather than the center, out of the direct line from the door, the saber range better used from an angle than head-on.

Sophie accepted this without comment, which was Sophie understanding tactics rather than Sophie deferring. Carmen noted the distinction.

Carmen listened. She assessed the plan. She found it adequate for the available resources, which was the most she asked of plans in situations like this — not elegant, not certain, but executable with what they had. She offered two modifications, which Matt accepted without argument because they were improvements and he was someone who accepted improvements without making the acceptance a thing.

She checked the revolver again. Three rounds. She checked the butterfly knife. She looked at Sophie's saber, which Sophie was holding with the particular ease of someone for whom it was a familiar object rather than an improvised weapon.

"That's yours?" Carmen said.

"My grandmother's grandfather's," Sophie said. "Cavalry officer. Franco-Prussian war."

Carmen looked at the saber. She looked at Sophie. She updated the Sophie file significantly.

"Can you use it?" she said.

Sophie looked at her with the expression she used when she found a question technically answerable but practically redundant. "I have been fencing for eleven years," she said. "To control my temper."

Carmen thought:

of course you have.

She thought:

of course it's for the temper.

She thought, with a quality she identified as appreciation:

I have been underestimating Sophie.

"Good," she said.

Outside, the town held its quiet. The gas lamps burned. The dry mud held its condition. Somewhere in the dark beyond the chapel wall, O'Donnell was moving through the night with a shoulder wound and whatever remained of his plan, and the man she'd hit with her vehicle was not where she'd left him, and the deputy had disappeared from a doorway she'd been watching, and none of these things had explanations she was ready to give them.

She held the revolver and waited for Matt to give the word.

The word came.

They moved.

ELEVEN

Providence

Emma --- Greenbriar Gulch, Nevada, 1886

Emma — Greenbriar Gulch, Nevada, 1886

She had been expecting O'Donnell. She had not been expecting two men in strange clothes who smelled of rain and the road and something else she could not name — a faint metallic quality, like coins held too long in a warm hand, which she had never encountered before and which she filed away in the part of her mind that kept the things she didn't yet understand.

She heard the boots on the porch and her hand went to the desk and then she stopped herself, because the rifle was in the corner and reaching for it before she knew what was coming was the kind of response that could not be taken back, and she had learned over five years of running the Drunken Coyote that responses that could not be taken back were best reserved for situations that were past the point of ambiguity. She was not yet past that point. She smoothed her dress. She went out.

Two men. Young — thirties, both of them — with the travel-worn quality of people who had been in a vehicle for several hours, not a horse and not a wagon but something she had no category for yet, something that produced a particular kind of tired that was specific to long enclosed spaces and limited movement. She filed this without naming it.

She told them the saloon was closed. She heard her own voice and it was steady, which was what she had aimed for.

The taller one apologized. He apologized in the way that people apologized when they meant it — directly, briefly, without embellishment. She had noted, over five years of receiving apologies for everything from unpaid tabs to broken chairs, that the ones who meant it said less rather than more, as though they understood that the apology was a practical correction rather than a performance requiring an audience.

She listened to their explanation. The road, the mud, the storm. She looked at their boots and their clothes and the particular quality of their discomfort, which was not the discomfort of deception but the discomfort of people who were cold and wet and genuinely uncertain what to do next.

She asked if they were alone.

The shorter one — the one with the easy quality, the one who looked like the kind of man who arrived at parties already knowing half the room — said his girlfriend and her friend were waiting at the car. She did not know the word car in the way he used it and she filed this too, in the same compartment as the metallic smell, under:

unknown, address later.

She said: coyotes run these flats at night. It is not safe for women out there alone. She said it because it was true and because she needed to move this conversation forward and because getting two more people inside a building she could manage was preferable to having two women outside it in the dark where O'Donnell might find them.

And then she looked properly at the tall one. She had been looking at him since they came in — not obviously, not in the way that drew attention to the looking — but with the peripheral efficiency she had developed for assessing the people who came into her saloon. She had looked at him and she had seen: large, composed, economy of movement, the kind of physical confidence that did not require demonstration. She had categorized him as:

straightforward, low risk, functional in a crisis.

And then she looked at him properly and the categorization dissolved.

She knew his face.

This was not possible. She had never seen him before. She was certain of this in the way she was certain of things she had catalogued carefully — she remembered faces, she had always remembered faces, it was a professional requirement and also a personal habit and she had not seen this face before today. And yet she knew it. She knew it the way you knew a tune you couldn't name — present and complete in some part of the mind that operated below the naming faculty, below the categorizing faculty, below everything she trusted as reliable.

She said: you look very familiar to me. Have we met before?

He said he didn't think so. He said he would have remembered.

He said it without thinking, which was how people said the things that were simply true.

She smiled. She felt it happen — the real smile, not the working one — and she did not try to stop it because stopping it would have required a deliberateness she didn't have at that particular moment, her resources being directed elsewhere.

She brought broth because it was what she had and because they looked as though they needed it. She had made it that morning from the stock she kept going through the week, replenishing it each day with whatever the kitchen produced — bones, vegetable ends, the parts of things that had more use in water than on a plate. It was not remarkable broth. It was the broth of a woman who understood that unremarkable things done consistently produced a reliable quality of life, which was its own kind of remarkable.

She sat down at the table with them.

She did not generally sit with customers. She managed from behind the bar or from the doorway of her office, maintaining the particular professional distance that kept her in a position to see the room rather than be in it. But these two men were not customers — they were people who had walked into her building in a storm, soaking wet, with women on a dark road outside, and she had decided within the first three minutes that they were not a threat, and the decision came with an instinct she had learned to trust, which was: when a person is not a threat, meet them rather than manage them.

So she sat.

The shorter one — Charles, she thought of him as Charles almost immediately, because he had the quality of someone whose name arrived ahead of them, the name being the person in some specific and hard-to-explain way — Charles drank the broth with the absorbed pleasure of someone who had decided that the broth was the most important thing in the room and was treating it accordingly. He said very little. This was, she would come to understand over the short and violent hours that followed, one of Charles's most sincere forms of appreciation: silence, and full attention, and the slight forward tilt of someone who has found exactly what they needed.

Matthew asked questions.

This was the other thing she noticed about him: the questions were not conversational. They were genuine. He asked about Leatherman Peak with the interest of someone who had thought about the specific mountain and had specific thoughts. He asked about base jumping in a way that assumed she could follow the explanation and would not require it simplified, which was a form of respect so automatic in him that she doubted he was aware of extending it.

She asked what base jumping was.

He explained it with care. He used the right number of words — not too many, not so few that the explanation failed — and when he was done she understood what he was proposing to do and she said: that sounds either very brave or very foolish, and he said those weren't always different things, and she agreed, and they looked at each other, and she was aware that they were having the kind of conversation she did not have often, which was a conversation in which both participants were fully present rather than managing their presence.

She could feel herself responding to this. She noted it with a kind of interest that had nothing to do with judgment and everything to do with recognition — she had not felt this specific thing for a long time, this particular aliveness in the presence of another person, and she was old enough and honest enough to call it what it was rather than what was convenient.

"I have a mind to spend the rest of my days with you," she told him, later, in the lamplight of the saloon after the deputy had gone and they were briefly alone.

She had not planned to say this. She had planned to say something practical about going — they needed to go, the situation was deteriorating and going was the correct response to deterioration. She had planned to say this.

Instead she had taken his face in her hands, which was also not planned, and had said the other thing.

He had said it didn't sound ridiculous.

She had thought: no. It doesn't. That is what is remarkable about it.

But before all of this — before the lamplight and the things said in it — there was O'Donnell.

She heard the horses when she was in the back with Charles and Matthew, and she felt the hearing in her body before her mind processed it — a tightening, a gathering, the physical vocabulary of a person who had expected something and here it was. She had sent George for the sheriff. The sheriff was two miles out. Forty minutes if Patterson rode fast.

She had approximately forty minutes.

She came out with the coffee and she saw them and she did not show what she felt, which was a clarifying cold terror, not the kind that locked you up but the kind that made everything very precise, the edges of the room sharpened, the distances exact. She had felt this once before — the morning James died, when the doctor came in from the field hospital with the expression that preceded the words — and she had learned then that this kind of terror was information rather than an obstacle, and the information was: this is serious, and you know it, and now you can proceed accordingly.

She set the mugs at Matthew and Charles's table. She went behind the bar. She kept her back straight.

O'Donnell spoke to her in the voice he used — the reasonable voice, the voice with the courtesy sitting on top of the threat the way a skin sat on top of a wound. Irish underneath the American, she had been right about that from the first evening. The Irish was not an affectation. It was geology — the layer below the surface layer, laid down early, permanent.

She answered him in the working voice. She kept moving.

When he reached across the bar and took her arm she had known it was coming for approximately eight seconds, which was not enough time to do anything useful about it but was enough time to decide that she was not going to flinch, and she did not flinch. She had in those eight seconds also made the calculation about the rifle — in the office, too far, the distance made it a different problem than it would have been if it were behind the bar — and she had arrived at the conclusion: not available. And then he had her arm and she slapped him because it was what the situation had become and she was not going to be what O'Donnell required her to be, which was someone who submitted to this.

She knew, when she slapped him, that the knowing was going to cost her. She knew it and she did it and then he hit her and she went down and the floor came up and she was on it.

She heard his voice from above her, and the particular quality of his voice when the politeness dropped away was like hearing a door fall off its hinges — not gradual, not a creak or a warning, just the sudden change from one state to the other. The Irish was very clear now. It was always clearest in the people she had known who carried it when the performance stopped.

She was on the floor. She was thinking clearly, which surprised her each time it happened in extremity — she had always thought, before the first time it happened, that extremity would cloud the thinking, and it did the opposite. She was thinking: Matthew will do something. She did not know why she thought this. She had known him for forty minutes. But she thought it with a certainty that had nothing provisional about it.

He did something.

The chair crossed the room with a sound she felt rather than heard — the displacement of air, the impact, O'Donnell going sideways into the bar and the bar giving slightly under him, the bottles. She was on her feet before she had consciously decided to stand, which was the body's knowledge operating ahead of the mind's, and Matthew had her arm and then they were running and the running was fast and real and she ran.

She knew the back door. She knew the alley. She knew the low building three streets over, the one that had been a chapel and still was in some technical sense even though no services had been held there in the eight years she'd been in Greenbriar Gulch. She knew every exit from every building on the main street, the way you knew such things when you had lived in a place for five years and paid attention.

She ran and Matthew ran beside her and she felt — even in the running, even in the rain and the dark and the particular weight of what was coming — the warmth of another person beside her who was moving at her pace and had decided, without discussion, that her direction was his direction.

This was not nothing.

She had been in Greenbriar Gulch for five years and she had built something real and she had been lonely in a way that the building did not entirely address, and she had made her peace with this, which was the peace of a practical woman with a practical life and no particular patience for the kind of mourning that didn't eventually give way to something useful.

And then: Matthew, running beside her, choosing her direction.

This was not nothing.

In the chapel she bound his wound with what she had, which was a strip of her own skirt because there was nothing else and the wound needed binding. She worked with the attention she brought to everything that required her hands, which was complete, and she was aware of him watching her hands work with the particular quality of attention he brought to things — as though the watching were itself a form of respect, as though seeing something done well was a thing worth seeing and not merely a thing preceding whatever came next.

She finished the bandage. She did not move away.

"I wish we'd met some other way," he said.

She thought about this. She thought about what another way would have looked like — a normal evening in the saloon, a man passing through, a conversation over the bar that had a different quality than the usual conversations over the bar. She thought about whether that version of the meeting would have produced this.

"I feel like we were meant to meet exactly this way," she said.

She said it because it was true and because she had stopped, somewhere in the last hour, caring about the protocol that governed what you said to strangers. He was not a stranger. She could not account for why he was not a stranger, but there it was — the fact of it, the specific warmth of someone known, which was not the warmth of someone liked, though that was present too, but the deeper warmth of recognition, the sense that this person existed in a category that had been waiting for its occupant.

She leaned against him. He put his arm around her. The chapel held its old quiet around them and outside, the horses moved somewhere in the dark, and somewhere O'Donnell was in the night with his arithmetic and his plans, and she was afraid, and she was also — she acknowledged it — happy. These two things coexisted. She had learned that they could.

Charles was looking at them from across the chapel with the expression of a man who was both moved and desperately trying to stay focused on the practical problem.

She liked Charles very much.

"Whatever happens," Matthew said, "I'm not going to let them hurt you."

She looked at him in the almost-dark.

"I know," she said.

She said it because she did know. Because she had known it from the first moment she had looked at him properly — the quality of him, the specific density of a person who meant what they said without requiring the words to carry extra weight because the words were sufficient. She had met very few such people. She recognized them when they arrived.

She leaned against him.

Outside, the rain.

Inside, the chapel's older quiet, and Matthew's arm around her, and the small sound of Charles at the window doing his best.

She allowed herself, briefly, to be exactly where she was.

TWELVE

The Gallows

Sophia

Sophia

The lasso took her off her feet before she understood what was happening.

One moment she was running — the horsemen appearing from the dark, Carmen going down hard, Matt grabbing Charlie, the whole situation collapsing from alarming into something she had no framework for, no language for, something that moved too fast for language — and then the rope dropped around her waist and snapped tight and she was moving through the air horizontally and then she was on the ground and the ground was moving past her face in the dark and she understood that she was being dragged.

The dry mud of the main street was cold against her cheek. She got her hands under her — the rope was at her waist, not her hands, her hands were free — and she pushed and managed to get upright enough to run rather than be dragged, half-running and half-pulled, her feet finding purchase and losing it and finding it again while the horse moved at a trot and the rope kept its pressure and somewhere behind her she heard Charlie calling her name.

She heard him calling her name and she could not answer because she was using everything she had for the running.

The voice went smaller as the distance between them grew. She felt this — the specific diminishment of a known voice moving away from you, going from full presence to something thinner, to the edge of audible, to gone. She had heard this once before: James, calling for her across a crowded platform in Lyon, her train already pulling away, his voice following the train for as long as it could. She had thought about that moment many times in the three years since, the way the voice went — present, present, thinning, gone.

She put it away. She ran.

★ ★ ★

The gallows were at the far edge of town, which she registered as information and also as the particular absurdity of the situation — that there were gallows, that they were in use, that she was being taken to them. In Paris she designed interiors for galleries and private collectors. She had been in Nevada for approximately five hours. There were gallows.

The large man — Frog, she would learn his name later, Frog — hauled her up the wooden steps with a competence that was the most disturbing thing about him. Not his size, not his willingness, but the competence: the way his hands moved as though this were familiar work, as though gallows platforms and struggling women were in a category he had extensive professional experience with and had long since stopped finding remarkable.

She fought. She was not trained for this — not the way Carmen was trained, not with the muscle memory of someone who had learned to fight as a discipline — but she was stronger than she appeared and she was also furious, which was something she had learned about herself over eleven years of fencing: that fury, properly directed, was not an obstacle to precision but a fuel for it. She had always been taught that passion impaired technique. She had never found this to be true. The passion gave the technique somewhere to go.

She got an elbow into his ribs. She felt it land with the satisfying density of bone meeting bone. He absorbed it the way he absorbed the fighting generally — without particular acknowledgment, as though her resistance was a weather condition rather than an opposition, something to be managed and moved past.

He tied the rope around her neck.

This was when the fear arrived as a distinct and separate thing from the urgency she'd been managing. Not panic — she had never, in her life, panicked, and she did not panic now, though she understood that this was a category of situation that justified it — but something that arrived through her chest like a door opening onto cold air, a recognition of genuine extremity so complete that for a moment everything else receded and there was only the rope at her neck and the drop below and the enormous specific fact of mortality.

She reached for the rope with both hands. She got her fingers between the rope and her neck and pulled, creating fraction of an inch of space, breathing against the constriction, working. The rope bit into her hands. She kept working.

Charlie's voice. From below. From somewhere.

"Charlie!" The word came out wrong — thin, wrong register, the voice of someone being strangled doing its best. She wasn't sure he could hear her. She kept pulling at the rope.

"Shut up," Frog said, and pulled.

The platform left her feet.

The two gunshots came from somewhere above and to her left and she did not hear them so much as feel them — the concussion of the rope, the sudden release, the drop and the impact of the platform boards against her knees as she came down. She was on her hands and knees on the gallows platform and the rope was no longer taut and she understood, without yet understanding how, that the rope had been cut.

A third shot. She heard Frog make a sound and fall.

She pulled the rope off her neck with shaking hands. The rope burn was real — she could feel it, a ring of fire around her throat, specific and present and something she would feel for days. She pulled the rope off and dropped it on the platform and looked at where Frog had fallen and then she looked at the rooftop across the street.

In the lightning — she had not noticed the lightning was still happening, she had been too occupied to notice the lightning — she saw him. A silhouette on the rooftop, the rifle barrel still elevated, the figure already moving back from the edge with the deliberateness of someone who had done what they came to do and was leaving before they could be seen doing it.

The lightning closed. The rooftop was dark and empty.

She looked at it for a moment. She was on her hands and knees on the gallows platform with a rope burn around her neck and shaking hands and she was looking at a dark rooftop where a man had been a second ago, a man with a rifle who had shot two ropes from that distance in two shots, which was a level of marksmanship that required a word she didn't have yet, which was something beyond skill, which was something that had been doing this for a long time.

She got to her feet. She was steady enough. She got down from the platform.

She walked back toward the gas lamps.

★★★

She had expected the crowd to feel anonymous.

She had been in crowds before — the Paris crowds, the press of bodies at the Marché d'Aligre, the specific compression of the Métro at rush hour, the collective warmth and smell of a lot of people in a small space — and she had always experienced crowds as impersonal, as a condition rather than a collection of individuals. She had expected this crowd to feel the same.

It didn't.

The people who had gathered at the edge of the gas lamp light were watching her with the quality of people who were genuinely uncertain what to do. Not all of them. There were several who had the easy viciousness of people who found other people's suffering entertaining, the ones who would always gather at any extremity, and she could identify these by a particular quality of enjoyment in how they stood. But the others — and there were more of the others — were watching with expressions she could read even in the partial light, which were expressions of discomfort and of a kind of paralysis, the expressions of people who were witnessing something they did not want to be witnessing but who did not know, or had decided not to know, what doing something about it looked like.

She looked at them. She made herself look at them, one face at a time, because looking away would have been a concession and she was not prepared to make concessions. A woman in a grey dress near the back looked away first. An older man near the front held her gaze for a moment and then dropped it, and in the dropping of it she could see — she could actually see — the specific moment when he chose the passive option, the choosing written clearly in his face and then covered over with the expression of someone who had decided they were not responsible.

She thought: I know what you are choosing.

She thought this clearly, without heat, the way she thought about fencing form — with precision and without the part of anger that was waste. The anger that was useful was here, directing her hands, keeping her fingers between the rope and her neck, keeping her upright when Frog's grip shifted. The anger that was waste she set aside. She did not have the energy for waste.

The rope was rougher than she had expected. She had never had a rope around her neck and she had no framework for what the texture would be, but she had somehow imagined it as more uniform, and it was not uniform, it was composed of individual fibers, and the fibers were abrading the skin of her throat in a way that she was going to feel for days. She noted this with the cool part of her mind that was always noting things and filed it under: survivable, address later.

The platform swayed slightly. She could feel it in her feet — the give of the boards, the structural flex of something that had been used before and had absorbed previous weight and was absorbing hers. She did not want to think about what it meant that the platform had been used before. She filed this also.

Charlie's voice. From below. From somewhere.

The sound of her own name in his voice — not the social sound of it, not the easy warmth of Charlie saying her name across a table or a phone call, but the urgent and frightened version, the version she had not heard before and which reached her through all the noise and the height and the rope's pressure as a specific frequency, the frequency of someone who knew her and was afraid for her.

She thought: he cannot see me. The angle was wrong from the street below. He was calling into the dark and the height on the chance that she could hear him.

She could hear him.

"Sophie!"

His voice going thinner as Frog dragged her toward the edge. The platform's edge. Below it, she had looked once and not again — the distance was enough, she had calculated it the way you calculated distances when the distance mattered, and the calculation had been sufficient and she did not need to look again.

Frog's hands moved. She felt the rope shift. She kept her fingers between her throat and the hemp and she breathed against the constriction and she thought about Carmen, who had been on her back in the street below and who was the best-prepared person she had ever met and who would find a way, if there was a way, and there was always a way if you had enough information and Carmen was always collecting information.

She thought about the saber in the cargo area of the SUV.

She thought: that was a very impractical thing to bring camping.

She thought this at the wrong moment, in the wrong register, and it produced in her, despite everything — the platform, the rope, the crowd, Frog's competent terrible hands — something that was very nearly a laugh, which was both inappropriate and also, she understood, exactly who she was. She was someone who found the wrong thing funny at the wrong moment, and this had not changed because she was on a gallows platform in 1886, and it was not going to change, and she found this fact briefly and unexpectedly stabilizing.

She was still herself. The rope had not taken that.

The platform shifted.

Then the shots came.

★ ★ ★

She was thinking about the rope.

Not the rope around her neck — she was going to stop thinking about that one, she was putting it in the file under: happened, survived, address later — but the other rope, the one she had not thought about in several years, the one that had started as a practical consideration and had become something else.

Her instructor at the Université — Maître Delacroix, seventy years old when she started, with the hands of a man who had been doing the same thing for fifty years and the patience of someone who had learned that the thing which took a long time to get right was always the thing most worth getting right — had told her, at the end of her first year, that she was technically proficient and emotionally closed.

She had asked what he meant.

He had said:

"You fence like someone who is trying to win. The best fencers fence like someone who is trying to say something."

She had thought about this for six months and then she had gone back and said: what am I supposed to be saying?

He had smiled — the particular smile of an old teacher who has been waiting for the question — and said:

"Whatever you are not saying anywhere else."

She had been saying it ever since. She did not always know what it was. Sometimes it was the particular frustration of a day that had gone wrong in ways too small to justify the frustration. Sometimes it was the larger frustration, the one that didn't have a day attached to it, the one that lived in the gap between the life she was living and the life she had expected to be living by now — not wrong exactly, not failed, but somehow adjacent to what she had imagined, as though she had gotten off at the right station and then walked in a direction that was close to correct but not quite.

She had been fencing it out for eleven years.

She thought about this walking back through the dark streets of Greenbriar Gulch with the rope burn on her neck and her hands still shaking. She thought about what the fencing was for and whether it had worked, whether the eleven years of saying the unsaid thing in footwork and blade had discharged it sufficiently or simply managed it, kept it at a level that didn't impair the rest of her life without actually addressing the thing itself.

She thought about January. Olivier's apartment. The understanding she'd had across a dinner table.

She thought about Charlie.

She thought: you know what the fencing is for. You have always known what the fencing is for. It is for the distance between knowing what you want and doing something about wanting it, and the distance has been there for three years and it has been your choice to maintain it and tonight there are men with guns and gallows and a rope around your neck and tomorrow there might not be a tomorrow and you have been walking around Paris for three years deciding when to close the distance.

She heard her name.

Charlie's voice — close now, urgent, coming from the dark ahead of her, and she called back and his footsteps accelerated and then he was there, running toward her through the lamplight of the main street, and he found her in the dark at the edge of the lamplight and she was crying, which she had not been doing a moment ago but was doing now, and his arms came around her and she let him hold her.

He said nothing useful. He said her name twice. He held her.

This was the right thing. She had always known he knew the right thing.

She stopped crying. She was not someone who cried at length — it was not a quality she judged in others but it was not her quality either, the extended grief, the extended anything. She felt things fully and then she moved through them, which was sometimes a virtue and sometimes a way of not stopping long enough to understand what she felt.

Tonight she let it be a virtue. She stopped crying and she stayed in Charlie's arms for another moment — she was deciding how long to stay, which was itself information, the fact that she was deciding — and then she stepped back and looked at him.

His face in the lamplight was the face she had been looking at for three years. She had looked at it across tables and across distance and through screens and she had made, she understood now, a taxonomy of it: the social face, the thinking face, the face he wore when he was happy and the face he wore when he was managing his happiness because the management of happiness was something he had learned to do in her presence, because her happiness was sometimes uncertain and uncertainty was contagious and he had learned to manage his in order not to add to hers.

She had taken this for granted.

Not without gratitude — she was not without gratitude, she was not without feeling for him, she had never been without feeling for him — but she had taken it for granted the way you took for granted the things that were always there. The light in a room you spent every day in. The warmth of a person who was always warm.

"Are you alright?" he said.

She touched his face. He went still — not surprise exactly, but the stillness of someone receiving something they had stopped expecting.

"I need to tell you something," she said.

"You don't have to —"

"Not now," she said. "I know it's not now. But I need you to know that I have something to tell you and that I will tell you when there is a moment that is not this moment, and I need you to hold that."

He looked at her. He was very good at looking at her — had always been very good at it, the quality of the looking, the specific attention that was not analysis but simply seeing. She had always found this both warming and slightly frightening, to be seen that completely.

"Okay," he said.

"Okay," she said.

She took his hand. They walked back toward the saloon through the gas lamp light, and the town was quiet around them with the quiet that came after violence and before whatever came after the violence, and she held his hand and she thought:

you already know. You have always known. The only question has ever been when.

She had thought, walking back through the empty streets with the rope burn livid on her throat and the gas lamps burning their amber on the dry mud, that she was going to arrive at some tidy understanding. That the extremity of the night would produce the kind of clarity that people in stories extracted from extremity — the near-death revelation, the moment of knowing. She had always been skeptical of this as a narrative device. She was, walking back through Greenbriar Gulch in 1886 with Charlie's hand warm in hers, skeptical of it still.

What she had instead of clarity was an inventory.

She went through it methodically, the way she went through inventory: the rope, the platform, the crowd's faces, the specific quality of Frog's competence, the two shots from the rooftop that had come from a rifle at distance in the dark and had cut the rope precisely. She went through all of it and what she arrived at was not revelation but information, and the information was: she had been more afraid than she had known. She had been, in the moment the platform left her feet, genuinely and completely afraid, and she had not panicked, and she had not given Frog the satisfaction, and the fear had been real and present and she was still alive and it had not been bigger than her.

This was not a small thing.

She had fenced afraid before — had fenced with an audience watching, had fenced in competitions where the outcome mattered, had fenced through the particularly specific fear of a bout against someone she believed was better than her. She had found in all of these cases what Maître Delacroix had told her she would find, which was that the fear, properly directed, became fuel. That the passion gave the technique somewhere to go.

She had not, until tonight, known how much fuel she had.

She walked through the gas lamp light with Charlie's hand in hers and she thought about eleven years of fencing and what the eleven years had been building toward, what it had been saying in the language Maître Delacroix had taught her, and she understood — not for the first time but more completely than before — that it had been saying: I am not going to disappear. The fencing had been eleven years of insisting, in the private language of footwork and blade, that she was a person who persisted, who did not go away under pressure, who found, in the giving of full attention to a full opponent, something that could not be located anywhere else she had tried to find it.

Charlie looked at her.

She looked back at him.

His face in the lamplight was doing several things at once, which was the face she had always found most like him — the warmth and the worry and beneath both of them the steadiness, the specific steadiness of a person who was afraid and was not going to let the fear be the loudest thing in the room. She had thought, in the three years she had been with him, that this steadiness was a character trait, something he had been born with, the temperament of someone to whom equilibrium came easily. She was revising this now. She was revising it in light of tonight, in light of the sound of his voice in the dark below the gallows platform, which was the voice of someone who was very afraid and was calling her name anyway.

The steadiness was not the absence of fear. It was the decision to proceed regardless. She had been mistaken about this for three years and she was correcting the mistake now, in real time, walking through a mining town in Nevada in 1886.

"Are you alright?" he said again.

"Yes," she said. And then, because she was done with the version of honesty that left the important parts out: "I will be."

He nodded. He did not say anything else immediately, which was right. She had always been, in her interior life, a person who needed a moment after a true statement before she could move through it to the next thing, and he knew this, though she had never told him. He had simply learned it, in the way that people who paid attention learned the rhythms of the people they were paying attention to.

She thought: he has always been paying attention.

She thought: I have not always known what to do with that.

She thought: I know now.

She had not been wrong about what she needed from the desert. She had needed to be accurately sized. She had thought she needed the size to find the courage to end something.

She understood now that what she had needed the size to find was the courage to begin.

TWELVE AND A HALF

What I Want to Tell You

Sophia

Sophia

They found a doorway.

This was what there was: a doorway on the side of a building that faced the alley rather than the main street, set back from the gas lamp light enough to be in shadow, a recessed threshold with a wooden overhang that kept the last of the rain off. Charlie found it. He had found it the way he found things — not by looking for the specific thing but by being in motion with an awareness of what the situation required, his attention on her but also on the periphery, the way his attention always worked, broad and accumulating without being diffuse.

"Here," he said.

She went into the doorway with him. The wood of the door at her back was old and solid and smelled of the desert and old lumber and something she couldn't name, something that was specific to this town, this time, this air that was not the air she had grown up in. The rope burn on her throat was still warm. She became aware, in the doorway's shelter, that her legs were shaking — a fine and private tremor, not the kind that was visible, the kind that lived in the muscles and was the body's way of processing what had been spent.

Charlie put his hand on her face.

He cupped her jaw carefully, his thumb against her cheekbone, not pressing, simply there — the presence of his hand on her face, warm and steady. She covered his hand with hers and they stood in the doorway in the shadow and she breathed.

She breathed.

"You don't have to —" he started.

"I know."

"I just want you to know that whatever you were going to tell me —"

"Charlie."

"Yes."

"I know you know. That's what I've been trying to figure out how to say for three months. That I know you know."

He was quiet. She felt his hand still against her face, steady, not withdrawing.

"I came here to end it," she said.

She said it directly because she had decided, on the gallows platform when the fear arrived as a distinct and separate thing and the only inventory she'd been able to take was the inventory of what she had not yet done and not yet said — she had decided that the version of honesty that left the important parts out was over, and that what came after it had to be the complete version.

"I know," he said.

"You knew?"

"January. You called on a Thursday evening. You were different."

She looked at him. In the shadow of the doorway his face was mostly planes and angles, the gas lamp light at a distance catching only the edges of him — the jaw, the brow, the particular way he held his head when he was being careful with something.

"You didn't say anything."

"No."

"Why not?"

He thought about this. She watched him think about it, the quality of his consideration, the unhurried way he sat with a question before answering it.

"Because I didn't want to say the thing that would make it happen faster," he said. "And I didn't want to say the thing that would make you feel you couldn't. Both of those things seemed — unkind. So I just — waited."

She absorbed this. It had the specific weight of a thing that was both true and more generous than she had understood.

"I was wrong," she said. "About what I needed from this trip."

"Tell me."

"I thought I needed the desert to remember that I could be without you. That I was a full person with a full life and the distance was real and the geography was real and the ambivalence was real, and I needed to be in a large enough space to see all of it clearly and make a clear decision."

"And?"

"And tonight a man put a rope around my neck."

He made a sound that was not quite a laugh and not quite grief, something between the two.

"And it turns out," she said, "that the clarity I needed was not the clarity about whether to leave. It was the clarity about why I stayed. Which I have been treating as a problem to solve instead of a fact I was already living inside."

He took her other hand. He held both of her hands in both of his, in the doorway, in the shadow, with the gas lamp burning its amber twenty feet away and the streets of Greenbriar Gulch quiet around them and somewhere in the town the remaining business of the night still unfinished.

"I have been so afraid," she said, "of being someone who stayed because she didn't know how to go. Who built a life around someone by default rather than by choosing. I have watched people do that — watched my mother do that, watched women in Paris do that, watched the architecture of a life that was shaped by the absence of a decision rather than the presence of one — and I have been so afraid that I was doing the same thing that I made the fear itself into a reason to leave."

"And now?"

"And now I am standing in a doorway in Nevada in what I believe is 1886, and I have just been on a gallows, and I am thinking about what I would have not said if the rope had —"

She stopped. He waited.

"I would not have told you," she said. "That is the fact. I would have gone to Nevada and found the right moment and ended it kindly and flown back to Paris and I would have spent the rest of my life knowing that I had made a decision without understanding what I was deciding."

She looked at him. His face was very clear to her, even in the shadow, even in the unfamiliar light of a gas lamp in a town that should not exist. She had been looking at this face for three years and she had made, without knowing it, a complete study of it — every version, every register, the social face and the thinking face and the face he wore in the specific moment of understanding something he had been waiting to understand. She knew all of them.

She did not know the face he was wearing right now.

It was not the face of relief. It was not the face of someone receiving the answer they had been hoping for. It was quieter than that — a stillness that was not the stillness of containment but the stillness of something that had been true for a long time and was now acknowledged rather than arrived at, the way a season didn't arrive but was simply, one morning, present.

"I love you," he said.

Three words. Said without preamble, without decoration, without the management of how they might land. Just the words, and him, in the shadow of the doorway.

She felt them.

She had heard these words from him before — had heard them at the end of phone calls, in the warmth of the specific shorthand of people who had said a thing enough times that it became fluent, and she had said them back with the same fluency, and they had meant something. They had always meant something.

They meant more now. She understood, hearing them in this doorway in this terrible and improbable night, that the words had been accumulating meaning across three years of being said in the easy register, and the accumulated meaning was here in this version, in the version said in a doorway in 1886 with the rope burn still on her throat, and it was larger than she had known it would be, and she was grateful for the size of it.

"Je t'aime," she said.

The French came first. It always did, when she meant something completely — when the thing she was saying needed to come from the deepest available layer, the first layer, the one laid down in childhood before English, before the years of living in an international register. The French was the language underneath the language. She had told him this once and he had remembered it, the way he remembered things.

She saw him receive it.

"What I want to tell you," she said, "is that I know what I chose. I know I chose it and I am choosing it and I am sorry it took me three years and a gallows to arrive at saying so."

He kissed her. Not the version from earlier tonight, the deliberate declaration of it, the first real one — that had been true and it had been hers to give, and she had given it. This was different, this was the version that came after the declaration, the quieter version, the one that assumed the thing was real and was simply the physical fact of two people who had just confirmed something and were here together in the immediate aftermath of it.

She kissed him back.

When she stepped back she was crying, which surprised her, because she had not been crying a moment ago and she had not felt the onset of it. The tears were simply present, which was how she cried — without announcement, without the preliminary warning that it was coming, just suddenly there, the evidence of something that had been moving in her and had found the only available exit.

She wiped her face with the back of her hand. He watched her do it.

"We need to go back to the others," she said.

"We do."

"In a minute."

"In a minute," he agreed.

They stood in the doorway for a minute. The town was quiet around them and the gas lamps burned and somewhere to the east the storm was receding, its thunder growing infrequent, the sky lightening fractionally at the edge where the clouds had pulled apart. She leaned against him. He put his arm around her.

She thought about the telescope in the back of the SUV. Charlie's telescope, packed for a trip to a mountain they hadn't reached, with a list of things he wanted to show her, which she had found on his phone weeks ago and had not told him she'd found. The list had made her cry then too, in a way she hadn't expected — not for sadness but for the specific quality of it, the careful and private excitement of a person planning to show someone something they loved.

stars for Sophie.

She had thought, reading it, that she didn't deserve it. That she was planning to end things with the person who had titled his notes *stars for Sophie* and she did not deserve the telescope or the list or the patient planning of someone who had been, for three years, quietly preparing the world to be more beautiful for her.

She thought now: this is correctable. Not the three years of ambivalence — those had been real, and she would sit with them honestly, and she would not pretend they had been something else. But the correctable part was the future, which was unwritten, and she was going to write it differently.

"Andromeda," she said.

He looked at her. "What?"

"On your list. On your phone. Stars for Sophie." She felt him go still. "I found it three weeks ago. I should have told you."

"You read my list."

"I read your list."

He exhaled. Then, in the tone she loved best in him, the tone that was both genuine and slightly absurd at the same time: "Okay. Well. Then you know the plan."

"Andromeda last," she said. "Build to it."

"Exactly."

"Except you wrote: actually show her first. The others are practice."

A pause. She heard him, in the dark of the doorway, trying not to laugh.

"I may have changed the plan," he said.

"I thought so."

She took his hand. She stepped out of the doorway into the gas lamp light. The rope burn on her throat was still warm and would be for days, and the town was still dark beyond the lamp circles, and there was still whatever remained of the night to get through. But she was here, and he was here, and she was not going to let either of those facts pass without knowing that she knew them.

"Come on," she said.

They walked back toward the chapel and the others, her hand in his, through the lamp-lit dark of Greenbriar Gulch.

THIRTEEN

The Gold

Matt

Matt

The sheriff's instructions were simple and Matt was glad of it, because his leg had been bleeding through the bandage Emma had tied in the chapel and simple instructions were the kind he could execute on a leg that was bleeding through its bandage.

Go with Emma. Get the gold. Hide it in the mines. Come back.

Four steps. He could do four steps.

He fell in beside Emma as they came out of the chapel and the street received them — the gas lamps, the dry mud, the particular quality of the silence between gunshots, which was the silence of something paused rather than something ended. He kept his weight on the good leg. He kept his eyes on the buildings on either side because Tommy Boy was somewhere and so was Frog and O'Donnell was somewhere with a shoulder wound that would not improve his disposition.

Emma moved quickly. She knew the distance between every building on the main street — he could see this in how she moved, the way she cut the angle at each corner and kept close to the walls without being told to, the body knowledge of someone who had been navigating this specific geography for five years and had long since integrated it below the level of thought. He matched her pace. His leg informed him of its condition with each step. He noted this and kept moving.

The deputy came out of the dark to meet them halfway. He was carrying a lamp and he had the revolver holstered and his hands were low, which was the universal posture of a man trying to communicate that he was not an immediate threat. He walked with them to the saloon without speaking, which Matt appreciated.

He still had questions about the deputy. He had many questions about the deputy. He filed them under:

later, when later is possible.

The Drunken Coyote at night with no customers was a different room than it had been an hour ago with the gang at the back table. The absence of the gang did not make it feel safe — it made it feel the way a room felt after a large animal had recently passed through it, a residual alertness in the air, the sense of something having been present that had not been benign.

Emma went to her office. He followed. He watched her cross to the desk and open the desk drawer and take out nothing — she was not taking anything from the drawer, she was using the motion of opening it to check something he couldn't see from his angle, something the angle of her body suggested was on the far wall. She closed the drawer. She moved to the back wall.

The clay flower pot was large — the largest thing in the small office, and the most incongruous, the kind of object that occupied its position with such settled assurance that it stopped being noticed, which was, he understood now, the point. Emma moved it with the ease of someone who had moved it many times, tilting it rather than lifting it, rolling it on its base in a practiced arc.

Behind the pot: a wooden panel at floor level, set flush into the wall with the craftsmanship of someone who had intended it to be invisible and had succeeded. He had looked at that wall when he'd been in the office earlier — had registered the panel as part of the wall's texture, had moved on. He would not have found it. Nobody would have found it who was not looking for it specifically, and nobody would have known to look for it specifically unless Emma had told them.

She pressed the panel in three places — a sequence, three specific points, in an order that mattered. He watched her fingers find the points without hesitation, the muscle memory of a combination she had pressed enough times that her hands knew it without her mind needing to direct them. The panel swung inward.

Inside: a wooden box. Not large — the size of a small case for documents, or a wide Bible. But made with care: the joinery tight, the brass fittings polished, the wood a dark reddish grain he didn't recognize. It had been somewhere before it was here. It had a past.

She lifted it out and the deputy took it and the deputy said something to her, low, and she nodded, and then the deputy went and they were alone.

★ ★ ★

He should have said: we need to go. He knew this. The situation was active, Sophie and Carmen were in the chapel without them, O'Donnell was in the night with a plan that was not finished, and the deputy was outside with the box and they needed to move. He knew all of this.

He stood in the lamplight of Emma Rose's office and did not say it.

She stood at the window — the small window that faced the alley — and she was looking at something outside or possibly at nothing, possibly at her own reflection in the glass, which would have shown her a woman in the lamplight of her own building on the worst night of the last five years.

"I don't want your gold," he said.

She turned.

"Whatever's in that box is yours. Five years of work. Whatever you've been saving toward — I don't want it."

She looked at him. The lamp was on the desk and it threw its amber light up at her face from below, which was not the most flattering angle for anyone but which for Emma produced something exact — the lines of her face in relief, the set of her jaw, the quality of her eyes which was the quality he had been trying to name since he'd first seen her and which he still could not name, which was something between steadiness and knowing, the look of someone who had been paying attention to the world for a long time and had arrived, through the paying of attention, at a set of conclusions she trusted.

"Nothing would please me more than for you to have it," she said.

"That doesn't make sense."

"It makes complete sense. You came into my saloon tonight in the middle of a storm and you threw a chair at a man twice your size on behalf of a woman you'd known for eleven minutes, and you did it because it was what the situation required and because you are the kind of person for whom what the situation requires and what you do are the same thing without any deliberation in between. I have not met many such people. I would like you to have the box."

He looked at her. He thought about the traverse — the sixth move, the sloper, the question of whether the failure lived not at the point of failure but earlier in the sequence. He thought about his sister's question:

maybe you're thinking about it wrong.

He thought: I have been thinking about a great many things wrong.

"I have a mind," she said, "to spend the rest of my days with you. I know that is a remarkable thing to say to someone I met this evening. I am saying it anyway because the evening has been of a kind that makes the usual protocols seem beside the point, and because I am old enough to know that the things left unsaid have a way of staying unsaid past the point when you can say them, and I would rather say a true thing at the wrong time than not say it at all."

He thought about Sophie on the train platform saying

yes, alright to a man she loved across a restaurant table in October. He thought about Carmen not calling. He thought about the people who moved through their lives with the things they meant arranged in some interior order, waiting for the right moment, and how the right moment and any moment were not always the thing he'd assumed they were.

"It doesn't sound ridiculous at all," he said. "It sounds like the most sensible thing anyone's said to me in years."

This was true. He was aware of it being true in the way he was aware of the six moves of the traverse — in his body before his mind had the language, as a fact about the configuration of things rather than an argument toward it.

She crossed to him. She took his face in both hands — her hands were warm, warmer than the room, and they were steady in the way everything about her was steady, with the steadiness of someone who had decided something and was in the act of doing it. She looked at him.

He held very still. He was good at holding still.

"We should go," she said.

"Yeah," he said.

Neither of them moved for a moment.

He thought: I know her face. He had thought this from the first moment in the saloon, the recognition that had no rational basis and that he had set aside because setting things aside was what he did when he didn't know what to do with them. He had set it aside and kept setting it aside through the whole of the evening and it was still there, under everything, the specific warmth of someone known.

He thought: I do not believe in things I cannot account for.

He thought: I cannot account for this.

He thought: I believe it anyway.

She released his face. She took his hand to lead him to the door and then something moved in the back room — a sound, faint, the sound of someone trying not to make a sound and not entirely succeeding — and her hand tightened on his and they both went still.

Tommy Boy was in the back room.

He could hear him now — the particular sounds of a search conducted by someone who was looking for something specific and not finding it and becoming less careful about the not-finding as the frustration accumulated. Bottles moved. A crate scraped against the floor. Something fell and was not picked up.

He looked at Emma. He kept his voice below a breath: "Stay here."

She grabbed his arm. She said his name — Matthew, the full name, which she had used from the beginning and which in her mouth had the quality of a word that meant something more than his name, the way certain words acquired additional meaning through specific use. She said it and she pulled his face down to hers and she kissed him — fully, deliberately, with the intention of someone who had decided to do this and was doing it and was not managing it but giving it — and then she released him.

"Be careful," she said. Barely audible.

"Yes ma'am," he said.

He went through the door.

Tommy Boy was at the shelves, pulling things down with the systematic efficiency of a man who had done this before and who would not stop until he found what he was looking for or ran out of places to look. He didn't hear Matt come in, which was information — Tommy Boy was focused inward, in the grip of the task, his attention directed at the shelves and not at the room. This was a mistake that people made when they were frustrated and Matt noted it and used it.

He waited. He positioned himself beside the doorframe, out of the lamp's direct light, and he waited for Tommy Boy to turn and come through the door because Tommy Boy was going to come through the door eventually when the shelves yielded nothing, and when he came through the door, Matt would be there.

He thought about the traverse. The heel hook hypothesis. His sister's question.

He thought about Emma in the lamplight with her hands on his face.

Tommy Boy came through the door.

Matt swung the chair.

The chair connected solidly — the kind of connection that communicated itself through the arms in a way that was distinct from the connections that glanced or partially landed, a full transfer of force from the chair to the recipient that sent Tommy Boy into the wall and sent his revolver across the floor. Tommy Boy came off the wall already swinging, which meant he had taken the hit and organized himself faster than expected, which was the kind of information you needed to have and preferred to acquire early.

They fought.

Matt was athletic and trained and operating on the specific clarity that came from necessity, the narrowing of everything extraneous until only the immediate problem remained. He also had a leg that had been shot an hour ago and was communicating this fact with increasing urgency. The leg was a variable he was managing rather than ignoring — he kept his weight distributed, he used the good leg for the movements that required power and the bad leg for balance only, he was compensating in real time for a compromise in the system.

Tommy Boy noticed the leg. Of course he noticed the leg. It was the kind of thing that a person like Tommy Boy would notice in the first thirty seconds because it was the kind of person Tommy Boy was — experienced at assessing opponents, long accustomed to finding and exploiting the available weakness. He shifted his attacks to the left, pressing Matt's bad side, forcing the weight transfer that cost the most.

Matt was losing ground.

He heard the front door and then Charlie was in the room.

Charlie came in the way Charlie did most things in a crisis, which was with the energy of someone who had been running toward the situation and had not quite formulated a plan for what to do when he arrived. He was not trained and he was not large and he was not, in any combat sense, prepared. He was also Charlie, which meant he threw himself at Tommy Boy with the complete and utter commitment of someone who had decided that the situation required this and was not going to let the absence of a plan be an obstacle to acting.

It was not elegant. It worked.

Tommy Boy lost his footing. Matt swung the chair. It was a different chair than the one from the saloon — he had picked this one up from the back room floor without thinking about it — but the principle held. The chair connected and Tommy Boy hit the floor and was quiet.

Charlie looked at the unconscious man on the floor. He looked at Matt.

"Why is it always a chair with you?" he said.

Matt looked at the chair in his hands. He had thrown a chair tonight, this being the second one, and he had not in either case planned to throw a chair — it was simply what his hands had found at the relevant moment. There was something about this that felt like information, like the traverse question, like maybe the right instrument was the one that presented itself rather than the one you'd planned for.

"They work," he said.

He set the chair down. He looked at Tommy Boy on the floor and then at the back room door, where a moment ago Emma had been standing. She was gone — she had understood, without being told, that the thing to do when a fight ended was not to be in the room where the fight had been.

He found her in the office. She was at the window again. She had her back to the door and she did not turn when he came in, which meant she had heard him before she could see him and had decided it was him and had decided not to turn.

He stood in the doorway.

"He's down," he said.

She nodded. She was looking at the alley window. He could see her face in the glass — reflected, amber-lit, composed.

"The box," she said. "The deputy has it."

"I know."

"If anything happens to me —"

"Emma."

"Matthew." She said it the way she'd been saying it — with the weight of something that meant more than his name. "If anything happens to me tonight, I want you to have it. I already told the deputy. He's given his word."

He looked at her reflection in the window. He thought about what to say to this and could not find anything adequate, which was a situation he occasionally encountered and which he generally addressed by not saying the inadequate thing.

"Nothing is going to happen to you," he said.

This was not adequate either. But it was what he had, and she heard it the way she heard most things — fully, without requiring it to be more than it was.

"No," she said. "I don't imagine it will."

She turned from the window. She looked at him across the small office — the desk between them, the lamp throwing its amber light, the rifle still leaning against the wall where it had been all evening, loaded, the thing she hadn't needed yet.

She said it the way she said things she meant but did not require him to respond to immediately — with the patience of someone who had learned that silence sometimes contained a better answer than any answer she could prompt.

He looked at her.

She was standing at the alley window with the lamp below her face and the rifle against the wall and five years of a life she had built and run and been proud of all around her, and she was composed, and he thought: I have never met anyone like this. He had thought it several times over the course of the night and he thought it again now, in the lamplight of the small office, with the sounds of the town still settling outside and O'Donnell somewhere in it.

"The box," she said.

"Emma."

She turned to look at him. Her expression had a particular quality he had been cataloguing all evening — the working composure, the professional surface, and then underneath it, visible only in certain moments, the person who was managing the working composure rather than the person who simply was it. The managing took effort. He could see the effort, and he could see that she did not want him to see it, and he could see that she knew he was seeing it anyway, and that she had decided this was acceptable.

"It will take care of itself," he said. "The box. Whatever's in it — it'll find its way."

She looked at him steadily. "You cannot know that."

"No. But you built this." He gestured — at the office, at the saloon beyond the thin wall, at the town, at the five years of decisions she had made that had produced a woman who stood at an alley window with a rifle and a box of saved gold and the composure of someone who had decided that what she had built was worth keeping. "Whatever happens tonight, you built this. That's yours."

She was quiet for a moment. He watched her receive it — not accepting it without examination, which was not her way, but considering it in the precise manner she considered most things.

"Yes," she said, finally. "I suppose it is."

He did not say: I wish we'd had more time. He did not say: I will come back, which he believed but could not promise. He said:

"The traverse. The thing I told you about. The problem in the fifth move."

She looked at him. "What about it?"

"I think I understand it now. I've been setting it up wrong for three years. The sixth move isn't the problem. The problem was in what I was assuming in the fifth."

She tilted her head. "What were you assuming?"

"That the obvious choice was the right one. The obvious footwork. The obvious weight distribution."

"And it wasn't."

"The obvious choice was setting me up wrong for the sixth. I was solving the wrong problem. Every time."

She looked at him with the expression he had catalogued as: not commenting yet, still processing.

"This is not about the traverse," she said.

"No," he said. "It is about the traverse. And also other things."

She almost smiled. Not the working smile — the other one, the real one, the one he had first seen over the broth at the table in the saloon and that had produced in him, very clearly, the thought: there you are.

"Matthew," she said.

"Yes."

"Whatever comes after this —"

"Emma."

"I am going to say it."

"Alright."

She looked at him across the small office. The lamp between them. The rifle. The window with its dark alley beyond.

"Whatever comes after this," she said, "I am glad you came in from the rain. I am glad it was your saloon."

He held this. He held it the way he was learning to hold things that were too large for their category — not analyzing, not requiring language, simply receiving.

"My saloon," he said.

"My saloon," she agreed. "For tonight."

She smiled.

"Come on then," she said. "We have work to do."

He followed her out.

FOURTEEN

It's Going to Be Alright

Charlie

Charlie

He had never been so frightened in his life and he was, underneath the fear, almost entirely fine.

This was a thing he had not known about himself until tonight: that he could be afraid at a level that was genuinely new — the fear of gunshots, the fear of Sophia dragged away on a rope, the fear of a man in a black hat who had looked at him across a saloon with the expression of someone taking inventory of a problem — and still be, underneath all of it, essentially himself. Still be someone who found the situation clarifying rather than obliterating. Still be someone who, in the gaps between the worst moments, noticed things: the smell of the chapel's old wood, the quality of Emma's composure, the specific relief on Sophie's face when he found her by the gallows, which was the relief of someone who had been afraid and was no longer afraid and was letting the relief happen rather than managing it.

He had not known he was this person. He had suspected, in a theoretical way, that he was not a coward — he had done a few things that required nerve, in a small and ordinary way, the small and ordinary nerve of a person navigating a small and ordinary life. But he had not known that his nerve had this particular quality, which was not the nerve of aggression or of indifference to danger but something quieter: the nerve of someone who, when things got genuinely bad, found that the self he had been carrying around all this time was still present and still functional and was, if anything, more itself under pressure than it had been when the pressure was ordinary.

He thought: Sophie's hands were shaking when I found her. He thought: I held her and they stopped.

He thought this with a quiet completeness that had nothing to do with pride. She had been afraid. He had been afraid. He had held her and something in the holding had been useful, and that was all, and that was enough.

★★★

In the chapel they had the plan. The sheriff had given them instructions and the instructions made sense and the sheriff was someone Charlie had an immediate and complete confidence in, of the kind he usually reserved for people he had known for years and had watched under pressure. He had watched the sheriff for approximately forty minutes. He trusted him completely.

He had always been this way — fast to trust, which most people experienced as naivety and which he had spent considerable time examining to determine whether they were right. He had concluded, at some point in his early twenties, that fast trust was not the same as undiscriminating trust. He did not trust everyone quickly. He trusted specific people quickly — people who had a quality he could not name precisely but which had something to do with the alignment between what they appeared to be and what they were, the absence of a gap between the performance and the person. The sheriff had this quality. Emma had it. Matt had always had it. Sophie had it, with the specific caveat that Sophie's gap ran in the opposite direction from most people's — she appeared more reserved than she was, appeared less warm than she was, appeared more certain than she was, and the actual Sophie underneath the appearance was larger and warmer and more uncertain, which Charlie had always found both moving and very Sophie.

The plan: go with Emma and the deputy to retrieve the gold. He and Carmen and Sophie would stay in the chapel. When the gold was secured they would move together toward the edge of town.

He agreed to the plan. He understood the plan. He sat in the chapel and he thought about Sophie.

He thought about what she had said to him, after the gallows, on the dark street between the gas lamps. She had said: I have something to tell you. She had said: not now. She had said: hold that.

He had said okay. He had meant it. He was holding it.

He knew, with the certainty of someone who had been paying attention for three years, that the something was large. He knew that the something was the thing he had been sensing since January, the change in the register of her that he had noticed and named and refused to examine too closely because examining things too closely was sometimes the thing that made them resolve in the direction you were afraid of rather than the direction you were hoping for.

He was not, sitting in the chapel in the middle of everything, afraid.

He was holding the something she had asked him to hold and he was not afraid of what it contained, because she had touched his face when she said it. She had touched his face and the touch had the quality of someone reaching for something they had decided to reach for rather than reaching for something out of habit, and there was a difference, and he knew the difference, and he had felt it.

He thought: whatever she has to tell me, she is going to tell me.

He thought: I can wait.

He had been thinking about Sophie since January.

Not in the way he sometimes caught himself thinking about her, which was the way you thought about the person you loved in the ordinary mode of loving someone — the ambient awareness, the small and continuous accounting of where they were and how they were and what they needed. He had been thinking about her in a different mode since January, the mode of someone who had noticed a change and was deciding what it meant.

The change was small. It was in the register of her calls, the slight increase in the care with which she chose her words, the quality of the pauses before she said things she had apparently decided to say after deciding not to say them. He had catalogued these the way he catalogued everything about the people he loved — carefully, without requiring the catalogue to produce a conclusion before it was ready. He had catalogued them and he had not pressed and he had waited.

He understood that most people would have pressed. Most people, in possession of evidence that the person they loved was managing something they were not sharing, would have asked directly, would have said: Sophie, what's happening, talk to me. He had considered this. He had decided against it, not because he was afraid of the answer but because pressing prematurely was, in his experience, the thing that collapsed the space a person needed to arrive at their own conclusion. Sophie was someone who arrived at things on her own schedule. His job, when Sophie was arriving at something, was to be present and patient and to not make the schedule about him.

So he had waited.

He had waited since January and tonight she had touched his face. In the dark street after the gallows, with the rope burn still livid on her neck and her hands shaking the fine shaking of someone who had just come through something and was still metabolizing it, she had reached up and put her hand on his face. Not for comfort — he was the one who wanted to offer comfort, who had been wanting to offer it since he'd heard the horseman take her, the specific terror of hearing her voice going smaller as the horse moved away. She had touched his face for some other reason, some reason of her own, and then she had said: I have something to tell you.

He was holding that.

He was holding it the way he held things he was not ready to examine but not willing to put down — present, carried, available when the time came for it to be more than carried. He did not speculate about what the something was. Speculation produced false arrivals, conclusions you then had to undo when the real one came. He waited for the real one.

He thought: she touched my face.

He thought: in the lamplight on the gallows street, with everything happening, she stopped and touched my face. And whatever is in the something she has to tell me, that was also in the touch, and the touch was true, and I felt it.

★ ★ ★

The storm had passed its worst by the time Matt and Emma came back. The rain was still present but lighter, the thunder far to the east, the sky beginning to show, in the gaps between the clouds, the specific dark of a sky that was clearing rather than deepening. Charlie stood at the chapel window and watched them come back through the street — Emma, Matt, the deputy — and he felt, watching them, the relief that he had always felt when the people he cared about came back from wherever they'd been.

He had always felt this. He had always felt the mild terror of people being not-present and the relief of their return. He felt it when Matt came back from climbs and when Sophie landed from flights and when Carmen came back from deployments. He felt it at a consistent level regardless of the severity of the absence, which he understood was probably an idiosyncrasy — that the same relief of Matt returning from a phone call and Matt returning from a climb in Kazakhstan was a category error that most people didn't make — but which he had never been able to correct because the relief was involuntary and preceded any rational accounting of the actual risk involved.

Emma and Matt were talking quietly as they came in. He observed this and updated the Matt-and-Emma situation assessment he had been running since the broth. The update was: significant. He did not interfere with significant.

He would tell Matt something, when there was time. He had been composing it in his head for the last hour:

she is the right one. I don't know how to explain why I'm sure, but I'm sure. Pay attention.

He would say this when there was time. There was not currently time. He filed it.

Sophie came to him. She put her hand on his arm and stood beside him at the window and they looked out at the street together in the way they looked at things together, which was the way of two people who had arrived, over three years, at a shared way of looking — not agreeing on everything they saw but knowing what each other was seeing and being comfortable with the knowing.

"How are you?" she said.

"Fine," he said. "You?"

She was quiet for a moment. "Better," she said. "I'm better."

He understood that better meant something specific. He was glad of it. He kept holding the something she'd asked him to hold and he kept it carefully, the way you carried something that mattered in terrain that required attention.

★★★

The gunfire outside changed the plan.

He heard it and his body registered it before his mind had language for what was happening — the specific quality of gunshots that were close and directed rather than distant and scattered, the kind of sound that meant someone was shooting at a specific target rather than shooting generally. He looked at Carmen, who was already assessing. He looked at Sophie, who had the saber in her hand and had positioned herself with the economy of someone who knew what she was doing with the thing she was holding.

He thought: I knew about the saber before tonight. He had not known about the saber before tonight. He updated this.

The sheriff had gone out to deal with O'Donnell. The deputy had gone with the gold. Matt and Emma were in the saloon. The four of them were in the chapel: himself, Carmen, Sophie, and the specific quality of a situation that had reached a new level of seriousness.

Carmen said: we can't wait here.

He agreed. He was going to check on Matt and Emma. He said this and Sophie turned to him and he was looking at her when she crossed the distance between them in two steps and kissed him.

Not the cheeks. The lips. Fully and deliberately, the way she had kissed him on the Tuesday in October three years ago when he had asked her, inarticulately, across a restaurant table in Paris, to be with him — not the same kiss, not a replica, but the same quality, the same deliberateness, the same absolute absence of performance in a moment that could have been performed and wasn't.

He stood very still. He received it completely.

When she stepped back she looked at him with the look she used when she was not managing her face at all, which was the look he had been waiting three years for in its complete form, which was the look of Sophie without the apartment in Paris and the considered deliberateness and the distance she maintained because distance was what she had always had and had not always known how to be without.

"I love you," she said.

He thought of all the things he wanted to say and said instead the truest one: "I've missed your kisses."

She almost smiled. "You won't have to anymore."

He went toward the door. He looked back at her once through the closing — her face in the lamp light, the saber in her hand, Carmen at her shoulder with the revolver. He thought: this is what she looks like when she has decided something. He thought: I will remember this.

He went out.

★ ★ ★

The night was quieter than it had been. The rain had gone from a curtain to a presence — still there, still cold, but no longer the driving thing it had been. The gas lamps were burning. He moved across the main street toward the saloon.

He thought about the Andromeda galaxy. He had been thinking about it since they left Las Vegas, in the background, below the level of the situation — the telescope in the SUV, the sky above Leatherman Peak that he had not seen and now would not see tonight, the list of things he had wanted to show Sophie. Andromeda. Two and a half million light years. The light that had left it before they existed, arriving now.

He thought: there will be other nights.

He thought: next weekend, or the weekend after. The Ruby Mountains. He had read about the sky there. Sophie had said she needed the desert. She was right that she needed the desert, though not for the reasons she had thought she needed it when she said it — he understood this now, he had understood it the moment she kissed him, the thing the desert had been for.

He thought: we will go back. Not to this place, to a better one. The hot springs we didn't reach. Leatherman Peak for Matt. The sky for both of them.

He walked toward the saloon and the night was quiet and the gas lamps burned.

Inside the saloon: a crash, the unmistakable sound of furniture and a person colliding with something solid. Matt. He broke into a run.

He came through the saloon door and found the fight already in progress — Matt and Tommy Boy, the back room, the sound of it reaching the main room and the sight of it visible through the doorway: two men, the specific ugly economy of two people trying to hurt each other, Matt losing ground because of the leg, the leg that had been bleeding all night and that was now demanding what it was owed.

Charlie went through the doorway.

He did not have a plan. He had never had a plan when he ran toward things — he had always had an impulse and then a running, and the plan had always arrived after the running had begun, from the territory rather than from the preparation. He grabbed Tommy Boy from behind, which was not elegant and was not trained and was what he could do, and he got his arms around the man's arms and held on and he heard Matt say something and saw something coming and Tommy Boy went down.

Tommy Boy was on the floor. Matt was standing, breathing hard, the chair in his hands.

"Why is it always a chair with you?" Charlie said.

Matt looked at the chair. "They work."

Charlie looked at the man on the floor. He looked at Matt. Something moved through him — not triumph, not relief exactly, something quieter than either of those, the feeling of having done something that needed doing and having done it adequately. He had not been trained for this and he had not been heroic and he had done the thing that needed doing.

He thought: I should call my sister tomorrow.

He thought: Sophie's hands stopped shaking when I held her.

He thought: I want to show her Andromeda. I want to be standing next to her when she understands how far away it is.

He thought: there will be time.

★ ★ ★

When they got back to the chapel the situation had changed again, which was how the night had been — a continuous redistribution of threat, each resolved situation generating a new one, the problem not fixed but migrating. He came in and found the room and updated his understanding and decided that the immediate requirement was Sophie, who had come back from somewhere with the saber bloody and Carmen at her shoulder, and he went to her.

He got his arms around her. She was shaking — a fine tremor, not the large shaking of someone in crisis but the smaller shaking of someone whose adrenaline was still present and had not yet been metabolized. He held her.

"I'm alright," she said, into his shoulder.

"I know," he said.

He didn't ask what had happened. She would tell him. She would tell him when she was ready and he would listen and it would be enough for right now to stand here with her in the aftermath of whatever it had been and be the person she was shaking against.

The sheriff returned. There was a plan. They moved through the town — all of them, the sheriff and the deputy and Emma and the four friends — toward the jailhouse to lock up Tommy Boy before whatever came next.

Then Frog and O'Donnell on horseback, coming out of the dark, and the world reorganizing again.

He ran. They all ran. Up the steps of the Town Hall and the door barricaded and the gunfire outside and the smoke beginning, the orange light at the base of the walls, the smell of it.

He thought, in the middle of this: Sophie's hands stopped shaking.

He thought: Matt and Emma, in the saloon, in the lamplight.

He thought, with the clarity that the smoke and the heat were producing, which was the clarity of a situation that had removed all the non-essential things and left only what mattered: I have had a very good life. It has not been very long but it has been very good. I have loved the people who deserved to be loved and I have been loved by people I did not entirely deserve. I have had seven years of Matt's friendship and three years of Sophie's and a decade of Carmen's and the specific unrepeatable quality of all of it and none of it has been wasted.

He thought: the telescope is in the SUV.

He thought: Sophie will figure out how to use it.

The trap door. The deputy's voice from below. Sophie going down, Carmen going down, Emma running across the room, the building fully engaged above them.

He sat on the floor at the edge of the shaft and he braced the trap door with his back and he reached up for Emma's hand. He could feel the heat of the floor through his clothes. He could feel the beam above him shifting in its brackets, the structural sounds of a building that was deciding whether to hold.

Emma's hand found his.

The beam fell.

It was not dramatic. This was the thing he registered — in the half-second after the impact, before anything else — that it was not dramatic. He was on the floor with the burning weight of the beam across his back and his face pressed to the boards and he could feel the heat of both, the beam from above and the boards from below, and Sophie was still below him in the shaft and her hands were on his arms and Matt's hands were on his arms and he was looking down at Sophie's face.

He tried to smile at her.

He thought: this is going to be alright.

He thought this the way he had always thought it — with the complete and involuntary conviction of someone who had, for as long as he could remember, believed that the things that needed to be alright would be alright, not because the world guaranteed this but because something in his constitution refused to accept the alternative as the permanent state. It had always been this way. He had always slept well. He had always woken expecting the day to be good. He had always found, in the specific configuration of people he loved arranged around him in the world, a sufficiency that was not complacency but genuine gratitude, the gratitude of someone who understood that this was not the default condition and was lucky to have it.

He thought: it's going to be alright.

He thought: Sophie.

He said: "It's going to be alright."

He heard the shot.

Part Three: Fire

FIFTEEN

The Tunnel

Carmen

Carmen

She ran.

This was what you did when the roof was coming down and bullets were coming through the floor and the person beside you had just gone still in a way that people only went still one way. You ran. You took the burning timber from the wall bracket because the dark without a light source was not survivable and the light source was the burning timber and you ran.

The tunnel was not wide. She ran close to the wall, one hand trailing the rock to keep orientation, the other holding the torch and trying to hold it in the position that cast the most useful light forward rather than back. Behind her she heard Matt running — she knew his footfall by now, the specific compromise he was making with the leg, the step-and-compensate rhythm that had a particular sound — and behind him she could hear Sophia.

She did not think about Charlie.

She thought about the tunnel. She thought about the distance and the air quality and the question of whether the tunnel's ventilation was passive or actively compromised by the fire above it and whether the fire's oxygen consumption would affect the tunnel before or after they reached the exit. She thought about the deputy's words: the tunnel goes to the mine, there's air all the way through, it comes out on the north side. She thought: north side. She oriented.

She did not think about Charlie.

The tunnel curved left and then straightened and the torch threw shadows that lurched with each step, the walls coming close and then opening up slightly, the ceiling varying, the floor uneven with the particular unevenness of a mining tunnel — not built for human comfort but for extraction, the floor graded for water runoff rather than walking, her boot finding the low center of it and using it.

She did not think about Charlie and she was also, with the part of her that she could not fully direct, thinking about Charlie continuously, the way you thought about the thing you were not thinking about.

★ ★ ★

Matt stopped.

She heard it before she saw it — the change in the sound of his running, the step-and-compensate rhythm dropping out, replaced by the sound of a person who had stopped and was breathing against a wall. She came back to him. She held the torch up.

His face was grey. Not fear — she knew the face of fear and this was different, this was the face of a body that had been running on the adrenaline reserve and had come to the end of it, the look of someone who had been using more than they had and were now being asked to account for the difference.

"Come on," she said. "Let's go."

"They killed my friend."

She heard it. She received it. She did not look away from it — looking away would have been a kind of lie, and she had learned over three deployments that lying to people in extremity, even through the mechanism of the averted eye, cost more than it saved.

"I know," she said.

"He was my best friend. He was—"

She waited. She watched his face. The torch burned beside her and the tunnel held its silence around them and behind them, far away, she could hear the sound of the building finishing its collapse, the sound of things settling into their final positions.

She thought: Torres. Second from the left in the back row. The laugh receding from his face.

She thought: I know what it is to have that number in your count.

She did not say this. It was true and it was hers and it was not what Matt needed from her right now. What Matt needed from her right now was to move.

"We are going to do something about it," she said. "I promise you that. But right now, this moment, the only thing you can do for Charlie is get out of this tunnel. So come on. Lean on me and come on."

He looked at her. She could see the calculation happening behind his eyes — the assessment of the statement, the check against available options, the conclusion that she was right and that being right was both true and beside the point and that he was going to do it anyway because Charlie would have told him to do it anyway.

He got his arm over her shoulder. She took his weight.

They moved.

Sophia walked behind them.

She had not cried in the tunnel. Carmen had expected tears — had expected the immediate and full grief response of someone who had just watched the person they loved die in front of them — and it had not come. What had come was something quieter and, in some ways, harder to be near: a quality of silence that had weight, a presence that was not grief expressed but grief contained, held under such pressure that it had changed state and become something else, something that was going to have to come out eventually through whatever opening presented itself.

She had seen this before. The grief that came fast and loud was easier, in some ways — it moved, it expressed, it spent itself and resolved into the next thing. The grief that came slow and dense was the kind that had to be waited out, and the waiting was not passive but active, the continuous work of a person managing something very large in a very small space.

She heard Sophia start to speak.

"He really loved me," Sophia said. Not a question. "Didn't he."

"Yes he did," Carmen said.

The tunnel held the words. Carmen kept moving, kept Matt moving, kept her attention divided between the torch and the ground and the sound of Sophie behind them and the distance to the exit which she was estimating from the deputy's words and the rate of travel and the air quality, which was still adequate.

"And I wasted so much time," Sophie said.

This was the statement that required the most precision in response, because it was true and because it was not the whole truth and because telling Sophie it wasn't true would be a lie and telling Sophie it was true would not be useful and what was needed was something that was neither of these things.

She said nothing.

She had learned this — learned the specific value of saying nothing when nothing was the only honest option — over years of being the person in rooms who could be relied upon to provide the accurate assessment. Accuracy sometimes looked like silence. She had learned to be comfortable with that.

Sophie said: "He always said that. You know? Everything's going to be alright. Every time. Even when it obviously wasn't."

"That's who he was," Carmen said.

"I kissed him," Sophie said. "Tonight. I finally kissed him. And I told him I loved him and then twenty minutes later —"

She stopped. Carmen felt Matt go slightly heavy against her shoulder — not his body failing but something else, something that moved through him at Sophie's words and had weight.

She gave them the silence. She walked in it with them and held Matt's weight and kept the torch pointed at the ground ahead.

"He knew," Carmen said, after a while. She said it carefully, the way she said things she meant completely. "Before tonight, before the kiss. He knew. Some people just know."

Sophie did not respond. Carmen heard her breathing change — not crying, not yet, but the breath of someone who was very close to the edge of something and was deciding whether to go over it.

"I was going to end it," Sophie said. "This weekend. I came to Nevada to end it. That was the plan."

Carmen had known this. She had known it since January, since the change in Sophie's register when she talked about Charlie, the slight increase in the carefulness of what she said. She had known it and she had said nothing because it was Sophie's to say and Sophie's to resolve and the resolving had happened in the gallows street when Sophie had touched Charlie's face in the dark and asked him to hold something.

"And then I remembered why I loved him," Sophie said, "and it was too late."

Carmen thought: it was not too late. She thought: you kissed him. You told him. He went out with that. He went out carrying the real version of it.

She thought these things and did not say them because saying them would sound like consolation and consolation was not what Sophie was asking for. Sophie was asking to be heard. Carmen was hearing.

The torch flickered. She angled it. The flame steadied.

Ahead, the air changed — barely perceptible, a fraction of a degree cooler, a slight movement in it that was different from the tunnel's flat air. She knew this change. She had come out of tunnels before, in different countries, for different reasons, and the air always changed before the exit was visible, and the change always felt the same: like something opening, like the world resuming.

"It's getting lighter," Sophie said, behind her.

Carmen dropped the torch.

The light at the end was real.

She came out first. The morning hit her — pale, cold, the sky the grey-blue of an hour before the sun cleared the mountains, the desert stretching away in every direction still wet from the storm, the scrubland glistening. She stood in it and breathed. She breathed the air that was not tunnel air and was not smoke air and was simply the air of a Friday morning in the Nevada desert and she breathed it and did not think about anything for ten seconds.

Sophie came out beside her. They stood together.

Sophie was shaking — the fine deep tremor of someone who had been holding something for a long time and had reached the exit and could feel the holding beginning to give. Carmen put her arm around her. Sophie leaned into it.

They held each other in the morning air.

Carmen thought about Charlie and let herself think about him — not the thinking she had been managing in the tunnel, the constant suppression, but the actual thinking, the actual fact of him. She thought about the dinner party in his apartment. She thought about the way he answered his phone on the first ring whenever it was someone he was glad to hear from, and on the fourth ring when it was anyone else, and she had always been in the first category and had taken this for granted the way she took for granted most things that were constant. She thought about the way he laughed — the full-body quality of it, the laugh of someone who had decided, somewhere early in his life, that laughter was not a private transaction but a shared one, a thing to be given rather than guarded.

She thought: he is the only person I have ever met who made me feel, specifically and reliably, that the world contained more goodwill than I had independently estimated.

She thought: I am going to have to revise that estimate now.

She heard Matt coming.

He emerged from the tunnel slowly, one hand on the rock wall, the leg finally getting what it was owed. In his hands — she had not seen him pick it up, had not noticed him taking it — a small wooden box. Simple, cedar, brass fittings. Emma's box, which the deputy had placed on the boulder just inside the exit, keeping the word he had given.

Matt stood in the morning and looked at it. He looked at the sky, at the column of smoke rising from the direction of town, at the box in his hands.

He looked at the smoke for a long time.

She went to him. She stood beside him and she looked at the smoke with him because that was what the moment required — not words, not instruction, not comfort precisely but presence, the specific kind of presence that meant: you are not standing here alone.

He was not, she noted, crying. She had expected it — had expected that the tunnel and the morning and the box and the smoke would be the combination that broke through whatever he was managing. It hadn't. He stood in the morning with his face very still and his hands on the box and she understood, standing beside him, that his grief was going to work the way his everything worked: interior, private, organized below the surface into something he would carry with him rather than express.

She understood this. She carried things this way herself.

She thought: we are going to be okay. Both of us. Not today, and not quickly, and not in a way that didn't leave marks. But okay.

She did not say this. She stood beside him.

The morning came on around them — the light strengthening, the colour returning to the scrubland, the smoke from the town rising straight in the still air. Sophie was a few feet away, sitting on a boulder with her arms around herself, looking at nothing in particular with the concentrated look of someone doing interior work.

Carmen looked at Matt.

He turned and looked at her. His eyes were dark and clear and entirely themselves — no softening, no performance, just Matt looking at her with the directness he brought to everything and that she had been filing under:

interesting, not acted upon, for two years.

She thought: there will be time for that. Not now. But time.

"Something went very wrong," he said.

"Yes," she said.

"Emma."

"Yes."

"They needed her alive — she's the only one who knew —"

He was already moving, already turning back toward the town, already working the next problem with the focused intention of someone who had put the grief somewhere it would keep and was now engaged with the only thing available to him, which was action.

She fell in beside him.

"Let's go," she said.

They went.

★★★

She came back.

She could not have said exactly when she made the decision — it happened in the same continuous processing she always ran, the assessment of the situation against the available resources, the constant revision of the plan based on what the plan encountered in the territory. Emma. Emma who had been in the Town Hall. Emma who had not come through the tunnel.

She came back because the math was simple: the tunnel went to the mine. They had come out on the north side. Emma had been in the Town Hall when the ceiling went. The Town Hall was a hundred yards from the mine entrance, on the surface, in a town that had gas lamps but no fire services and a street plan she had memorized over the course of the night.

She told Matt she was going back. He started to say something. She said: stay with Sophie. He looked at her. She looked at him.

He nodded.

She went.

★★★

The town from the north side in the early morning was a different proposition than the town from the road in the rain. The rain had stopped entirely now. The sky in the east was the specific grey-blue of dawn at altitude, lightening at the horizon, the dark not gone but going. She moved through the scrubland and then onto the main street from the north end and she moved fast, the way she moved when she had a clear objective and the time to reach it was uncertain.

The Town Hall was burning at its base and structural in the middle and gone at the top. She could see this as she approached — the fire at the foundation, the walls still standing but compromised, the roof open to the sky. The smoke was real and present and she moved upwind of it and she looked at the building and she made the assessment in approximately five seconds, which was: the building was still standing, barely, and the structure would hold for a while yet, and Emma was not in it.

She knew Emma was not in it the way she knew most things she knew quickly — from the accumulation of evidence rather than from a single clear fact. The door was open. The fire at the base was burning inward. If Emma had been in the building she would have gone through the door, or through a window, or she would not have come through anything at all, and the not-coming-through-anything version produced a specific quality of stillness in the building that she did not feel from here.

The building was not still. The building was burning and settling and making the sounds of a structure in the late stages of a process. Emma was not in it.

She went to the Drunken Coyote.

The saloon was undamaged. The fire had not reached it — the wind had been wrong for it, or the distance, or something else she couldn't account for. She stood at the door of the Drunken Coyote and she looked at it and she knew, before she reached for the latch, that she was not going to find what she expected to find on the other side of it.

She had been accumulating the evidence all night. The clothes. The gas lamps. The dry mud. Tommy Boy, who had gone fifteen feet and then walked. The deputy, who had been in a doorway and then been nowhere at all. She had filed all of it and she had kept moving, because filing and moving was what you did when the evidence produced a conclusion you didn't yet have the architecture to accept.

She had the architecture now. She had built it in the tunnel, in the dark, in the space between running and thinking, from the available materials: everything she'd seen tonight, everything that didn't fit, everything she'd been refusing to name.

She put her hand on the door of the Drunken Coyote.

She pushed it open.

The saloon was quiet. The oil lamps were burning, which they should not have been burning — she noted this with the part of her that was still noting things, the part that never stopped. The chairs were straightened. The bar was clean. The broken glass had been swept. The room had the quality of a room that had been set to rights by someone who had done so carefully and methodically, in the particular way of someone for whom the maintenance of the space was a form of meaning.

She stood in the doorway.

She looked at the room.

She thought: she is here.

She thought it with the certainty she reserved for conclusions that the evidence had fully supported, the kind of certainty that was not faith but arithmetic. Emma was here. She could not see her. The room was empty of any visible person. But Emma was here in the room the way a temperature was in a room — present, distributed, not located in one place but pervasive. The room smelled of broth and old wood and lamp oil and something that was specifically itself, the composite smell of a life lived attentively in a specific space.

She stood in it for a moment.

She had not, in three deployments and fourteen months away from the world she had grown up in, been in a room that felt this specific, this inhabited. The FOB had felt institutional. Her apartment in Las Vegas felt like hers, the accumulated result of her own preferences, but not inhabited in this way, not with this density of a particular person's attention.

She thought: Emma has been here. Emma is still here.

She thought: that is going to require a conversation I don't have time for right now.

She turned. She went back out into the street. The patrol cars were already coming — she could see the lights on the highway, the distant flash of red and blue, moving fast in the pre-dawn. She had approximately six minutes.

She went to find Matt and Sophie.

Part Four: After

SIXTEEN

The Window

Emma --- Greenbriar Gulch, Nevada, 1886

Emma — Greenbriar Gulch, Nevada, 1886

She understood before she could have said precisely when she had come to understand it.

This was how it arrived — not as a revelation, not as a single moment of clarity in which everything reorganized itself, but as a slow accumulation of a particular kind of evidence that her mind had been processing below the surface of the evening's events, filing and correlating while the rest of her was busy with the immediate requirements of the night. The clothes that were wrong. The word

car, used with such ease by both men and filed by her in the compartment she kept for things she didn't yet understand. The object Sophie had been carrying in the long wooden box — its name she now knew, she had asked the deputy while they were walking, and the deputy had given her a word that meant nothing to her and everything:

a saber.

But more than any of these: the quality of their confusion. She had been watching it all evening — the way they moved through the town with a kind of underlying disorientation that was distinct from the ordinary disorientation of strangers in an unfamiliar place. Strangers looked around; these people looked at things twice. Strangers asked for directions; these people asked questions that had a particular shape, the shape of questions asked by people who already knew the answer could not be what they expected. The dry mud. The gas lamps. The man on the horse they had hit with the vehicle and who was walking again. They had each encountered these things and had each, she observed, chosen not to examine them too directly — had filed them, one by one, in some interior compartment where inexplicable things were kept, and had kept going, because keeping going was what the situation required.

She had recognized this strategy. She had been using it herself for years — the filing of the things that didn't fit, the maintenance of a functioning life in the presence of the unfiled — though the things she had filed were different in kind from the things they were filing, and the unfiled things she carried were going to turn out to be larger than she had known.

She had understood sometime before the Town Hall burned. She was fairly certain it was before — that the understanding had arrived, quietly, while she was running through the street with Matthew, and that she had chosen not to examine it because examining it would have been the end of the running, and the running needed to happen.

The Town Hall had burned. She had not been in it when it burned.

She was in the saloon.

She did not know how she had come to be in the saloon. This was the strangest part — not the understanding itself, which had the quality of a thing that had been true for a while and was simply now acknowledged, but the gap between the last thing she remembered clearly and this: standing in the Drunken Coyote with the morning light beginning through the windows and the smell of smoke from the direction of the Town Hall and no memory of how she had gotten here.

She had been in the Town Hall. She knew this. The trap door, the shaft below, Matthew's hands, Charles at the edge of the opening. The beam. The beam was the last clear thing — the sound of it, the impact, the way Charles had looked at her as it took him.

And then she was in the saloon. Standing. The saloon was undamaged — the fire had not reached it — and she was standing in it in the early morning light with the certainty of someone who had been here for a while without knowing she had been here for a while.

She looked at her hands. They were steady. She was not afraid — she assessed this and found it true and also remarkable, because the understanding she had arrived at was not a small thing and not a comfortable thing and not the kind of thing that typically produced equanimity in the person arriving at it.

She thought: I am here. I am in my saloon.

She thought: I am going to be here for some time.

She thought, with the particular precision she had always brought to the examination of her own situation: I built this. This is mine. I built it from nothing and I have run it for five years and I have not wasted the years and I have been the person I meant to be in the place I chose to be it.

She thought: that will not stop being true.

She straightened the bar. She righted the chairs that had been overturned in the night's violence. She picked up the broken glass, which she could pick up, which meant her hands were adequate to the work. She lit the oil lamps, which she could do, and they burned the way they always burned — the familiar warm amber, the movement of the flame, the way the light shifted and breathed.

She went to the window.

The vehicles arrived at first light.

She watched them from the window of the Drunken Coyote — the two highway patrol cruisers, the fire engines, the ambulance. She watched them move through the main street with the particular weight of institutions arriving after the fact, the weight of the official world coming to account for what the unofficial one had produced. She watched the three of them — Matthew, Carmen, Sophie — emerge from the scrubland to the north and be received by the men in uniform, and she watched the conversations that she could not hear and could read, after five years of watching conversations through windows she could not open, with reasonable accuracy.

She watched them learn.

This was the hardest part to watch — not the arriving, not the official activity around the smoldering ruin of the Town Hall, but the specific moment when the tall man in the uniform of the highway patrol said what he said to the three of them and she watched their faces receive it. She watched Matthew's face. He looked at the uniform and he went very still and she could see, even at this distance, through the glass, the quality of his stillness — not the stillness of someone receiving information but the stillness of someone receiving confirmation of something they had half-known and had not wanted to confirm.

She pressed her palm flat against the glass.

She had done this before — pressed her hand to glass, to the membrane between herself and a world that was moving in directions she could not follow. She had done it on the morning James died, at the hospital window, watching the orderly wheel the empty gurney back down the corridor. She had done it on the train platform in Lyon when Linda's train had pulled away in the summer of 1869 and she had watched her sister's face in the window going smaller, going to the edge of visible, going to gone.

She pressed her palm to the glass and she watched Matthew learn that she had been dead for a hundred and fifty years.

She thought: he knows I was real. He will always know that. Whatever they tell him, however they explain it, he will know that the broth was real and the warmth in the chapel was real and the conversation about brave and foolish was real and the kiss — she allowed herself to think about the kiss, which was the last thing she had expected and the last thing she had done and which had been, for all its briefness, entirely true.

She thought: he will go away now. He will go out of the perimeter of this town and into the world where he came from and he will carry this with him, the way you carried a thing that had been real when no one else had been there to confirm it was real.

She thought: I hope he makes the traverse.

She thought this with complete seriousness. She did not know what the traverse was in any technical sense — she had understood that it was a sequence of movements on a wall of rock and that the sixth movement was the one that had defeated him eleven times and that he believed the failure lived not in the sixth movement but earlier in the sequence, in some assumption he was making in the fifth movement or before it that compounded forward. She had understood this much from the conversation at the table and she had filed it, as she filed most things he said, with the particular attention she gave to things that told her who a person was rather than merely what they did.

She thought: he will make it. Not soon, but he will. He is the kind of person who figures out eventually where the mistake is.

She watched the ambulance. She knew Charles was in it. She did not watch the ambulance for very long.

She had been standing at the window for a long time.

The convoy had left. The last of the vehicles had rounded the edge of town and the main street was empty again, the way it had been empty on five hundred mornings before this one — the gas lamps dark in the growing light, the dry mud holding its permanent condition, the buildings on both sides silent with the particular silence of things that had no requirement to make noise.

She had watched the ambulance the whole way to the turn. She had not looked away.

She had, over five years of running the Drunken Coyote, developed the habit of watching things through to their end. Not out of morbidity. Out of a conviction, arrived at through experience, that the things left unwatched had a way of remaining unprocessed, and that unprocessed things accumulated in a person the way debt accumulated — quietly, in the margins, until one day the accounting came due and the amount was larger than you had been prepared for. She had watched James die, sitting beside the bed through the long hours because leaving the room had seemed like a form of abandonment that she could not justify to herself. She had watched the train platform until Linda's face was too small to see and then until the train itself was a moving line and then until it was gone. She had watched because watching was what she had to give and she had always given what she had.

She watched the ambulance until the turn.

Then she turned from the window and looked at the room.

Her room. The saloon she had bought for four hundred dollars from a man named Grover who had given up on it, who had run it without attention or affection for seven years before her and had let the floors go and the bar go and the reputation go, and who had looked at her with the expression of a man who was skeptical that she could make something of it. She had made something of it. She had made it into the best saloon in Elko County, which was not a large claim in 1886 but was a real one — the cleanest, the most reliably stocked, the one that women could enter without incident and men could leave without shame. She had built that from nothing. She had built it four hundred dollars and five years and ten thousand small decisions at a time.

She looked at it.

She thought: I am not going to leave this.

Not with bitterness — she was not a person given to bitterness, which was a quality she had examined in herself and found genuinely absent rather than repressed. The absence of bitterness was not the presence of peace; she was clear-eyed about the distinction. What she had, standing in the saloon she had built on a morning in 1886 with the understanding of her situation fully arrived, was not peace but clarity. The accounting was complete and the balance was known and she was looking at it without flinching.

She had loved James. She had come to Nevada and built something. She had been lonely in the specific way of a person who had a full life and a company of people she genuinely liked and no one to be the other kind of quiet with. She had managed this with the grace of someone who had decided that the managing was the project and that the managing could be done well. She had done it well.

She had, last night, looked at a man's face across a table in her own saloon and known it in the way you knew things before you had the language for them.

She thought about that.

She thought about the conversation at the table — the questions he'd asked about Leatherman Peak, the care with which he'd explained base jumping, the way he'd received her assessment of brave and foolish without any of the small defensiveness that men usually brought to assessments of their chosen risks. She thought about the chapel, the warmth of him beside her, the arm around her, the way he'd said whatever happens as though whatever was simply a weather condition they were sharing rather than a threat to be managed.

She thought about the kiss, which had been entirely hers to give or not give and which she had given with the full deliberateness of someone who had decided.

She pressed her palm against the glass one more time.

She thought: he will make the traverse. She thought this with the certainty she had been developing for him all night, the specific confidence in a specific person that was not the confidence of hope but the confidence of recognition. He would solve it the way he solved things, which was by examining what he was assuming, by looking at the problem from the angle he had not yet tried. He would solve it and he would know, when he solved it, exactly where the mistake had been.

She hoped he would have a moment of it. A moment of the summit, before whatever came next.

She stepped back from the window.

She straightened a chair that was already straight. She ran her hand along the bar — the polished wood, the grain she knew with her eyes closed, the particular worn smoothness at the near end where the regular drinkers rested their elbows. Five years. Ten thousand hours. A life.

She went to her office. She sat at her desk. She picked up the pen.

She thought: Linda. I have been putting off this letter.

She dipped the pen. She began.

Charles arrived beside her without sound.

This was how it happened — not dramatically, not with the apparatus of the supernatural as she had occasionally imagined such things might work, not with cold air or the displacement of lamp flame or any of the other signs that the stories promised. He was simply not there and then he was there, standing beside her at the window of the Drunken Coyote with the morning light coming through the glass and the convoy visible in the street below.

She looked at him.

He was translucent in the way of things seen through very clean water — present, detailed, entirely himself, but with the light passing through him rather than stopping at him. His face was the face she had catalogued over the course of the evening: the easy quality, the quickness to warmth, the expression that was already halfway to a smile even in repose. He looked at her and she looked at him and neither of them said anything immediately, because immediately was not the right register.

He looked down at himself. Then back at her.

"Well," he said.

"Well," she said.

He almost smiled — the specific one, the smaller one, the one that happened before the composure could arrange itself. She had seen it once, very briefly, at the table over the broth, when Matthew had said something in a tone that she had only caught the edge of. She had catalogued it then. She recognized it now.

"I'm sorry," he said. "About all of this."

"Don't be," she said. "None of it was yours to be sorry for."

He looked at the street. At the convoy. At the ambulance.

"Sophie," he said. It was not a question.

"She's alright. She was alright when they walked out. I watched her."

He nodded. He absorbed this the way he absorbed things — fully, with the complete attention she had observed him giving to everything that mattered to him, which was most things.

"She's going to be sad for a while," he said.

"Yes," Emma said. "She is."

"And then she'll be alright."

Emma looked at him. He was not asking. He was stating — with the conviction that had animated him all evening, the conviction that she had catalogued under:

unreasonable and possibly correct.

"Yes," she said. "I believe she will."

He looked at the convoy again. The vehicles were turning, beginning to leave the main street. The ambulance moved slowly, with the particular care that ambulances moved at the end of things.

She watched his face watch it.

She had thought, when she understood what her own situation was, that the hardest thing would be the permanence — the understanding that the perimeter was absolute, that the town was the whole of the world available to her now and forever, that the things she had planned and the things she had deferred and the things she had meant to do eventually were simply not going to happen. She had thought the permanence would be the hard part.

It was not the hardest part. The hardest part was watching the people she had come to care about leave. Watching them go through the perimeter and back into the world that moved, the world that had days in it and years and the full ordinary weight of time passing, and knowing she would watch this — the leaving of people — for as long as the town had people to leave it.

She pressed her palm harder against the glass.

Beside her, Charles was watching the ambulance until it turned at the edge of town and went out of sight. Then he was watching the empty street.

Then, slowly, he stepped back from the window.

She looked at him.

He was looking at the place where the ambulance had been. His face had the expression she associated with someone who has made a decision and is in the first moment after making it — not relief and not grief but something that was both of these and neither, the expression of someone who has chosen their own condition rather than having it chosen for them.

"This is yours," she said. Not a question.

"This is mine," he said.

She understood. The perimeter was not a prison if you chose to be inside it, which was not the same as saying it wasn't a perimeter. She had been inside it since September of 1886 and she had not chosen it, which was a different condition entirely, and she was not going to pretend otherwise for his comfort or her own.

But he was choosing it. He was standing in the saloon she had built and he was choosing it with the same unreasonable conviction he brought to most things and she was, she found, not going to argue with him about it.

"I have been here a long time," she said. "You will have questions."

"I have questions already," he said.

"Good. I have answers to some of them and not to others, and I will tell you honestly which is which."

He looked at her. The almost-smile again — settling into the full version now, the social one and the real one arriving together, which was the version of Charlie's smile she had not yet seen and which was, she found, considerable.

"You're going to be a good person to be stuck with," he said.

"I have been managing this saloon for five years," she said. "I am an excellent person to be stuck with."

He laughed. It was the full-body kind, unguarded, the laugh of someone who had decided that laughter was not a private transaction but a shared one. She had not heard it before — had seen, at the table, the residue of it in his face as the shutter caught it, but not the thing itself. The thing itself was warm and present and entirely Charlie and it filled the morning saloon the way it must have filled every room he'd ever been in.

She found herself smiling.

Outside, the street was empty. The last of the convoy had gone. The gas lamps were dark in the morning light, their work done. The dry mud of the main street held its condition, as it always held its condition, as it would hold it when the next people came — and there would be next people, there were always next people — who drove off the road in a storm and followed a sign and walked toward the lights.

She stood at the window with her hand against the glass and looked at the street she had made her life in, and beside her Charles stood with the morning light coming through him, and she thought: the town always keeps what it takes, and it has taken us both, and we are what it has, and we will make of that what we can.

She thought: it is not nothing.

She thought: it is, in fact, quite a lot.

She turned from the window.

"Come on then," she said. "I'll show you the town."

SEVENTEEN

Rose

Matt

Matt

The hospital in Elko was forty minutes from Greenbriar Gulch. He knew this because the highway patrolman had told him, in the particular tone that highway patrolmen used for information they needed you to have and were not sure you were in a condition to retain. He retained it. He was in a condition to retain most things — the shock had not taken his processing capacity, had taken instead something harder to name, a quality of presence that meant he was functioning completely and also not entirely here.

The drive was in the back of the second patrol car. Sophie on one side of him, Carmen on the other. No one spoke. The desert went past the windows in the early morning light — the scrubland going gold, the mountains very clear after the storm, the sky the specific blue that followed rain in the high desert, washed and depthless. He looked at it. He had nothing useful to think that he wasn't already thinking, and the thinking was not going to change anything, and looking at the desert was what was available.

He thought about Charlie.

He thought about Charlie the way he thought about the traverse — not as a problem to be worked but as a fact to be absorbed, the way you absorbed a fact that your body knew before your mind had caught up to it. The beam had fallen. He had seen it. He had had Charlie's hands in his for one second and then he hadn't, and the one second and the not having were both present simultaneously in the way of things that had just happened and had not yet organized themselves into memory.

He thought: seven years.

He thought: he called during the climb because he always called during the climb and I always answered on the fourth ring and I told him it was fine every time and it was always fine. I told him it was fine on Tuesday morning on the wall east of Wells and he told me about the camping trip and

I said it's fine, Carmen's fine, the trip will be fine. I said it with the conviction I usually felt when I said it.

He looked out the window at the desert.

He thought: the last thing he said to me was why is it always a chair. He said it the way he said everything that was slightly absurd — with the warmth of someone who found absurdity a form of affection rather than a critique. He meant it as affection. I know he meant it as affection.

He held the wooden box in his lap. He had not put it down since he picked it up from outside the mine exit. He was not sure he was going to put it down for a while.

The Elko Regional Medical Center was a modest building set back from the highway with the particular institutional certainty of buildings that existed to process difficult things and had been processing them long enough to have arrived at a specific efficiency. He went through the automatic doors on the leg that the paramedic had properly bandaged — better work than Emma's strip of skirt, he thought, and then thought about Emma, which he was not going to be able to think about completely right now, which was a thing he was going to have to address eventually and not yet.

The admitting nurse was brisk and competent and asked him questions that he answered correctly. He sat in the chair she indicated. Sophie and Carmen were somewhere in the building — Sophie had been taken to a different part of the ER, Carmen had gone with her. He was alone with the fluorescent light and the linoleum and the wooden box on his knees and the particular quality of an emergency waiting room at seven in the morning, which was a quality he had no framework for and which seemed, in some way he couldn't articulate, appropriate to the situation.

A doctor came. She was younger than he expected and had the quality of someone who had been awake for a while and was managing this efficiently and without drama, which he found he was grateful for. She examined the leg with the focused attention of someone for whom a gunshot wound was a technical problem rather than an occasion for reaction. She said: clean through, no arterial involvement, you're going to be fine. She said it with the specificity of someone who meant

fine in its medical sense and understood that the other sense of the word was not her department tonight.

He said thank you.

She said: someone's going to come and ask you some questions in a few minutes. He said: I know. She nodded and moved on to the next person requiring her competence.

He sat in the chair she had indicated and he waited.

The waiting room had the quality of all waiting rooms, which was the quality of time disaggregated from purpose — time that was not being used for anything, that was simply passing, the specific texture of hours spent in a state of suspension between the thing that had happened and whatever came next. He had been in waiting rooms before: the hospital in Elko when his father had the knee surgery, the urgent care in Vegas after a bad landing, the ER in Reno when Charlie had broken two fingers on a camping trip three years ago and they had spent four hours in a room exactly like this one while the on-call orthopedist made his way in.

He thought about that night in Reno. Three in the morning. He and Charlie in the waiting room, Charlie managing his broken fingers with the equanimity he brought to physical inconvenience — this was not, Charlie had said, the worst thing that had happened to him, and he was aware that he had a very good life if this was the worst thing. He had said this genuinely. He had not been performing. Matt had looked at him and thought: I know a lot of people and I don't know anyone quite like you, and he had not said this because saying it would have required Charlie to receive it and Charlie received sincere things with such complete openness that it was sometimes easier not to give them.

He had not said it in Reno. He had said: your fingers are not that bad. Charlie had said: they're not. He had said: you'll be fine. Charlie had said: I know. And they had sat in the waiting room at three in the morning and Charlie had told him, at length and with great enthusiasm, about the Andromeda galaxy, which he had been reading about for reasons that had something to do with Sophie, and which was two and a half million light years away, and which was the most distant object visible to the naked eye.

Matt had listened. He had learned something about Andromeda. He had thought, listening: this is what you do. This is the specific version of what you do, which is to be interested in things and to make the interest available to people who are sitting next to you in places where there is not much else to do.

He sat in the Elko waiting room and he thought about the Andromeda conversation and he held the wooden box in his lap.

The box was cedar. He had established this from the smell, which was faint and specific, the smell of cedar that had been in an enclosed space for a long time and had given most of its scent to the air around it but had kept some, the way old wood kept things. The brass fittings were solid, not decorative. It had been made with care by someone who understood that care was not the same as ornament.

Emma's name was inside the lid. He had found it when he first opened the box in the mine tunnel, just before Carmen had said something and he had closed it again. Her name in the same careful cursive he now recognized from the photograph: Emma Rose, with the year below it, 1876. Ten years before the night they had met. Ten years of carrying this.

He held the box and he did not try to think useful thoughts. There were no useful thoughts available right now and the attempt to produce them was a form of waste. He let the fluorescent light be the fluorescent light. He let the linoleum be the linoleum. He let the wooden box be the wooden box, warm in his lap from his own body heat.

Sophia was somewhere in the building. Carmen was somewhere in the building. Sophie had the rope burn on her throat dressed by the paramedic on the road. Carmen had been assessed functional by the EMT with the confidence of someone reading from a familiar chart. They were both in the building and both alright and this was what he had and it was not nothing.

He looked at the rectangle of the window across the room. The Nevada morning outside it was getting lighter at the edges. Full dawn coming.

★ ★ ★

The woman who came to ask the questions had a notepad and a lanyard and the particular quality of controlled curiosity that he had come to associate, over a working life spent around athletes and their injuries, with people who were very good at their jobs and who kept most of what made them good at their jobs invisible. She was not a highway patrol officer. She was something else — she introduced herself with a title that he caught the shape of but not the specifics, something that had the word investigator in it and implied a governmental rather than law enforcement context. He filed this without pressing.

She sat down across from him. She had the notepad but she did not open it immediately.

She said: can you tell me your name and where you're from.

He told her. She wrote it down.

She said: and the names of the people with you.

He told her. She wrote them down, asking him to spell each one. When he got to Carmen's last name she paused — the pen moving more slowly, a slight adjustment in the quality of her attention, subtle enough that he would not have noticed it if he had not been, since sometime before the broth, paying close attention to the qualities of people's attention.

She asked Carmen's last name again. He repeated it.

"And she's in the building?" the woman said.

"Down the hall somewhere. She came in with Sophie."

She made a note. She moved on.

He answered the rest of her questions with the economy he brought to all communications — enough detail to be useful, not enough to invite elaboration he wasn't ready to give. What happened, in order. How they ended up in the town. The men who had been there. O'Donnell's name — she wrote this carefully, the pen moving with deliberateness. The deputy, whose name he did not know and said so. The building that had burned.

He did not talk about Emma. He mentioned a woman who had helped them, who had been in the building, who had not come out. He left it at that. He could feel the investigator receiving this incompleteness and deciding, with the professionalism of someone who understood which details to press and which to allow to remain incomplete for now, to let it stand.

She closed the notepad.

"Mr. Cavanaugh," she said, "I want to ask you one more thing, and I want to be clear that it's not part of the formal questioning."

He looked at her. He waited.

"The town," she said. "Greenbriar Gulch. The buildings, the lamps. The condition of the place." She paused. "Did it seem to you like a place that had been recently occupied, or a place that had been — preserved somehow. Maintained."

He looked at her. He thought about the dry mud on the main street. He thought about the Drunken Coyote — the clean bar, the trimmed oil lamps, the broth that had been on the heat all day. The piano, polished. The sign above the door with EMMA ROSE in letters that had not faded.

"Maintained," he said.

She made a note that was not in the notepad — a slight adjustment in her expression, a thing settled into a different position. Then she stood.

"My name is Dr. Charlotte Rose," she said. She extended her hand.

He shook it.

He held the handshake for a half-second longer than necessary. He was looking at her face. She was perhaps forty-five, with dark hair that had some grey in it and the kind of face that had been somewhere and come back — not aged, but experienced, the face of someone whose attention had been through things and had organized them.

"Rose," he said.

"Yes." She received the word without expression. She had received it before.

"Is that — are you related to someone in —"

"My family has been in Nevada for several generations," she said, in a tone that was not quite an answer and not quite a deflection, a tone he recognized as the tone of someone who had a great deal to say about something and had decided that now was not the time. "I'll be in touch, Mr. Cavanaugh. Please rest."

She left.

He looked at the wooden box in his lap. He thought about the name on the box — Emma had written her name inside the lid, he had found it when he first opened it, small and exact in the same hand as the back of the photograph. He thought about the woman who had just left the room with the same name.

He thought: maintained.

He thought about the dry mud on the main street. He thought about the piano and the lamps and the broth. He thought about the way Emma had moved through her saloon — not the way a caretaker moved through a place they were preserving but the way a proprietor moved through a place they ran, with ownership, with the particular confidence of someone in their own space doing their own work.

He thought: she has been there all this time.

He thought this and sat with it and did not do anything with it because there was nothing to do with it, not right now, not in an emergency waiting room in Elko with the leg and the box and the fluorescent light and the seven years that were yesterday and were also gone.

Carmen appeared in the doorway. She looked at him with the comprehensive look.

He gave her the small nod that meant: functional.

She gave him the small nod that meant: understood. She came and sat beside him. She did not say anything. She was Carmen — she understood that silence was sometimes the most accurate response to a situation, and that offering silence was not the same as having nothing to offer.

He held the box.

Outside the window — there was a window, small, high on the wall, showing a rectangle of Nevada morning — the sky was the colour of something beginning rather than something ending. He looked at it for a while.

He thought about Emma at the window of the Drunken Coyote, watching the convoy leave. He thought about her hand against the glass. He thought about the broth and the lamp and the way she'd said

Come on then. We have work to do.

He thought: she is still there.

He thought: I know where she is.

He thought about the gear list.

This was not a productive thing to think about and he knew it was not a productive thing to think about and he thought about it anyway, because grief in the first hours did not run on productive, it ran on available, and the gear list was available.

The gear list had been Charlie's. He had sent it in a group text on Wednesday morning, three days before the trip, a text that had arrived while Matt was at work and which he had scrolled through and acknowledged without reading carefully. He had read it carefully now, in the back of the patrol car, because Charlie's phone was in his jacket pocket — he had picked it up from the ground outside the mine entrance without thinking, just picked it up the way you picked things up that belonged to someone, the instinct preceding the reasoning — and the gear list was on it. He had opened the list because it was there.

sleeping bag, rated to 30, check. tent stakes extra, always. the wax cheese things Sophie likes (confirmed: Vons Eastern has them). extra phone cable Carmen never has hers. trail mix, not the kind with only raisins, the other kind. ibuprofen two bottles Matt's knees. headlamps x4 because last time. coffee for Emma? bring the good stuff.

He had stopped at the wax cheese things Sophie likes and he had read it twice and he had understood, reading it twice, something he had not previously understood in quite this way, which was that Charlie had written this list the way he approached most things that involved the people he loved, which was with a particular attention to what each of them specifically needed rather than what people generally needed. The sleeping bag was practical. The wax cheese things were Sophie's. The cable was Carmen's. The ibuprofen was his knees.

coffee for Emma? bring the good stuff.

He had not known that Charlie knew Emma's name. There was no way Charlie had known Emma's name. And yet it was on the list, which had been written three days before the trip, and he had no explanation for this, and he was not going to look for one right now.

He was going to hold the phone and sit in the back of the patrol car with Sophie and Carmen on either side of him and look at the gear list and let it be what it was, which was the last thing Charlie wrote before something he didn't expect, which was a list of the specific things the people he loved would need.

This was who he had been.

Matt had known this. He had known Charlie for seven years and he had known this — had known that Charlie's attention to the people around him was not performance, was not social skill, was not the cultivated warmth of someone who understood its strategic value. It was simply who Charlie was. The attention was as natural to him as breathing and as continuous, and it produced, in the people he applied it to, the particular feeling of being genuinely seen, which was different from being noticed and different from being liked, and which was rarer than either.

He had not taken it for granted. He had been aware of it, had been grateful for it, had thought, in the seven years of their friendship: I am lucky to know this person.

He had not said this to Charlie. This was the thing he was sitting with in the back of the patrol car on the highway to Elko, the thing beneath the shock and beneath the leg that had needed real stitches, the thing underneath everything: that he had known and had not said. That the accounting had been done internally and never externalized, and the failure to externalize was not catastrophic — Charlie had known, the way Charlie knew most things about the people he loved, he had known without being told — but the not-saying was present now, a small and permanent fact that he was going to carry alongside the larger ones.

He thought about seven years.

He thought about the first camping trip, four years ago, before Carmen — just the three of them, Matt and Charlie and Sophie, a long weekend in Zion, a trip that had been Charlie's idea in the way all their trips were Charlie's idea and that had gone, in the way of all their trips, somewhat sideways and entirely right. The rain on the second night. The tent that turned out to have a slow leak. Charlie's completely unhelpful suggestion that they simply embrace the rain, delivered with such genuine equanimity that it was impossible to be actually irritated with him, which Sophie had said was the most annoying thing about him, and they had all laughed and the tent had leaked and the morning had been very clear.

He thought about the drive back from Zion, Charlie in the front passenger seat doing the playlist, which he took very seriously, treating it as a curatorial problem to be solved rather than a background task. He had spent twenty minutes on the question of whether to follow the Tom Waits with something that continued the mood or something that broke it intentionally. He had decided to break it intentionally. He had played something that made Sophie roll her eyes and Matt grin, and Charlie had watched the grin in the rearview mirror and looked satisfied in the specific way of someone who had gotten exactly what they were aiming for.

He thought: seven years of being grinned at in a rearview mirror.

He thought: I am going to miss him for the rest of my life, and this is not an exaggeration and not a thing that is going to resolve into something more manageable, and the appropriate response to this is to sit with it and not require it to be anything other than what it is.

He looked out the window. The Nevada desert received him in its usual manner, which was without particular acknowledgment, the sage and the scrubland going past at highway speed, the mountains present at the horizon with the permanence of things that had been there long before any of this and would be there long after.

He thought: that is not nothing.

He held the box and looked at the rectangle of Nevada morning and let that be, for now, enough.

EIGHTEEN

Etiology Unclear

Rose

Rose

The first file was a hiker.

Her name was Patricia Weiss, twenty-nine years old, a graduate student in geology from the University of Nevada, Reno. She had gone into the Ruby Mountain foothills on a solo backpacking trip in the summer of 1974 and had come out four days later from a direction that was not the direction she had gone in. She had presented to the Elko Regional Medical Center with a cluster of symptoms that the attending physician had documented as: metallic taste in mouth, persistent visual disturbances described by the patient as peripheral light flashes, cardiac arrhythmia, and a fatigue that the physician had characterized, with the clinical economy that Rose had come to recognize as the hallmark of physicians confronting things outside their category, as

profound and of unclear etiology.

The symptoms had resolved within forty-eight hours of the patient leaving the area. The physician had noted this. The physician had attributed it, in the final summary, to dehydration and stress.

Rose read this file twice. She set it aside.

She had been reading files for three weeks, in the two-bedroom rental in Elko that she had extended month to month because extending month to month was more honest than committing to something she didn't know the duration of. The files were photocopies, mostly — the originals were in county archives and in hospital records rooms and in the Elko county historical society, which had a small grey building on the edge of town staffed by a woman named Mrs. Halverson who had been there for twenty-two years and who had, on Rose's third visit, stopped asking her to justify her research requests and simply brought whatever she asked for.

Rose was grateful for this. She had spent a career cultivating the quality of a person who eventually got what she was looking for without requiring anyone to understand why she was looking, and Mrs. Halverson had recognized this quality and had responded to it appropriately.

The second file was a couple. 1981. Same symptom cluster — the metallic taste, the peripheral lights, the arrhythmia. Different attending physician. Same attribution: dehydration, stress, exposure. Resolved upon leaving the area.

Rose wrote in her notepad:

Case 2. 1981. MT, PL, AR. Resolved on departure. Attending attributes to environment. Inadequate.

She had developed, over the three weeks, a shorthand. MT for metallic taste. PL for peripheral lights — the phosphene-like visual disturbances that every case described in some variant of the same phrase,

like something at the edge of my vision that wasn't there when I looked directly.

AR for the arrhythmia. These three symptoms appeared in every case she had found so far. There were, as of this morning, seventeen of them.

★★★

She had come to Greenbriar Gulch because of the fire.

Not initially — initially she had come because of Matt Cavanaugh, or more precisely because of the name he had given as a group member: Carmen, last name spelled out letter by letter, which was a name Rose had been carrying in a different file for six months. Carmen had done three deployments. Rose worked in the intersection of environmental exposure and military medicine, a corner of the federal research apparatus that had no clean name and a mandate that could be summarized as: find things that are happening to people that nobody has categorized yet.

Carmen was not the reason she had stayed.

She had stayed because of the town itself. Because of the word Matt Cavanaugh had used when she asked him about the condition of the place —

maintained — and because of the specific way he had said it, with the weight of someone who had more to say and had chosen not to. Because of the building that had burned, which the fire marshal had dated at approximately 1875 in construction, which was not in any record she could find, which should not have had an intact roof. Because of the oil lamp she had photographed in the ruins, which was not a reproduction.

She had pulled the Elko county historical records. She had found, in the property assessments from 1882 to 1895, a Greenbriar Gulch. Population at peak: 214. Primary industry: silver mining. A post office. A church. A saloon called the Drunken Coyote, operated by one Emma Rose.

She had sat with that for a long time.

Her name was Charlotte Rose. Her grandmother had been Linda Rose. Her grandmother's grandmother — born in Georgia in 1851, moved west in the 1870s — had been named Emma.

She had sat with this for a longer time.

The county archive was where she found the church records.

Mrs. Halverson had brought the box without comment — a wooden box, genuinely old, the kind of archival container that preceded the manila folder by half a century, containing loose papers and a ledger and a small collection of items that had been in the church at Greenbriar Gulch when the mine closed and the town was abandoned, which the county records placed at 1891.

She put on the cotton gloves Mrs. Halverson set beside the box. She opened the ledger.

The handwriting was careful and regular, the handwriting of someone who had understood that the ledger was a record rather than a journal and who had written in it accordingly — dates on the left margin, entries spare and factual. Births. Deaths. Marriages. The ordinary inventory of a small congregation in a frontier town, the stuff of which history was mostly made: not the dramatic events but the accounting of ordinary time.

She turned pages. She was looking for the entry she had found a reference to in a county record — a burial in

September of 1886, a woman, proprietress of the saloon. She found it.

Emma Rose, aged 41 years, departed this life the 14th of September, by violence. She came to us from Georgia five years past and conducted herself with grace and industry in all the time she was among us. The town is diminished.

Rose read this paragraph three times. She read it as a document and then she read it as something else — as a fact about a specific woman, the specific woman whose name she had been carrying all her life without knowing she was carrying it, the woman whose saloon had still been maintained a hundred and thirty-five years after she died.

She read on.

A peculiar season. The Morrison family departed for Salt Lake three weeks past, without farewell, which is unlike them. The Hendrickses left the week prior. I count seven families gone from the congregation in the past month, which is more than any comparable period since I came to this place.

She wrote in her notepad:

Population flight. Sep 1886. Seven families in one month. Cause unclear. Possible relationship to events of 9/14.

Brother Thomas tells me he has had a persistent bitter taste in his mouth these past weeks, which he attributes to the water from the north well. I have had the same, though I had not mentioned it. Old Harlan the assayer has been unwell — a strange fatigue, he says, as though the weight of the air has increased. I have recommended rest.

She stopped reading. She picked up her pen.

She wrote in her notepad:

MT. 1886. Two subjects. Priest + Brother Thomas. Bitter taste attributed to water source. Third subject (Harlan) presents with fatigue — "weight of air." Not dehydration. Not stress. Not in the modern population. In 1886.

Her hand was not entirely steady. She noted this and continued.

I have seen lights on the valley floor at night, three occasions. Low, amber, not fire. I cannot account for them. I have prayed for discernment and found none forthcoming, which I take to mean the answer is not yet available to me.

She wrote:

PL. Valley floor. Amber. 1886. Priest as observer. Not attributed to subject — priest observing externally. Consistent with EM emission pattern.

She looked at what she had written. She looked at the priest's ledger. She looked at her shorthand for the eighteen cases she had assembled — MT, PL, AR, running across three decades, each case filed as dehydration or stress or exposure, each resolved upon departure, each clustering within a radius that she had been trying to establish from incomplete records and which was beginning to resolve into a shape she could almost see.

The priest had seen it in 1886.

He had written it down because he was a man who understood that the correct response to things you could not explain was to record what you observed while you waited for the explanation, and he had waited, and the explanation had not come to him, and he had kept writing.

★ ★ ★

She went back to the hospital records that evening.

She had the eighteen cases spread across her rental's kitchen table, arranged chronologically, the symptom cluster present in each one, the resolution upon departure consistent across all. She added a nineteenth column to her timeline: the priest's account, September 1886, annotated in her own shorthand, the same symptoms in different language, the same pattern in a different century.

She sat with this for a long time.

She was a scientist. She had spent twenty years operating in the specific space between what was documented and what was true, the space that most people found uncomfortable and that she found clarifying — the space where the evidence existed but the category did not yet, where you could see the shape of something before you had the name for it. She had learned that the shape was trustworthy. She had learned that the name came later, and sometimes not at all, and that the absence of a name was not the same as the absence of the thing.

She thought about Emma Rose. She thought about the saloon that was still maintained. She thought about the dry mud on the main street that Matt Cavanaugh had described, the gas lamps, the broth on the heat. The quality of occupation rather than preservation.

She thought about the deputy in the interview — the interview she had conducted three days after the incident, the deputy who existed in no county record she could find, who had given his name as James Patterson, who had described the events of that night with a specificity and a composure that she had been turning over ever since. The composure of someone for whom the events were not surprising. The specificity of someone who had been there before.

She wrote in her notepad:

What is the town doing to them?

She underlined it. She looked at it.

She added below it:

What is it keeping?

She turned the page. She began a new section. At the top she wrote the date, and below it, in the careful regular hand she used for things she was committing to the record rather than merely noting:

Greenbriar Gulch, Elko County, Nevada. Active investigation. Electromagnetic anomaly, valley floor, radius TBD. Symptom cluster: metallic taste, peripheral visual disturbance, cardiac arrhythmia. First documented case: September 1886. Most recent case: current. Population effects: unclear. Mechanism: unknown.

She looked at what she had written.

She thought about the handshake in the hospital — Matt Cavanaugh's hand in hers, the half-second longer than necessary, the way he had said

Rose with the weight of someone who had just understood something. She had seen it happen. She had watched the understanding arrive on his face the way understanding arrived — not as revelation but as recognition, the feeling not of learning something new but of knowing something you had always known.

She understood that feeling. She had been having it, at intervals, for three weeks.

She wrote one more line in the notepad. She wrote it in her own name, not in shorthand, not in the careful regular hand of the committed record, but in the slightly different hand of something she was still deciding how to say:

She was there.

She closed the notepad.

She made herself a cup of tea. She stood at the window of the rental and looked at the Nevada night — the mountains very black against the stars, the stars very clear after another day of wind. The Milky Way was visible, which meant it was a good night for a telescope, which was a thought she had had many times out here and had not acted on, because acting on it had always seemed, until recently, beside the point.

She thought: I am going to go back to the town.

She thought: not yet. But I am going to go back.

She thought: she has been there all this time, and she knew — the whole time she knew she was my — she knew and she wrote

To my dear sister Linda and she sealed it and she left it on the desk and she never sent it, because there was no longer time.

She stood at the window for a long time.

Then she went to her desk and opened her laptop and began to write the first formal report.

She would not include everything. She was a scientist, and scientists reported what the evidence supported, and the evidence supported: electromagnetic anomaly, symptom cluster, historical continuity of the phenomenon, population effects, mechanism unknown. That was enough. That was what she could document.

The rest — the saloon, the broth, the maintained lamps, the woman who had conducted herself with grace and industry and had not been found in the ruins — she wrote in the notepad. In her own hand. For herself.

The county archive was in a converted ranch building on the north side of Elko, a low structure with the institutional beige of something that had been functional for a long time without anyone having thought hard about it. She had been here three times. The archivist, a man named Wallace in his late sixties who wore reading glasses on a lanyard and had the compressed patience of someone who had spent decades watching people mishandle primary sources, knew her by now.

She spread the county land records across the table and went through them methodically, one item at a time, no skimming. The records for Greenbriar Gulch stopped in 1891. This she already knew. What she had not previously examined carefully were the records immediately before 1891 — the final two years when the town had been actively operating, filing its taxes and its permits and its mineral claims through the county office.

She found the transfer on page seven of a property ledger from October 1889. A transfer of the deed to the Drunken Coyote Saloon from Emma Rose to an entity she did not recognize: the Greenbriar Gulch Town Trust.

She looked at this for a long time.

She went back to the beginning of the ledger. The Trust appeared three times in the 1889 records and once in 1887, in a filing that established its existence and listed its original trustees: the sheriff, the barkeep, and the deputy — whose name she had not previously known was George Aldridge.

She wrote the name in her notepad: *George Aldridge. She trusted them. She planned for this.*

She went to find Mrs. Halverson.

Agnes Halverson was eighty-one years old and had lived in Elko County her entire life except for four years at the University of Nevada and a summer in London in 1967 that she referenced approximately once per conversation. She was on the county historical society board. She had boxes.

The boxes were in her garage, which had not contained a car since 1994, and which now served as the physical archive of forty years of collecting every piece of paper that pertained to Elko County's mining history. She moved fast and talked faster and she had already made coffee before Charlotte had finished explaining what she was looking for.

"Rose," Agnes said immediately. "Emma Rose. The Drunken Coyote."

"You know her?"

"Know of her. She's in the county records, the church records — the Methodist church in Wells had a contribution she made in 1888, which is unusual, a Catholic woman contributing to a Methodist church. But that was Emma Rose, apparently. Pragmatic." Agnes was already moving between boxes. "There's a photograph. 1886, the county photographer did a circuit of the mining camps that summer. Here."

She set a folder on the workbench and held the contact prints toward the overhead bulb one at a time.

"That's her," Agnes said.

Charlotte took the print.

A woman sitting alone, facing the camera, in a pale silk dress that was finer than anything else about her suggested she wore regularly. Her hands in her lap. Her face composed. In her eyes something the composure had not quite reached — a quality of genuine looking, as though the camera were something she was deciding what to do with rather than something being done to her.

Charlotte looked at the photograph for a long time.

She thought: I have been inside the building she ran. I have stood at the bar she polished.

She thought: she was my — and stopped, because the word was both accurate and strange, the genealogy spanning a hundred and thirty-five years.

"May I photograph this?" Charlotte said.

"You may have it," Agnes said. "I've got the negative stored properly. That's a duplicate."

She looked at the old woman. Agnes was watching her with the expression of someone who understood that something was happening that was not purely archival and had decided not to ask.

"Thank you," Charlotte said.

The priest's ledger was the last piece.

She found it not in the county archive but in the basement of the Methodist church in Wells — the one Emma Rose had contributed to in 1888. The pastor, a young man named Elliot who was genuinely pleased that anyone was interested in his church's historical records, led her to the basement with the air of someone being useful in a new way.

The ledger ran from 1886 to 1891. The final entry was dated September 14, 1886. Two days after the fire.

A burial record.

She read it twice. Then a third time, her pen still above the notepad.

The burial record listed two names. The first was James O'Donnell. The second was Emma Rose.

She set the pen down.

She sat in the basement of the Methodist church and understood several things simultaneously that she had been understanding separately. Emma Rose had been in the Town Hall when it burned. The record was clear, corroborated by two witnesses written in the margin: the sheriff and George Aldridge.

Emma had not come through the tunnel.

And yet.

She thought about Matt Cavanaugh with the wooden box in his hands. She thought about the maintained oil lamps and the warm broth and the woman at the window pressing her palm to the glass, watching three people emerge from the scrubland in the early morning.

She thought: *the town is keeping her.*

She wrote it in her notepad, in her own hand. Then she wrote below it, in the careful regular hand she used for things she was committing to record:

She was there.

She wrote:

Follow up.

NINETEEN

Leatherman Peak

Sophia

Sophia

She went back to the mountain three months later.

Not because anyone asked her to — Matt had not asked, had in fact said very little about the mountain since Greenbriar Gulch, had said very little about most things that didn't have a practical resolution, which was his way of carrying what he carried. But she had known since the morning they walked out of the mine tunnel — since she had stood in the early light with rope burns still livid on her neck and understood, with the clarity that extremity produced, what the fencing had always been for — that she was going to come back. Not to complete someone else's task but to complete her own.

She had made a decision in Nevada. She needed to be somewhere large enough to stand inside it.

The drive from Las Vegas took four hours. She had borrowed Matt's jeep — he had offered it without asking why, which was Matt, and she had taken it without explaining, which was them — and she drove it north on the empty highway with the windows down and the desert doing its thing in the early October light, the colors richer than they had been in March, the scrubland gone amber at the edges, the mountains cleaner against the sky.

She thought about Charlie for most of the drive. She had been thinking about Charlie every day since September, which was accurate and insufficient as a description — thinking was not quite the right word for what she did with him. It was closer to carrying. She carried him the way you carried something that had been given to you and that you were not sure yet what to do with, that you were not sure would ever resolve into something you knew what to do with, that you had simply accepted was yours now and would be yours for a long time.

She had not cried very much. This was not a decision — she was not someone who decided about crying — but it was a fact about how the grief had moved through her, which was slowly and internally, the way water moved through rock rather than over it. The rock changed. It just took longer.

She arrived at the Leatherman trailhead at noon. She put on the pack. She started up.

★ ★ ★

The mountain was everything Matt had said it was and also not at all what she had imagined from his descriptions, which was the usual gap between language and landscape. He had described it accurately — the approach through the pines, the transition zone where the trees gave out and the real climbing began, the summit ridge that required hands as well as feet in the final stretch. He had described all of it correctly and she had formed an image that was correct in its components and entirely wrong in its quality.

The quality was the thing that language could not carry. It was the quality of altitude — the thinning of the air, the specific silence that lived above the tree line, a silence that was different in kind from the desert silence, less ancient, more exposed, the silence of a place that did not particularly want to be visited and received visitors anyway with the complete indifference of something that had been here much longer than any visitor and expected to be here much longer after.

She climbed.

She was not a climber — had never been a climber, had in fact spent considerable energy over the years finding polite ways to decline Matt's invitations to various vertical surfaces. But she was fit, fencer-fit, which was a particular kind of fitness — not the endurance runner's fitness or the lifter's fitness but the fitness of someone whose body had been trained for sudden complete exertion followed by stillness, the body of someone who could sustain a great deal of precise effort over a long period and who understood, at a physical level, the difference between moving with intention and moving without it.

She moved with intention.

She did not think about the summit specifically. She thought about the next section, the next handhold, the next transition. She thought about her breathing, which she had to actively manage at altitude, the breath coming shallower and requiring more effort. She thought about the light, which was changing as the afternoon moved toward the low-sun hours, the shadows on the rock going long and the rock itself warming from gold to amber in a way that reminded her — not painfully, but with precision — of the gas lamps on the main street of Greenbriar Gulch.

She thought: he would have loved this.

She thought it and kept climbing.

The transition zone came at eleven thousand feet, where the trees gave out entirely and the mountain became what it was rather than what it approached — no more pines, no more the soft silence of a forest at altitude, just rock and sky and the specific exposed quality of a place that did not offer shelter and had never pretended to. She stopped at the tree line and looked up.

The final stretch was hands-and-feet territory, which Matt had told her and which she had understood intellectually and was now understanding physically, which was a different kind of understanding. The rock was good — she could feel this in her hands when she reached for holds, the grip of it, the way it communicated its own texture to her palms, not trying to deceive her about what it offered. She thought about Matt, who had been reading rock faces for years the way she read rooms — instinctively, with the body rather than the mind, the information arriving below the level of thought.

She climbed.

She found, in the climbing, something she had not expected to find, which was a relationship to her body that was different from the relationship she had in the fencing salle. Fencing was vertical movement, lateral movement, the controlled explosion of the attack and the precise retreat of the recovery. The mountain required her to think in three dimensions, to plan the next three moves while executing the current one, to assess not just the hold in front of her but the position it would leave her in for what came after.

She was learning it, which was different from not knowing it.

She thought about Maître Delacroix's hands. The way they had moved when he demonstrated — the economy of it, nothing wasted. She had asked him once, in her second year, how he thought about the blade. He had said: I don't think about it. I think about where I want to be. The blade goes there because it knows how.

She thought: I want to be at the summit.

The wind was picking up above the tree line — not the filtered, softened wind of the forest but the unmediated wind of an exposed ridge, coming in at angles and changing its angle as she moved. She leaned into it. She found the correction instinctive after the first few minutes, the body learning the wind's logic the way it learned any repeated condition.

She stopped on a ledge at twelve thousand feet and looked at the valley below.

The valley was enormous. She had known this from the drive up and from Matt's descriptions, but knowing it from below was different from knowing it from twelve thousand feet. The valley floor and its roads and its occasional buildings were small in a way that was not diminishment but accuracy. This was what it actually was: small. The scale was always there, always this ratio of human things to the landscape that contained them. She had just needed the altitude to see it correctly.

She thought about the Valley of Fire. Three years ago. *Accurately sized.*

She had needed that then and she needed this now, and the need was the same need — to be in a place large enough to contain what she was carrying without the carrying taking up all the available space. She had been carrying Charlie for three months in Paris, in apartments and cafés and the narrow streets of the sixth arrondissement, and the carrying had been too large for the containers.

Here the container was the right size.

She allowed herself to carry him here.

She thought about Charlie on this mountain. She thought about him in the SUV saying *Leatherman Peak — Matt's thing* with the tone of someone who had already decided that Matt's thing was his thing too, because that was how Charlie related to the things people he loved loved. He absorbed them. He found the specific quality of attention that made someone else's passion legible, and then the passion was accessible to him and he was genuinely glad of it.

He had done this with her fencing. He had asked questions she hadn't expected — about the philosophy of it, about what it felt like when the technique and the intention were fully aligned. She had told him: it feels like saying something true. He had said: yes. That's what I thought.

She picked up her pack. She kept climbing.

She reached the summit as the sun was clearing the mountains to the west, which put a specific quality of light on the world — horizontal, amber, throwing everything into sharp relief. She sat on the summit and looked at the view, which was the Ruby Mountains in every direction and the valley below and the sky above and the full enormous scale of a landscape that was not interested in human scale and which she found, as she had found the Valley of Fire three years ago, correctly sized.

She had brought the telescope.

It had been in the back of Matt's jeep, in its leather case, exactly where Charlie had packed it for a trip that had not gone as planned. She had not asked Matt if she could take it. She had taken it because it was Charlie's and because she was going to the mountain he had wanted to reach and because it seemed right that the telescope should be there, should see what it had been brought to see.

She took it out of its case. It was a four-inch refractor — she knew this because she had spent two evenings watching amateur astronomy videos on her laptop, learning enough to use the thing correctly, which Charlie would have found both touching and faintly hilarious, she thought. He would have offered to teach her. She had wanted to learn it herself first.

She set it up. She made the adjustments she had learned from the videos. She aimed it at the sky above the eastern horizon, which was where it needed to be aimed, and she let the eye of it find the sky.

She looked.

Andromeda was not difficult to find. This surprised her — she had expected it to be elusive, the way difficult things were elusive, requiring patience and technique and the willingness to look for a long time before finding. But the sky above Leatherman Peak was the sky Charlie had described, almost no light pollution at this altitude, and the galaxy was there in the eyepiece with a clarity that felt like something being given rather than found.

She looked at it for a long time.

She thought about what Charlie had said — had told anyone who would listen, had texted her about at eleven o'clock on a Tuesday evening three years ago with enough detail that she had read the text twice and then put her phone face down because the detail was beautiful and she was not ready for beautiful. Two and a half million light years. The light that had left it before humans existed, arriving now. The most distant thing visible to the naked eye.

She looked at the light that had left it before humans existed.

She thought about Charlie in his office on a Tuesday morning, minimizing the booking confirmation because he didn't want to jinx it by looking at it too directly. She thought about Charlie at the camping supply store buying the emergency kit that Carmen had restocked without comment. She thought about Charlie's voice on the fourth ring, patient, without urgency, the voice of someone who had time for you because he had decided you were worth having time for.

She thought about his face in the lamp light through the closing door. The saber in her hand and Carmen at her shoulder and Charlie going out to find Matt and the look on his face, which was the look she had been waiting three years for in its complete form, the look of someone who has been fully seen and knows it and is not afraid of it.

She thought: I told him. He knew. He went out carrying the real version of it.

She had been telling herself this for three months, holding it the way Carmen had said to hold things that were true — with both hands, without requiring it to be enough, simply not putting it down.

She looked at the light from two and a half million years ago.

She thought: he would have been standing right here. He would have been so pleased with himself for getting us here.

She thought: he would have talked for twenty minutes about the light travel time. He would have explained it three different ways to make sure she understood it, and she would have understood it after the first way and she would have let him explain it three ways because the explaining was the point as much as the understanding.

She thought: I would give a great deal to hear him explain it right now.

She did not say this out loud. There was no one to say it to. The mountain held its altitude silence around her and the telescope held its eye to the sky and the galaxy held its two and a half million light years of distance between itself and her and none of it asked her to be anything other than what she was, which was someone looking at something very far away and very old and feeling, in the feeling of that distance and that age, the specific smallness that was not diminishment but its opposite — the feeling of being accurately sized, which was what she had needed the desert for, which was what the desert had finally given her, though not in the way she had planned.

A tear went down her face. Just one, and slow, the kind that came not from the acute grief but from something below it — from gratitude, possibly, or from the specific texture of loss when it had been in you long enough that it had settled into something you could almost hold without dropping.

She let it go. She kept looking.

The stars came out fully as the sky went dark, which was faster at altitude than in the city, the dark arriving with a completeness that she had never experienced in Paris and which she had experienced twice before in Nevada and which still surprised her — the way the dark was not the absence of light but a presence, the sky going from blue to the specific dark that was full of things rather than empty of them.

She moved the telescope. She had Charlie's list — she had found it on his phone, which Matt had retrieved, the note titled

stars for Sophie, which she had read twice and then put the phone face down because the detail was beautiful and she was not ready and then she had picked it up again because she was going to have to be ready eventually. The list was: Andromeda first, then the Orion nebula if it was visible, then the Pleiades, then the double cluster in Perseus. The list had a note at the bottom in the informal shorthand of someone writing to themselves:

save Andromeda for last, build to it. Actually show her first, the others are practice.

She had shown herself Andromeda first. She thought Charlie would have understood.

She worked through the list. She found the Orion nebula — the fuzzy smear of it, the cloud of gas and dust where stars were being made, which was the kind of thing that sounded like a metaphor and was simply true. She found the Pleiades, the cluster of blue-white stars that she had always been able to see with the naked eye as a faint smudge and that through the telescope resolved into individual points, each one its own sun, each one with whatever it had around it. She found the double cluster in Perseus, two open clusters side by side, the telescope showing them as two distinct families of stars with the particular beauty of things that were separate and close at once.

She packed the telescope up carefully. She had learned how to do this from the same videos and she did it with the care you brought to something that was not yours to damage.

The mountain was cold at night and she was not adequately dressed for it, which was a thing Charlie would have anticipated and prepared for and which she had not adequately prepared for because she was Sophia and the practical details of outdoor things were not her specialty and this had not changed because Charlie was gone, which was something she was going to have to continue addressing.

She put on the extra layer she had remembered at the last minute. She sat on the summit for a little while longer.

She thought about January. About Olivier's apartment. About the thing she had understood across a dinner table — the specific quality of Charlie's attention, the particular kind of listening that was not strategic but complete. She had flown to Nevada to end something and instead she had found the courage to begin, and then there had been no time, and she had told him anyway, and he had heard her, and he had known.

She thought: it is not a tragedy that I was almost too late. I was not too late. I was exactly in time and then time ran out and those are different things.

She thought this carefully, the way she thought about things she needed to be precise about, because precision was the only way she knew how to make peace with things that were not tidy.

The stars were very clear.

She looked at them for a long time without the telescope — just her eyes, the unmediated sky, the way it looked when you didn't look too directly at any one part of it but let it be the whole thing, the full dark field, the way Charlie had told her to look at things you wanted to see all of at once.

She said: "Thank you for the list."

The mountain received this without comment, which was appropriate.

She picked up the pack. She started down.

TWENTY

And Stay Down

Carmen

Carmen

She had gone back because the work was not finished. This was the complete explanation and she was aware it was also not the complete explanation, but the other parts of the explanation required more examining than she had done so far, and the work was not finished, and the work not finished was sufficient.

The fourth deployment was different from the first three in ways she had expected and in ways she had not. The ways she had expected: the heat, the dust, the quality of the light in the late afternoon that was specific to this part of the world and that she had missed without knowing she had missed it, the way you missed things that were part of a rhythm your body had learned. The operational tempo, which was higher than the last deployment and which required more and left less room for the kind of thinking that did not directly serve the mission. The particular community of people who were doing the same work — not friends, necessarily, but colleagues in the deepest sense, people who understood the specific demands of the thing you were all doing without requiring explanation.

The way she had not expected: Charlie.

She had not expected to carry him here. She had expected, in the way she had always managed grief, that the carrying would remain interior and organized — filed, maintained, present but not intrusive. She had not expected that here, specifically, in this landscape, the carrying would be different.

It was not heavier here. That was the thing she found hardest to explain to herself. It was not heavier — it did not impair her function, did not slow her thinking, did not affect her work in any way she could measure. It was simply more present. As though the landscape, which was so far from anything Charlie had known or loved or been interested in, was itself a kind of contrast — the specific clarity of a loss measured against an entirely alien background, the way you saw certain colors more truly when they were set against colors that had nothing to do with them.

She thought about him in the intervals. Not constantly — she was not someone who thought constantly about anything except the work, and even then the thinking was organized rather than obsessive. But in the intervals between the work, when the kind of quiet that was not the quiet of her apartment but the quiet of a place where quiet was also information, she thought about Charlie.

She thought: he would have hated it here.

She thought: he would have found something to like. He always did.

★★★

The mission was a night operation. She could not describe it in any detail that she would be willing to put in writing, but its broad outlines were: four hours, three objectives, a team of eight, the kind of work that required absolute clarity at every decision point because the cost of a wrong decision at any point was not recoverable. She had done this kind of work before. She did it the way she did all work: with full attention and no wasted motion, the focus narrowed to the immediate thing and then the next immediate thing and the next, the sequence of present moments that was the only way through something that could not be survived by looking at it whole.

It went correctly. This was not always the case. She was grateful when it was the case and she was realistic about the ratio, which was better than it had been earlier in her career and which would never be as good as she wanted it.

They came back in before dawn. She did the debrief. She ate. She cleaned her equipment, which she did after every operation regardless of the hour, because equipment that was not maintained was equipment that failed at the worst possible time, and the worst possible time was always the next time.

She had carried Torres differently.

This was the comparison she kept arriving at and then setting aside and then arriving at again, because it was useful and because it was also not quite right and the not-quite-rightness was information she didn't fully have the language for yet.

She had carried Torres — had been carrying him for eight months now, the specific weight of a twenty-four-year-old on a road they'd driven seventeen times before without incident, a weight that was made of particular things: his laugh in the photograph receding, the letter she had written to his parents, the specific way he'd moved under pressure which was the way she'd wanted everyone on the team to move, fast and clean and without the half-second of hesitation that cost you. She had carried him the way she had learned to carry people she had lost on deployment, which was quietly, in the interior, organized and managed so that the carrying did not impair the function.

Charlie was different.

Charlie was not a casualty. This was the obvious difference and also the wrong way to think about it, because the wrong way to think about it produced the wrong accounting, and the wrong accounting was — she could feel this — going to cost her something she couldn't yet identify.

Torres had died because of the specific logic of the work. The road, the device, the fraction of a second. The logic of the work had killed people she had known before Torres and she understood the logic of the work and she had made her peace with the understanding in the way you made peace with things that were not peace but were the closest available approximation.

Charlie had died because he had gotten on his knees on a floor in a burning building and held a trap door closed so that the people he loved could go through it. This was not the logic of the work. This was the logic of Charlie, which was: the people he loved, and everything else second. He had held the door until the beam came. She did not believe he had been surprised.

She was carrying this differently because it required a different kind of carrying.

She thought: he would have been terrible at this deployment.

She meant this affectionately and also literally. He would have found the heat excessive and would have commented on it repeatedly, with the equanimity he brought to things he found excessive, which was not the equanimity of someone who didn't feel the excess but the equanimity of someone who had decided the feeling was not going to be the main thing. He would have been interested in the food — genuinely interested, not performatively, the way he was genuinely interested in most things that were specific to a place. He would have spent an afternoon asking the interpreters about the regional variation in particular dishes and would have taken notes.

He would have made the interpreters like him. She was certain of this. He had a quality that translated across almost any cultural register, which was the quality of someone who was genuinely curious about you specifically, as a person, rather than curious about the category you represented. People felt this. People responded to it.

She thought: what a waste.

She thought this with the cold precision she brought to waste in the operational sense, the waste of a resource that could not be replaced, the specific loss of a capability that had been unique and that the system did not have a redundancy for. Charlie had been irreplaceable in this specific way, this quality of genuine particular attention, and its loss was a loss that had consequences beyond the people who had known him, consequences that spread outward in the way that the loss of any irreplaceable thing spread outward, invisibly but really.

She did not say this to anyone. There was no one to say it to here who would have understood it.

She would say it to Matt eventually. Matt would understand it.

She thought: Matt is going to go back to the town.

She had known this since the morning they walked out of the mine — had seen it in the way he'd stood in the early light with the wooden box, the particular quality of his stillness, which was the stillness of someone who had made a decision and was living in the first moment after the making of it. She had not said anything. It was not the moment and also it was his to say, not hers.

She hoped he went soon. She hoped he went and came back and could tell her what he found. She had put her hand on the door of the Drunken Coyote in the pre-dawn and felt something on the other side of it that she had filed under a category she had not yet named, a category that sat between the explicable and the inexplicable and that she was going to need more information to close.

She wanted the information.

She wanted to know what Emma had built in there, in those five years and all the years after. She wanted to know what the town was keeping and why it was keeping it and whether the keeping was something that happened to Emma or something that Emma had decided. She had a theory. The theory involved the Trust established in 1887 with the barkeep and the sheriff and the deputy as trustees, the deliberateness of it, the careful practical arrangement of someone who had understood that her situation was permanent and had made the appropriate provisions.

She thought: Emma planned this.

She filed this thought carefully, in the category she was building, and she committed to continuing the filing when she got home.

She would get home. This she knew the way she knew most things she knew with certainty, which was from the evidence and from the specific kind of conviction that was not faith but the product of continuous accurate assessment. She would get home. She would see Matt and Sophie. She would sit in her apartment on the street in Las Vegas and drink her coffee and look at the street below.

She would call Sophie on a Sunday and Sophie would be in Paris because Sophie was going to go back to Paris, was already going back in every way that mattered except physically, which was the only way that had been changed by the desert and the town and the gallows and the decisions Sophie had made in a doorway in the gas lamp light. Sophie was going to go back to Paris and she was going to mourn Charlie in the way that was available to her, which was with the precision she brought to everything, the grief moving through her slowly and internally, and she was going to be alright. Carmen had promised this to Matt in a tunnel and she had meant it.

She would not go back to Greenbriar Gulch. Not yet. She did not yet know what it would mean when she did.

She took the first watch because someone had to take the first watch and she was not going to sleep yet anyway.

The desert here was different from Nevada. The same vast indifference, the same age in the rock and the sand, but a different quality of color — the palette drier, more beige than amber, the mountains lower and more distant. The sky was the same. The sky above the desert was always the same, she had found — the same darkness, the same depth, the same particular silence of a sky that had nothing between you and it.

She sat with her back against the vehicle and she looked at the sky.

She thought about Torres. She thought about Torres the way she always thought about Torres in the interval after a mission — not with grief exactly, but with the particular attention she gave to the people in her count, the people she carried differently from Charlie because she had been responsible for them in a way she had not been responsible for Charlie. Torres had been twenty-four and he had been caught mid-laugh in the platoon photograph and he had been on a road they had driven seventeen times before and the eighteenth time the road had changed.

She thought: I have been carrying people for a long time.

She thought: I am good at it. I have gotten better at it. I am going to keep getting better at it because the alternative is not carrying them, which is not available to me.

The sunset was extraordinary. This was not unusual — desert sunsets were always extraordinary, had always been extraordinary, she had watched them in three countries and found them consistently reliable in this one respect, which was that the sky in the last hour before dark did something that the rest of the day did not, organizing the light in a way that was almost architectural, the colors moving from gold to amber to the specific orange that had no name, and then to the dark.

She watched it and she thought about what Carmen had said — not said, thought, in the tunnel, in the dark, moving Matt toward the exit with the torch and Sophie's voice behind her. She had thought: I am going to have to revise my estimate. She had revised it. She was still revising it. The estimate of how much goodwill the world contained had always been a working figure for her, not a fixed one, and Charlie had been the primary source of upward revision for seven years, and she was learning what the estimate looked like without that source.

It was lower. Not catastrophically lower — she was not someone for whom catastrophic revisions happened without evidence, and the world had continued to provide evidence of goodwill in the months since September. Matt, who had called her from the wall on a Tuesday morning three months before the trip and who now called her on the first of every month, at nine a.m. Las Vegas time, without comment or explanation, in the way that people maintained connections they did not have language for. Sophie, who had written her a letter — an actual letter, handwritten, in French, which Carmen had read with the dictionary app and had then read again without it, because some of what Sophie wrote was meant to be understood through the rhythm of the language rather than the definitions. Mrs. Petrakis from the building, who had sent emails in the interval between deployments that contained photographs of the mail pile and brief inventories of its contents.

The world had continued to produce evidence.

She took her phone from her pocket. She opened it. She went to the contacts and she scrolled to M and she looked at Matt's name.

She had called him once since September. The day she found out she was being deployed again — she had called and told him, because he needed to know, and he had said

okay and she had said

okay and they had sat in the phone silence for a moment and then he had said

"be careful" and she had said

"always" and they had hung up. That was the last time.

She looked at his name on the screen.

The things she would have said, if she had been someone who said things: I think about you in the intervals. I think about what you said at the rest stop —

would you actually want that, someone there with you for it — and I filed it under interesting and I have not stopped finding it interesting. I think about the morning outside the mine when you turned and looked at me and I thought: there will be time for that. I still think that. I think the time is coming and I am not sure what to do with the fact that I think that, so I am doing what I do with most things I am not sure what to do with, which is to continue and wait for the situation to clarify.

These were not things she said. They were things she knew. The knowing and the saying were different categories and she had always operated more comfortably in the first.

The sky went from amber to orange to the particular dark that was not absence but presence.

She looked at his name on the screen.

She thought: not now. The situation is not yet clarified. The deployment is not yet finished. The distance between here and Las Vegas is real, and the distance between what I know and what I am ready to do something about is also real, and I have never been someone who did things before the situation was ready.

She thought: but I am going to call him.

She thought: when I am home. When the work is finished and I am back in the apartment and the quiet is legible again. I am going to call on a Tuesday when he is on the wall and I know he will answer on the fourth ring, and I am going to say:

I have been thinking about something and I think you should know what I have been thinking.

She thought: he will say okay. He will wait. He always waits.

She thought: that is enough. That is what I have. That is where we are.

She closed the phone. She put it back in her pocket.

The desert held its enormous dark. The stars were coming out — slowly at first and then all at once, the way they came when there was nothing between you and them, the way they came in a place that did not insist on its own illumination.

She watched them come.

She thought about the Andromeda galaxy, which Charlie had told her about seven months ago on a camping trip she had almost not gone on, in the back seat of the car between Wells and the town they had not intended to stop in. He had told her with the detail of someone who loved the subject and the audience equally, and she had listened with the attention she gave to people she found worth listening to, which was not everyone, and which was Charlie.

Two and a half million light years. The light that had left it before they existed, arriving now.

She was looking at a sky full of lights that had left before she existed and were arriving now.

She thought: Charlie knew how to be in the world. He knew how to receive it. I have been working on that my whole life and I am better at it than I was and I am not yet where he was and I am going to keep working on it because that is what you did with the things that mattered.

She thought: I should call my sister.

She thought this and noted it and filed it under:

Tuesday, when I am home.

She sat with her back against the vehicle and her face tilted to the sky and she let herself be accurately sized — not diminished, not overwhelmed, but precisely located in the scale of things, which was: small and present and alive and carrying what she carried and doing the work and going to call Matt on a Tuesday and going to call her sister and going to come home when the work was done.

The stars were very bright.

She watched them for a while.

She took the second watch too, because there was enough quiet and she wanted to be in it.

TWENTY-ONE

To My Dear Sister Linda

Matt

Matt

He had been in the house for four months before he went up to the attic.

This was not avoidance — he had been in the house for four months because the house needed to be sold, and the house needed to be sold because Charlotte Rose had told him what she could tell him, which was that the property records for Greenbriar Gulch listed a single surviving heir, and the surviving heir was Emma Rose's great-grandniece, and the great-grandniece was Charlotte Rose herself, and Charlotte had signed over a portion of the estate to him because Emma had instructed the deputy and the deputy had given his word and the word had been kept across a hundred and thirty-five years in ways that Charlotte had chosen not to examine too carefully in the formal documentation. The wooden box and whatever was in it were his. The house that went with the box — a small property in Elko county that had been in the Rose family since 1887 — was going on the market, but Charlotte had asked if he would look after it until the sale was final, and he had said yes.

It was the kind of house that had been built for a specific life and had accumulated that life in its walls — not large, not remarkable from the outside, but with the interior quality of a place where someone had done consistent and careful work for a very long time. Everything was in good repair. Everything was in its place. It had the quality of a place that had been prepared for an eventual departure rather than simply abandoned, and he found this, when he first walked through it, both moving and very Emma.

He had spent four months doing what the house required. Small repairs, documentation, the estate agent's visits, the particular bureaucracy of a property with an unusual ownership history that the estate agent had handled with professional tact, asking fewer questions than her expression suggested she had. He had lived in the house while he did this, sleeping in the small back bedroom and cooking in the kitchen and sitting in the evenings on the porch that faced east, watching the desert go through its changes in the hour before dark.

He had not been lonely. This surprised him — he had expected loneliness, had expected the specific quality of being alone in a house that wasn't his, in a county he had only known at the worst time of his life. Instead he had found, in the four months of the house, something he could only describe as company, though he could not account for the company in any way that would have survived examination. The house felt inhabited. Not haunted — he had no framework for haunted, and the feeling was not cold or wrong in any of the ways the word implied. Simply: inhabited. Maintained. The same quality Charlotte had heard when he said it, the same quality that had made her pen slow over the notepad.

He had thought about Emma every day. He had thought about her in the saloon and in the chapel and on the dark street and in the office with the lamp and the rifle and the kiss that had been brief and entirely true. He had thought: she is still there. He had thought: I know where she is. He had held this the way he held the things he couldn't change — not tightly, not loosely, just present, just carried.

The first month he had worked. This was what he did with things that did not have a clear resolution: he worked. The house was a 1920s ranch on a half-acre outside Elko that had belonged to a branch of the Rose family for sixty years and that needed the particular attention of a house that had been lived in by careful people who had grown old and whose careful attention had quietly shifted from maintenance to management. The roof was good. The foundation was good. The plumbing required a week of focused effort and one call to a plumber named Dave who did not ask unnecessary questions, which Matt appreciated.

He worked on the house during the days. He drove to the grocery store in Elko twice a week. He called his sister on Sundays. He did not go to the wall, because the leg still needed another six weeks and he knew it and he gave it the six weeks without argument, because arguing with a healing leg was the kind of thing that produced a leg that healed wrong. He went to a doctor in Elko who looked at the original stitches and said the work was clean, which it was. Emma's strip of skirt first and then the paramedic's proper bandaging, layered, each adequate.

He did not think about Carmen or Sophie in any systematic way. He thought about them the way you thought about people you trusted to be managing — with the background awareness of someone who knew they were alright, who had verified that they were alright in the immediate aftermath and who did not require continuous verification. Sophie had gone back to Paris. Carmen had gone back to deployment. They had stood in the hospital corridor and said what needed saying in the time available, which was not much time and was enough. He knew where they were.

He knew where Emma was.

This was the thing that had changed. He had spent the first week in the house — the week before the leg would let him do much more than sit at the kitchen table and drink coffee and look out the window at the half-acre of Nevada scrubland — with the specific quality of a person who knows something they cannot verify and is deciding what to do with the knowing. He had been in the Town Hall. He had been in the chapel. He had seen Emma at the window of the Drunken Coyote pressing her palm to the glass. He knew.

The house was on a rise that looked south toward the valley where Greenbriar Gulch was. Or had been. Or still was, in the sense that interested him.

He did not drive to Greenbriar Gulch. The highway patrol had it sealed pending investigation and Charlotte Rose's investigation was ongoing and he had agreed, in the hospital corridor, to stay out until she had what she needed. He was a person who kept his agreements. He stayed out.

He thought about Emma every day. He did not romanticize this — it was not pining, it was not the particular luxurious grief of an unrequited thing. It was simpler and more specific than that. He had sat beside her in a chapel with her shoulder an inch from his and the warmth of her in the cold dark, and he had kissed her in a saloon office with the lamp between them, and he had watched her press her palm to glass and understand something about her own situation with the same composure she brought to everything. He knew who she was. He knew where she was. He thought about both of these facts every day, the way you thought about things you were not ready to act on but were not willing to put down.

In the second month he found her books.

They were in a small room off the kitchen that the original owners had used as a sewing room and that subsequent occupants had used for various things — the evidence was layered, several categories of use, the most recent being storage. Against the back wall, behind boxes he moved carefully, was a low bookshelf. He had not expected it. He had moved the boxes for practical reasons and found himself looking at a shelf of books that were old enough to have the particular smell of books that had been in the same room for a long time, the smell of paper and age and the specific quality of something that had been handled.

He took them out one at a time. He read the title pages. Most were from the 1870s and 1880s, the kind of books that traveled west with the people who went west and that ended up in shelves in small rooms in houses in Elko County. A Bible. A volume of Tennyson, worn at the spine. A practical guide to mining claims. A novel in French — he turned it over in his hands, the pages still and cool — with a name written on the flyleaf in the handwriting he recognized by now.

Emma Rose, 1879.

He sat on the floor of the small room with the French novel in his hands and the afternoon light coming through the small window and the Nevada desert visible through the glass, and he held it for a long time.

She had been twenty-three in 1879. She had been in Georgia, or possibly already traveling west. She had been carrying this book, carrying it through the years of the journey and the years in Greenbriar Gulch, and it had ended up on a shelf in a room off the kitchen of a house in Elko that her family had lived in for sixty years after her, and it was in his hands now, in October, in the year she had been dead for a hundred and thirty-five.

He put the book back carefully. He put the others back. He went back to the kitchen and made coffee and looked out the window at the scrubland and let the feeling be what it was, which was not sadness exactly but not the absence of sadness either, the particular quality of a thing that was both present and past tense simultaneously and that did not resolve into either.

He thought: she is still there.

He thought: I know where she is.

On the fifth month, on a Tuesday morning with the autumn light coming through the east-facing windows at the angle that made the dust in the air visible and golden, he went up to the attic.

★ ★ ★

The attic was the attic of a house owned by careful people — organized, labeled, the boxes arranged with enough space between them to access each one without disturbing the others. He had brought a lamp. He had brought his phone for light. He used the lamp.

Most of what was in the attic was not relevant to him — the accumulated history of the Rose family across generations, the boxes and trunks of people he had not known, objects that had survived the particular winnowing of time through some combination of significance and luck. He moved through it with the respect he brought to all spaces that had belonged to other people, noting without touching most of what he passed.

The chest was at the back.

It was a traveling chest — the kind that had been made in the nineteenth century for people who were going somewhere and intended to keep going somewhere, built for use rather than display, the wood dark with age and use, the brass fittings tarnished to the particular brown-green of old metal that had been through weather. It was not locked. The latch was stiff but it moved when he pressed it, the mechanism releasing with the feel of something that had not been opened in a long time and that opened now without complaint.

Inside: folded clothes in the careful way of someone who understood that fabrics lasted longer folded than stored any other way. A small Bible, leather-covered, with a name inscribed inside the front cover in a hand he recognized from the box — Emma Rose, 1874. A ribbon, blue silk, faded but intact. A small mirror in a silver frame. And at the bottom, beneath these things, an envelope.

He picked up the envelope. It was sealed. The address on the front, in the same careful hand as the box:

Miss Linda Rose, care of Mr. Henry Beaumont, Savannah, Georgia.

And below the address, smaller, the same hand:

If found, please deliver.

He held the envelope in both hands for a moment. He looked at the address in the autumn light coming through the small attic window. He thought: she wrote this the morning she died. She put it in the envelope and addressed it and sealed it and set it somewhere she would see it, meaning to mail it, and then the evening came and O'Donnell came with it and there was no longer time and someone — George, probably, the barkeep, who had been loyal — had found it afterward and packed it with the rest of her things and it had traveled with the chest and the chest had traveled with the family and here it was, a hundred and thirty-five years later, unopened.

He opened it carefully, the way you opened things that had waited a long time.

★ ★ ★

The photograph came out first. He knew it before he turned it over — felt the stiff card stock, the specific weight of a period photograph, and knew. He turned it over.

She was in a pale blue dress, looking at the camera with the composed expression she had practiced, the expression he had seen her wearing in the saloon on the night they'd met and had recognized as the working version, the expression deployed when she needed to hold herself in. She was sitting. Her hands were in her lap. The camera had caught her at a moment when the composure was very nearly perfect — only in her eyes was there something that the composure hadn't quite reached, something that was present and looking out from behind the practiced surface.

He looked at her face for a long time.

He turned the photograph over.

To my dear sister Linda. Love, Emma.

The cursive was careful and small and entirely hers. He recognized it from the box and from the letter she had written in the office — the hand of someone who had been well-taught and who had kept the teaching alive through consistent use, who wrote the way she did everything: with attention and without waste.

He set the photograph down on the attic floor beside him. He unfolded the letter.

It was two pages, written on both sides of a single folded sheet, the ink brown with age but entirely legible. He read it.

He read:

Dearest Linda. I have been putting off this letter for three weeks because I could not find the right beginning, and I find now that the beginning is simply this: I am well. I am well in the way you asked about, the other kind of well, the kind that is harder to assess and easier to pretend to than the practical kind. I am well in that way too.

He read:

There is a man here. He arrived last night in the middle of a storm and threw a chair at someone on my behalf and I find I cannot account for him in any of the usual ways. He is not from here. He is not from anywhere near here. I do not know yet what to make of him except that he is entirely himself, which is a rarer quality than it ought to be, and that his face is known to me in the way that certain tunes are known before you can name them, and that this is something I am holding carefully because careful is the appropriate register for things you have not yet found the language for.

He stopped reading. He sat in the attic with the letter in his hands and the photograph beside him and the autumn light coming through the small window and the desert visible through it, the scrubland going gold in October the way it had gone gold in September the year before, the year before that, every year before that for a hundred and thirty-five years.

He sat with it.

He thought: she wrote this the morning she died. She wrote it after she sent George for the sheriff and before the gang came back the final time and she sat at her desk in the lamplight of her own saloon and she wrote to her sister about a man who had arrived in a storm and thrown a chair, and she used the word

known, and she put the letter in the envelope and addressed it and she was going to send it, and she didn't get the chance.

He thought: I was there. I was in that saloon. I threw the chair.

He thought: she was writing about me.

He held this. He held it the way he held things that were too large for their category — not analyzing it, not requiring it to be something he could account for, simply letting it be what it was, which was true and present and not going anywhere.

He read the rest of the letter.

I am going to be alright, Linda. I have always been going to be alright, which is either a character trait or a delusion and I have spent considerable time wondering which, and I have arrived at the conclusion that the distinction matters less than the fact that it has always been true. I have been alright in every circumstance I have found myself in, including the ones I did not choose. I expect I will continue to be alright in whatever circumstances follow these. I am not afraid.

I want you to know that I have been happy here. Not every day and not in every way, but in the way that counts, which is: I have been the person I meant to be in the place I chose to be it, and that is a thing not everyone gets to say, and I want you to know that I know I am lucky to say it, and I am saying it now so that if there is ever a time when it cannot be said, it will have been said.

Give my love to the children. Write when you can.

With all my love, your Emma.

He folded the letter. He set it beside the photograph on the attic floor. He looked at both of them — the photograph face up, Emma in the pale blue silk looking at a camera with the composed expression that was almost but not quite all the way there, and the letter folded beside it.

He looked at the photograph for a long time.

He thought: she is still there. He had been thinking this for five months and it had not changed and it was not going to change, and the not-changing of it was not a source of grief so much as a source of — he searched for the word and found, as he usually found when he searched for words, that the word was not available and that the thing itself was real regardless.

He thought: she is still there. She has been there for a hundred and thirty-five years. She is running her saloon and she has a companion now and she is doing what she always did, which is making the best of the situation she is in with the considerable resources she has for making the best of things.

He thought: I am going to go back.

He held this thought the way he held the six moves of the traverse — carefully, without requiring it to be more than it was, knowing it was going to take time and was going to require him to think about it from a different angle than he had been thinking about it. He did not know how you went back to a town that was not on any map, that did not appear in any record before 1882 and after 1891, that the highway patrol had sealed pending investigation and that Rose was still investigating with the focused intensity of someone who was not going to stop. He did not know how. He knew he was going.

He climbed on Saturday.

He had not been back to the wall since the Tuesday morning in March when Charlie had called during the climb and he had answered on the fourth ring and said it was fine and it had been fine and then it had not been fine. He had not been back in the seven months since. The leg had needed time and he had given it time and the leg was good now, and the wall had waited, as walls did — without patience or impatience, simply present, the traverse unsolved, the sixth move still the sixth move.

He drove to the trailhead in the dark and was packed and on the approach by first light. His body remembered the route — the approach, the base, the sequence of holds through the first two hundred feet that had become automatic over three years of repetition. He moved through them without thinking about them, the way you moved through things you had absorbed completely, his attention reserved for what was above.

He stopped below the traverse. He looked up at it. The six moves, the sequence he had been working for three years, the sixth move that had thrown him twelve times.

He thought about his sister's question, seven months ago on a Tuesday in March, the day before the camping trip:

maybe you're thinking about it wrong.

He thought about what Emma had written.

He is not from anywhere near here. I do not know yet what to make of him except that he is entirely himself.

He thought about the traverse. He thought about the assumption he had been making in the fifth move — the footwork, the smear he had been using because it was the obvious choice and the obvious choice had worked for the first five moves and had failed him at the sixth. He had been assuming the smear because the smear was what the terrain suggested. What if the terrain was wrong. What if the fifth move required a heel hook instead — a different weight distribution, the kind that committed the body correctly for the sixth rather than incorrectly for it, that made the sloper not a gamble but a consequence of being already in the right position.

He thought: I have been solving the wrong problem.

He thought: the problem was not the sixth move. The problem was the fifth.

He went up.

He moved through the first five moves in the sequence he had always used, and at the fifth he changed it — the heel hook, the weight shift, the different distribution — and he felt the difference immediately, felt it in his body before his mind confirmed it, the way you felt the right thing when you found it, which was not triumph but simply correctness, the feeling of something that had been slightly wrong becoming right.

The sloper was under his right hand.

He moved fast. He committed. He released the good hold and put his weight on the sloper and moved his left hand and the sequence completed, all six moves, the traverse done, his feet on the rock above it and the summit eighty feet above that.

He stopped. He held the wall. He breathed.

He thought: three years.

He thought: the problem was in the fifth move.

He thought: my sister was right.

He climbed to the summit. The desert spread below him in every direction — the valley floor, the mountains on all sides, the particular depth of the Nevada sky on a clear October morning. He had been here in his imagination many times, the summit that had been the goal, and it was exactly what he had imagined and nothing like it, which was always how summits were.

He sat on the rock at the top and he looked at the desert.

He thought about Emma at the window of the Drunken Coyote, watching the convoy leave. He thought about her hand against the glass. He thought about what she had written:

I have been the person I meant to be in the place I chose to be it.

He thought about Charlie walking out into the night to find him, going toward the saloon, looking back once at the closing door.

He thought: I am going to go back to the town. I do not know when and I do not know how and I do not know what it will mean when I get there, if I get there. I know she is there. I know she has been there. I know that the feeling of someone known, in the chapel in the dark, was a real feeling about a real person in a real place, and that real things persist, and that this one is persisting in a building on a main street in a valley I drove into in a storm on a Friday night.

He thought: she has been waiting a long time.

He thought: not for me specifically.

He thought about the letter.

He had read it eleven times. He knew this because he had counted, in the same way he counted traverse attempts — accurately, without sentimentality, because accuracy was how you tracked a thing that mattered. Eleven times. Each time he had read it he had arrived at the same word and stopped: *known.*

Her face is known to me in the way that certain tunes are known before you can name them.

He had been that word for her. He had walked into her saloon in a storm and thrown a chair at the man who was threatening her and somehow, in the space of a single night, he had become known to her in the deepest way she had for knowing things, the way below the naming faculty, and she had written it in a letter she meant to send to her sister and had not had time to send, and the letter had traveled from 1886 to a chest in an attic in a house in Elko County and from the chest to his hands in October, and the word was still there, still in her handwriting, still true.

He had been on the wall a dozen times since September. He had solved the traverse three weeks ago. He had stood on the summit once before this, alone with the desert below and the traverse behind him, and he had thought: I know where she is. He had come back a second time because the first time he had not been ready to think fully about what knowing where she was meant and what it required from him and what he intended to do about it.

He was ready now.

He thought about what Charlotte Rose had told him, in her careful and honest way, which was that the electromagnetic anomaly at Greenbriar Gulch was real and documented and that its mechanism was unknown and that the highway patrol seal had been lifted and that the town was, in the technical sense, accessible. She had told him this in the voice of someone who was giving him information and not making his decision for him. He appreciated this. He had made his decision without assistance.

He was going back to the town.

He did not know what he would find. He did not know whether the thing that was keeping Emma and the town in 1886 was a one-time occurrence or a door that opened in both directions. He did not know whether she would be visible to him, or whether the visit would be one-sided — him standing in the saloon of the Drunken Coyote, looking at the maintained lamps and the clean bar and the order that she kept over a hundred and thirty-five years of keeping things, knowing she was there and not being able to reach her.

He thought: I don't know. And not knowing is not the same as knowing the answer is no.

He thought about the heel hook. He thought about three years of solving the wrong problem, of making an assumption in the fifth move that compounded forward through the sequence until it expressed itself as failure at the sixth. He thought about his sister on the Tuesday morning in March: maybe you're thinking about it wrong.

He thought about Emma, reading the Tennyson in Georgia in 1879, packing it in her trunk to carry west, putting it on the shelf in a room off the kitchen where it had waited in the dark for forty years after her and another forty after that until a man from Las Vegas had moved the boxes in October and found it.

Things persisted. The things that mattered persisted. This was not a mystical statement. It was an observation, drawn from evidence, about the way that real things continued to be real regardless of the passing of time.

Emma was real. The night was real. The broth and the chapel and the two shots from the rooftop and the kiss were real. He had been there. She had been there. The reality of it did not stop being true because he had come out of the mine tunnel and been received by the highway patrol in the early morning.

She has been there and the town has kept her there and she has been running her saloon with a companion she did not expect and she has been making the best of it the way she made the best of everything. I am not her rescue. I am not the resolution of her situation.

He thought: but I know where she is. And I am going to go. And we will see what that is, when I get there.

He sat on the summit for a while. The desert held its enormous indifferent scale below him, the same scale it had held below him on every previous climb, unchanged and complete. The traverse was behind him. Charlie was behind him, in the specific way that people who were gone were behind you — not absent, not resolved, simply no longer in front. The wooden box was in the house in Elko, with the photograph and the letter. Charlotte Rose was in Elko, writing her report, adding a line to the notepad every few days when something new resolved.

The wall had waited three years for him to find the mistake in the fifth move. Some things required time to see correctly.

He thought: I know where she is.

He thought: I have the box and the letter and the traverse and the time.

He stood up. He prepared for the descent.

He looked at the desert one more time — the valley floor, the mountains, the sky, the particular quality of

October light on the Nevada rock, which was specific and unrepeatable and entirely itself. He looked at it the way Emma had taught him without knowing she was teaching him, which was: with the full attention it deserved, without requiring it to be more than it was.

He started down.

About the Author

Marco Antonio Varela was born in Mexico City, where he began studying music at the Artist Development Center at Televisa Studios. He came to Las Vegas to pursue a B.B.A. at the University of Nevada, Las Vegas — because even then, he understood that a life in the arts required someone who also understood a balance sheet. He began his professional career with the Seattle Opera, went on to perform recitals and concerts across Europe and Asia, recorded his debut album Trilogía, and became an active member of the American Guild of Musical Artists. For thirty years, he did what opera singers do: he stepped into other people's stories and made them feel true.

The move to storytelling on his own terms was, in hindsight, inevitable. A man who has spent a career inhabiting Verdi and Puccini — who understands that the largest human questions are best carried by the most precise formal structures — does not stop being a dramatist when he steps off the stage. He produced and co-wrote the short film The Last Call, recognized at the Nevada Women's Film Festival, and then kept going. At sixty-one, with six novels to his name — Sinter Klass, Soulblade, Bunker Hill, American Explorer, Across the Ages, and The Eternal Watch — he has found the form that contains everything the others were reaching toward.

An Echo in Time is his seventh novel.

About the Author

www.ingramcontent.com/pod-product-compliance
Lightning Source LLC
LaVergne TN
LVHW100528110826
845146LV00002B/813

* 9 7 9 8 9 9 5 6 4 2 8 7 9 *